One Among the Duggle Tree

Zach Perry

Library of Congress Cataloging-in-Publication Data:
Perry, Zachary, author.
One Among the Duggle Tree / Zach Perry.
Pleasanton, CA: Zachary Perry, 2021.
LCCN: 2021906792 | 978-1-7369714-0-6 (paperback) | 978-1-7369714-1-3 (ebook)
LCSH Fugitives from justice--Fiction.| Climactic change--Fiction. | Dystopia--Fiction. | Science fiction. | Detective and mystery stories. |
BISAC FICTION / Science Fiction / Cyberpunk | FICTION / Science Fiction / Crime & Mystery
LCC PS3616.E77 O54 2021| DDC 813.6--dc23

Cover Design by Raphael Ogunmuyiwa
10 9 8 7 6 5 4 3 2 1

Dedication

I would like to give a special thanks to George Perry, Daniel Reilly, Michael Collins, and Shaina Clingempeel for their contributions to the completion of this book.

To my mother and father, I can assure you that the tree flourishes well...

1

A small bedroom bakes in ferocious flames as ceiling rubble thunders down on a six-year-old child. It stabs the boy's wrist with a heap of splinters. Hand trembling in pain, the boy sees a giant 'X' shape scar sear his wrist, as he palms the greasy bedroom door knob. Smoke seals the door in place and leave it immovable. Losing his wits, he bolts over to a closed window across the room. Cloudy haze obscures safety to the outside world. Toxic fumes of carbon monoxide force the window shut. He crumbles to the floor with tears of disbelief. How did the fire start? Where are his mom and dad? The boy comes to no conclusion.

Tiny sparks corrode the metal off a night stand, while a burning wooden dresser topples over. The white paint that covers the plaster wall, oozes downward like melted butter. Smoke suffocates the boy's lungs. Flames seep through the crumbling wall, which could collapse at any moment. The bewildered child crawls to a partially burnt family portrait that lies shattered on the floor beside his bed. It holds a picture of the young child with two blotted out images of where his parent's faces once stood. Their loving faces float vaguely into his mind. He does not realize that their faces will soon fade from his memory.

He cries out desperately, "Somebody! Help me!" He hears no answer.

An axe crashes through the wall next to the window. The dazed and confused six-year-old hyperventilates, as he holds his soot-colored face between his wobbly knees. Flying wood chips bounce off him, while he whimpers.

"Little boy, can you hear me?" a gravelly voice hollers into the room. The boy remains unresponsive as loud cracks creek above him. He peers up to the caving ceiling that inches ever closer. A tall black man, dressed in his firefighter uniform, emerges by a large opening in the wall. He stretches out his hand as far into the room as possible. "Quickly! There is no time!"

Paralyzed with fear, the boy scampers back in repulsion from the stranger. The world closes in on the child. He feels trapped in a dark corner. He turns around.

"Take my hand!" the firefighter yells out in desperation. The pupils of the boy's brown eyes widen, as he realizes that help from the fireman is his only chance to escape the inferno. He must trust this stranger. The boy lunges for the opening in the wall with all his might. He coughs repeatedly, as he chokes on the smoke. Miraculously, the firefighter manages to grab hold of the child's bleeding wrist, and pulls him out to safety.

Firefighters shout and circle around the ball of fire that exudes through the house's collapsing foundation, and they fail to extinguish the flames. An imprint of the house address sign is barely visible along the wall beside the demolished garage. Broken fragments of the house address number lie clumped in a small pile hidden in the dirt where a well-furnished lawn once stood. In the middle of the driveway, a fresh pair of tire marks cover in overlapping patterns. An overwhelming smell of gasoline lingers near those marks.

The child slouches down to his knees in complete disbelief. He gazes mournfully across the unpaved street of his slummy neighborhood at his collapsing childhood home. The boy wonders if his parents survived and if they will come back for him. This floods his mind with great sorrow.

A pink healing wrap binds tightly around his frail wrist and leaves a lingering, burning sensation. The black firefighter comes over to the young child with a tight smile and a little twinkle in his eye. He wraps a faded grey blanket around the boy's body. "Come with me, little man. There's a better place out there for you," he says as he leads the wounded child to an ambulance. They climb into the back of the vehicle and slam the doors shut. The ambulance roars away from the violent firestorm.

***

Days later, with his wrist fully-healed, the boy plays with a toy truck on the kitchen table of a lavishly-furnished house. Portraits of vibrant flowers and dazzling colorful bushes decorate the tan walls. A tall grey refrigerator is against the far wall, and underneath, lies a small blue circular rug on the wooden floorboards. A middle-aged woman with an oversized apron stands still, transfixed by the lonely boy. She stands behind the doorway to the kitchen with her arms crossed. The aproned woman observes the boy's movements, while he races around the oval-shaped table with his toy car.

A younger woman, with her hair tightly wound in a bun, stands behind the aproned woman. She scrolls through pages on a clipboard in her hand. The aproned woman sighs as her heart melts at the sight of the boy. She swallows her tangled emotions before she speaks.

"And what is his last name, Heather?"

The young professional woman looks up. "We have no idea, Gladys. There are no documents or surviving records of the family that was living there."

Gladys' head snaps back with a quizzical look. "You mean he doesn't know his own last name?"

Heather skims over the last sheet of paper from her clipboard. "He says he doesn't remember."

Gladys wipes her trembling hands onto her apron. "What about his parents?"

Heather pulls out the first sheet of paper and hands it over to her client. "There are no remains of anyone else found in the house. Some tire marks were later identified in the driveway, but no other person was seen leaving the house. A couple neighbors reported seeing what looked like a family living there for a short period of time, but they denied knowing any of the family members personally. Whoever the parents or guardians were, they must have left without a trace."

Gladys' eyes watered.

A toy police car flies through the air and lands next to the brown-eyed boy's feet. Another boy enters the room. This other boy is slightly older with pulsating blue eyes. He wears long overalls, with one button intentionally unclipped. The blue-eyed boy slowly walks up to the other, as he holds up a stuffed T-Rex toy. They both stare curiously at each other, while they size the other one up.

The brown-eyed boy, who is shy and struggles to make new friends, stammers as he speaks. "Hi. My name is —"

The older boy interrupts, "You have my police car."

The brown-eyed boy looks down at the floor and spots the police car that lay gently at his feet. He hands it over to the older kid. "I'm sorry."

The blue-eyed boy smiles and throws the police car in the mouth of the stuffed T-Rex toy. He laughs hysterically. "Take that!" The T-Rex thrashes the police car from side to side. The blue-eyed boy makes loud chomping noises as the T-Rex launches the police car to the other side of the room.

Gladys, the blue-eyed boy's mother, smiles with delight. "We'll take him."

***

Thirty years later, darkness creeps through the misty sky, as the rain pelts down harder and harder into the night. An empty parking lot exudes the putrid smell of car fuel residue, which covers the abandoned space behind Tony's Bar. Nearby smoke stacks billow out toxic plumes of smog, which color the dismal skyline in ill-fated soot. Dark bulbs in street lights provide low illumination.

Heavy toxic pollution has destroyed the Earth for decades, largely due to mysteriously planted fires that have popped up all over the globe. Smoke clouds pile up low in Earth's waning atmosphere, which leaves a permanent dark stain in the sky that rain cannot wash away. Overconsumption plagues the streets of what were once prosperous cities, which includes this run-down metropolis. Factories have shut down due to outdated products and outsourcing to other nations. This bleak ecosystem lies in shambles. Machine parts lounge in cluttered heaps on every block corner from sidewalk to sidewalk. Once-essential equipment now seen as obsolete.

Dark shadows permeate abandoned buildings, which sit in scattered ruins. Other buildings remain functional with a dark sense of austerity. Gutters regurgitate unprocessed drainage from broken-down sewer systems that are now deemed as antiquated. The post-modern dump is a failing civilization that lay out with all its horror.

Gruesome clashes between civilians and law enforcement have led to substantial reforms, which has spawned the complete dissolution of the police department. Riots brew throughout every major city, as mounting frustration boils over, due to growing cases of police brutality. In response, the government mandated a well monitored militant authoritative sector, called the Detective Enforcement Office, or the DEO.

These specially-trained officers, much like private detectives, execute orders to arrest criminals. In addition, they perform more investigative background research on their prospective suspects before arrests. Every detail of each case is reported to ensure fairness to the public without prejudice. At first, it seemed like a perfect solution. Unfortunately, the full truth is never clear cut.

Meanwhile, a lone figure strolls out the back door of Tony's bar and gazes up to the sky. He itches the 'X' shaped scar on his wrist, a haunting reminder of his demoralizing childhood. He has a slick and slender build, as he fixes his mustard yellow and red colored tie while he waits outside. He wears a red-striped dress shirt under his dark grey, bean-boiled wool coat. Six black buttons stack in two rows on the coat's mid-section, which lead down to his soaked black dress pants. His fresh-polished boots do not feel so fresh anymore.

He checks his wristwatch, a thick round case with a wide screen as the centerpiece. It reads 8:22pm in red coding digital letters. He sighs impatiently. Two tumultuous clouds above him gather his full attention.

The rain drops suddenly freeze in place, as if they are suspended through time. A pair of large garish eyes project from the man's mind, amidst the blankness of the dimly lit sky. A familiar young man's voice rings out, "No, don't do it!" The sound of two bullets ring off in a half-faded memory, as the pair of judgmental eyes disappear.

The man's internal voice intervenes, "Hope...if I ever had a chance to change my life for the better, I will take back everything I did on that day. The pain and despair that soaks my worn-out shoes are the results of my untimely mistakes. We could have stayed as one happy and healthy unit. The same can be said for a lot of things. Maybe I could have saved those lonely people decaying to nothingness on the sidewalks. Maybe my existence could have led to a greater purpose. Maybe I could bring back fleeting emotions to those lost souls, as well as to my disappearing heart."

A woman's shriek rings from inside the bar. The man glides behind the back door, and draws a gun from the holster on his hip. It is an ultramodern-looking revolver, with a silver coding exterior in a compact amount of space. Sensitive heat sensor knobs lie on its backside, and it includes bullets that range from stun gun darts to paper-thin bullets. The grip handle folds parallel against the barrel, while the trigger slides away into a safety compartment. He snaps the grip handle upward, as the barrel and trigger lock into place in one quick click.

An overweight man with a brown leather jacket bolts out of the back door. A sturdy leg trips up the criminal's feet, and the large man tumbles to the pavement.

A rugged boot lands firmly onto the fat man's hand, and it applies pressure to the fugitive's wandering appendage. Weight from the boot stops his hand short of his jacket pocket. The futuristic revolver points at the large man's head, with the hammer knob cocked slickly back.

"Eight o'clock is a little late to cause a rumble on the bad side of town. Wouldn't you agree, Bryme?"

Bryme breathes out heavily as he glares up at the pistol. "What's it to you, bub?"

A wallet flashes out of the gunman's coat, which flaps open to reveal a Detective Enforcement Officer Badge. A saturated picture is next to physical listings of the detective in binary code lettering. Name: James Hunter Cazco. Height: 5'10 ½". Weight: 175 lbs. Eyes: Dark brown. Age: _36.

Bryme flares out his nose hairs, as he fumes with anger. "Screw you pig," he retorts back.

"Bryme, you're just the man I wanted to see. Are you coming in quietly? Or do I have to bury you next to a personal friend?" the detective poses mockingly. The unresponsive thug grimly stares back in silence.

Detective Enforcement Officer Ike Brooks, the much-younger partner in the fight against crime, sprints over to the two men from out of the back door of the bar. Ike dresses in a similar outfit to match his partner, though he is much taller, with a stronger build. A brown cashmere coat protects him safe from the relentless rain. Underneath, he wears a blue-striped dress shirt with a green and yellow mix tie. His long black dress pants complement his freshly polished boots.

The gunman, identifying himself as Detective Enforcement Officer Jim Cazco, grins while he keeps a watchful eye on the suspect. "Having trouble?"

Ike throws on a pair of rusty handcuffs on Bryme, then uses the bulk of his strength, as he hoists up the obese man to his feet.

"Little pest got a jump on me, Jim. But that's over now." Jim folds his gun back into its holster. "Get him in the car," he murmurs back.

2

Back at the officer's headquarters, the words stand in big golden letters outside the building's infrastructure: Detective Enforcement Office. The glass building towers over its colleagues like a looming giant.

Bryme taps his short bitten nails on a long marble table inside the interrogation room. The room is momentarily quiet, which leaves Bryme to his dreadful thoughts. Suddenly, the door bursts open as Jim and Ike enter the room. Jim takes a seat while Ike hovers over the table.

Jim massages out knots above his brow as he pulls out a small cylindrical container. Anxiety relief pills rest inside. He throws two yellow capsules down his throat, which relaxes his unsettled nerves. Sleep does not grace his troubled mind too often, at least not for the last several years.

Ike, Jim's younger partner, throws down a tan-colored envelope by the thug's hands. "Where is he?" Ike demands.

"Where is who?" Bryme inquires back nonchalantly.

Jim opens the envelope and slides over a picture of a large muscular man who wears a ripped-up vest. The muscular man's face lies half-hidden in shadow. "Your boss," Jim answers.

Bryme smirks sardonically. "I have not seen him in weeks."

Ike shakes his head. "Don't lie to us! We know your boss is involved with nuclear weapons. Past reports have confirmed this."

Bryme gazes at Ike's cold demeanor. "The company I work for builds chemistry labs. We're protected by a private sector. We create chemical compounds at our facility, not bombs."

Jim pulls out a testimonial document, and another picture of the same muscular man, as he shakes hands with two men in trench coats. "Your company, or network, has been built on fraud. A testimonial from a whistle-blower, Mr. Rhodes, indicates weapons and other supplies were purchased with no recorded transactions by your employer. Somehow, they made their way onto your company property. I have the pictures to go with that too. You see, we already done our research. We've concluded that around 40% of your entire workforce has criminal ties to either fraud or illegal distributions to weapons dealers. However, your elusive boss has no prior record of identification. I personally find this hard to believe."

Bryme blinks aimlessly to the back wall, emotionless. "Is your so-called testimonial supposed to represent some kind of warrant?"

Ike slams his fist on the table without warning. "DEO's don't need a written warrant! Or have you forgotten that? DEO's have government issued rights to execute the three principles of probable cause to solve crimes. We are the law."

Bryme yawns, unimpressed. "No person should have the right to take certain liberties away from other people, regardless of any random set of principles. Those laws won't last."

Jim slides the testimonial and one of the pictures back into the envelope. "The three principles are made for both of our benefits, Bryme. The first principle states that any case should have proper investigation, which means to investigate a suspect thoroughly. To track down any preceding arrest from our operating Drexwell System is paramount. Drexwell is our universal database that logs all information for the DEO's, so it's easy to access. It makes researching small snippets of information a walk in the park. Along with looking up prior arrest files, the DEO must look up the basic identity reports of the said person or people from the Department of Personal Records."

Bryme focuses his attention on the lone picture of the muscular man. He begins to tune out the meaningless lecture.

Jim takes notice of this as he continues, "The second principle of probable cause states that the authority unit must provide substantial evidence in a complete report of the situation and send it to the government heads for approval. It gives the chance for the accused, meaning you, Bryme, to either be convicted or exonerated after apprehension." The thug cantankerously sneers as his eyes meet back up to the officer. "And what would the wording for the third principle be, detective?"

Jim glares into the desolate eyes of his captive, finding no trace of care or reputable morals. "The third principle is the most protective piece of article for any suspect to obtain. Before apprehension, the DEO agent must give the accused a chance to give himself up. He does so in hopes of avoiding a messy situation with bullets and bloodshed." Brooks leans in, "Which means we don't shoot you without warning. Scumbags like you shouldn't receive such a luxury."

Bryme chuckles mockingly, "What a magical opportunity. So, what probable cause do you have for me? You have no damaging evidence here to pin on anybody."

Jim grins. "Quite the opposite, however, the investigation is still ongoing. You will have to pay a fine for fleeing a ranking officer. We will uphold the right to seize your firearm. It will cost you to repair the broken glass at the local bar. Lucky for you, Detective Brooks here didn't get injured in your scuffle, or I would have the right to hold you in prison with no chance of bail. After you pay your fines, you will be free to go...for now."

Bryme smiles as he slides the muscular man's picture back over to Jim. "You're playing a dangerous game amigo."

Jim pauses cautiously, "Tell me. Why do they call him Nevo?"

Bryme presses his hands together, "There is only so much I actually know about the man in the picture. To me, that man is an unsolvable enigma. But what I do know is that he is a man you do not want to cross. He is a huge man, with hands big enough to smash your head like a pumpkin. He is a cold-blooded character with no moral compass, and no care in the world. The one thing he does understand all too well is vengeance."

A drop of sweat rolls down Jim's forehead. "Do you know where I can find him?"

Bryme breaks out with a chuckle. He wags his finger. "No, no my dear DEO. That is not what you should be worrying about. What your biggest fear should be is what happens when he finds you." A moment of silence suffocates the air in the room.

Jim slides the envelope back into his pocket. "We'll see about that. Those are all the questions I have for today. Now, get out." Bryme grits his teeth as Ike escorts him out of the room. A shiver runs down Jim's spine, as his anxiety pills wear off way too soon.

***

Not long after, Jim's Bentley LX50 thunders down the roadway, as rainwater bounces off the windshield. Ike leans back in the passenger seat, then decides to break the silence, "We couldn't get much from that bum. I don't think we should have let him go."

Jim's hands tighten around the steering wheel. "You first got to reel in the minnows before nailing the big fish. Did you plant the tracker on him like I told you to?"

Ike nods his head. "On the back of his lapel, like you said. Two DEO's have eyes on his whereabouts as we speak. Last I heard, he was relaxing at some strip joint."

Jim checks the rear-view mirror to the empty road behind him. "That figures."

Ike turns his gaze to his mentor. "So where do we move from here?"

Jim replies, "Maxine Baker."

The befuddled young detective asks, "Wait, who's Maxine Baker?"

Jim replies keenly, "Before Bryme's arrest, I did some research on my own and learned that he picked up some mail at a house in the Stone Block District. Bryme must be staying there. Probably squatting, or something like that."

Ike asks, "Is Maxine Baker some sort of relative? You think we should go up to the house to ask her some questions?"

Jim answers, "Already looked up our suspect's personal record. Bryme has no living relatives in this area. There might not be a Maxine Baker at all. Her own personal record file is strangely minimal, only supplying a name and age."

Ike gazes at Jim quizzically. "Maybe Nevo is there. What time should we pay a house visit?" Jim shrugs, thinking off the top of his head for a time that works best for him. "We'll drive over at 3pm tomorrow. I'll give you a ride over." Ike nods his head, "Deal."

The brake lights brighten up the side of the road, as Jim parks in front of an oval-shaped house with a pristine garden that lines up the driveway. It's a one-story brick house with a coat of green and yellow paint.

Ike turns back to his partner, "How about this Thursday, man? Agatha is going to make pot roast with homegrown veggies. Why don't you come over for dinner? We would love to have you."

Jim takes a deep breath, while he drums his fingers on the steering wheel. "Maybe next time, kid. We'll see how this new case shapes up before making any more plans."

Ike chuckles. "How hard could it be? You can bring a date over when we do have dinner together. Agatha would like some company."

Jim brushes off the idea while the younger detective climbs out of the vehicle. They both wave at each other before Ike departs up the inclining driveway.

Jim glances down at his voice control system that resides above the car speakers, labeled as Drexwell. The Drexwell computer system consists of a large screen, four knobs, a slim scanner, and a spherical voice box. "Drexwell," the detective beams out. Three high pitch tone frequencies echo out of the voice box as the circular sphere lights up. "Yes sir," a calm female voice replies in return. "Give me the address of Maxine Baker. It's in the Stone Block District." Drexwell responds with two lower pitch frequencies. "Maxine Baker. Home address 323 Grayson Ave," Drexwell replies. "How many points of entry?" Jim asks.

Drexwell's screen displays a black and white outline configuration grid of the house. Fully descriptive measurements and diagrams of objects make up the whole structure.

Three entrances of the house are enhanced in the graphic framing. "Three main points of entry. Easiest point of access is the front door. The sliding gate leads to a closed-out backyard."

Jim memorizes the layout intently. "Give me a printout of the sliding gate dimensions." Drexwell broadcasts a brighter tone frequency beep. "It will pop out in a minute, sir. I would like to add that there is a minimal fourth point of access at the back window of the kitchen. Not a lot of space, but enough for an individual to fit on through. Should I include this with more data for blueprints?"

Jim nods his head. "Yes, include the kitchen window with the printout. That will be all, thank you." The scanner filters through a blue light. A line of paper spits out. Jim rips the paper out of the feeder, reading through it quickly before tossing the contents into the passenger seat. The Bentley speeds away and out of view.

***

A beautiful balcony branches elegantly out of a skinny, tall structure that makes up Jim's humble abode. Circular stepping stones incline upward to the front door. A tall metallic gate guards the secluded property on the outskirts of the city.

Jim dries off his hair after stepping out of the shower. He slips on pajama shorts as he brushes his crooked teeth. Steam circles the room like a giant mist, slowly fading away as Jim wipes the sink mirror clear. He vigorously brushes his teeth until he glares at his reflection in the mirror. A look of contempt reflects back, overwhelming his mind like an incurable disease.

Lights power down first in the bathroom, and darken down the elongated hallway through a spacious living room. Jim slides off his wristwatch and lays the device on a skinny wooden night stand. Lights on the watch start blinking a red flash with a 5:30am inscription. The detective smooths out his frizzy hair and jumps into his comfy bed. Maybe this time he could get some quality sleep. As the room fades to complete darkness, his anxiety for the upcoming day's uncertainties diminish to absolute nothingness.

3

A succession of five bullets rattle off in a huge commotion along the sliding gate door beside Maxine Baker's house, which pierces Jim's sensitive ears. The detective hyperventilates as he wipes off someone else's blood from his forehead. His heart races, as his fingers tightly grip the trigger of his unwieldy pistol.

Jim glances at the image that appears on his wristwatch screen. A clear visual from the watch's centerpiece gives full surveillance of the kitchen inside the house that now falls quiet. Usually such vantage points would be impossible to discover. However, with the help of his portable 360-degree lens camera that's attached on the kitchen's back window, the detective can obtain a complete view of the room. With a mere click of a button on his watch, he could shift around different angles of the lens to get a complete perspective of all objects into the room. He hopes that the device will expose all different corners of the room. At the moment, the image on his wristwatch shows no signs of life. Now is the time to close in.

The detective leans against the sliding gate of the shady house with adrenaline coursing through his veins. He raises his wristwatch close to his mouth and mutters, "Brooks, give me back up. I'm going in."

The dead body of a poor young thug, hunched over the broken glass frame of the sliding gate, leans inside the house. Jim shakes his head at the sight of the dead gangster's face, as he wipes off more blood from his temple disgruntledly. This youth couldn't even buy a beer, he reckons.

He pushes the bullet-ridden carcass off the gated door and onto the floor inside the house. Jim carefully glides his way through the cut-away glass hole of the doorway. A small, square-like table with four chairs sit undamaged in the middle of the small kitchen. As he sticks his gun out in front of him, the detective slowly reaches over to a dead body by the island counter space. Another dead body lies on the ripped-up carpet floor in the nearby living room. A young man in a flannel shirt, with a bullet lodged in his throat, lays in a pool of his own blood beside the detective. He never saw it coming. Jim checks the dead man's pockets. He pulls out a wallet, a metal bracelet with an image of an eye inside a pyramid insignia, and a letter. The detective starts to fish through the raggedy wallet, eyeing about a dozen business cards that lay inside.

A lone bullet brushes by Jim's earlobe and shatters a portrait that hangs on the wall. He drops to the floor and scampers behind the counter space, just as another bullet follows close by. Jim glances back at the image on the watch screen. The camera begins to shift around sporadically. He presses a couple buttons on his watch to locate the unwelcomed guest. The watch screen reveals the image of a gunman, as he reloads his gun behind a large dresser next to the back door. Jim quickly aims and fires his gun. He blasts off a rusty knob from the dresser. The gunman panics and bolts out the back door.

Ike slowly slides through the kitchen window and plops into the sink, which knocks empty bottles over the counter. "You alright, partner?" Ike asks.

Jim quickly points at the back door. "You have one on the run! He's getting away!" Urgency kicks the young detective into high gear. Ike catapults off the counter, as he darts past his partner. "Just a little head start, that's all." He turns the corner as the gunman climbs over the fence. Ike flings himself over the back fence while the assailant scrambles onto the rooftop of a neighboring house. The young detective leaps onto the rooftop with finesse and follows close behind. The chase leads them out of the neighborhood.

Jim paces back through the crime scene in the living room. He takes a couple deep breaths before he folds his gun back into its holster. The detective lifts his watch next to his mouth and shouts, "Drexwell, approach the front of 323 Grayson Ave." Two high pitch beeps ring out as the wristwatch blinks sporadically with a red flashing light. Jim reaches up to clasp the 360-degree lens camera off the kitchen window. His watch rings two beeps for an incoming call. "Give me a couple minutes," Jim replies to the voice box.

The detective strolls out from the side of the house and stops by the corner where he sees a cracked piece of glass. Jim slowly picks up the evidence and eyes it intently. He then glances around the front porch of the house. He cannot see the house address sign anywhere near the front porch. He realizes that the fragmented numbers in his hand must be what is left of the sign. While he slides the evidence in his pocket, he notices the hint of burning chemicals in the driveway. It is a strange mix of ethanol, rubbing alcohol, and benzene.

***

Daybreak hits the busy street on Grayson Avenue an hour later, as a dark orange sun illuminates the sky as it sets. The sidewalk fills in with heavy shade. Jim sits in his Bentley as medical personnel storm the house. They prefer to call themselves DEO Coroners, due to exclusive ties with the Detective Enforcement Office. Usually dressed in heavy duty Hazmat suits in order to not contaminate the crime scene, the DEO Coroners serve as the clean-up unit.

Jim gazes at the metal bracelet that bears the image of an eye inside a pyramid insignia. He pauses as he tries to recollect where he has seen it before. Probably off the wrist of another thug he put away, he reckons.

The detective then holds up the bracelet by his Drexwell box. "Drexwell, analyze." Three loud beeps go off as a ray of light from the circular sphere zaps through the bracelet. "Origins unknown. More data needed," Drexwell replies back.

Jim sighs as he rubs his thumb over the metal casing. "Analyze metal material. Is this aluminous copper?" he asks back to the machine.

Drexwell scans the bracelet once more. “Negative. Metal encasing is made of metallic silver with small traces of silver nitride.”

The detective stares back at the machine with perplexity, “Silver Nitride?” Drexwell continues, “Most factories refuse to make the stuff anymore, sir. But I can 100% confirm the material.”

Jim nods his head. “I see. That’s all I need. Thanks, Drexwell.”

The detective slides the thug’s letter in a separate compartment under the voice box for safe keeping. The screen to the Drexwell box materializes to the image of Chief Fred Brahm, the head of the Detective Enforcement Office. His thick grey goatee distracts from the look of fatigue that hangs on his face. He is a no-nonsense boisterous man, twisted with a brash sense of humor.

A low, booming voice projects outward. “Officer Cazco! Progress report!” Jim looks back at the screen, with its static breaking up slightly. “Four gunmen involved, chief. All resisting arrest, even after we displayed the probable cause principles. Three of them are dead. Detective Brooks is still chasing down the one remaining.” Chief Brahm pauses for a moment. “Did you recover a Maxine Baker?”

Jim shakes his head. “Negative, chief. No pictures, records, or any other proof of such a person ever existed in the house. Suggest freelance arsonist at work.”

Brahm nods his head in agreement. “Very well. Let me know about any updates. I will see you in my office first thing in the morning.”

Jim nods his head half-heartedly. “Aye, aye captain.” The screen turns blank to end the transmission.

A couple minutes later, Jim returns to the house to look for more clues. DEO Coroners crowd the place in their Hazmat suits, as they search every room to find some remote piece of evidence to save in tiny plastic bags. The three dead men lay next to each other in the kitchen, with body bags that rest on their backsides.

Wayne Smothers, a notorious news journalist, hovers over the counter space and analyzes the crime scene. He is a scrawny-looking man, with dark curls of hair. He only cares about getting his name under the next big headline. Wayne would sell out his own mother if he had to. The journalist has his notebook out and takes notes while he talks to the head DEO Coroner Examiner.

Wayne turns around and sees the detective walk into the kitchen with his 360-degree lens camera, as he takes pictures of the crime scene. A devious smile creeps upon the journalist's face. "Well, well, look what the authorities dragged in. A classic peacemaker."

Jim doesn't give any dignifying response. He faces away from the manipulative journalist.

Wayne persists. "What's the damage this time officer? Haven't you done enough to these poor kids already?"

Jim slides on a pair of gloves so he does not contaminate the crime scene. He keeps his eyes peeled away from his unholy rival. "I don't have time for your antics, Wayne. There is nothing for you here. Get lost."

Wayne chuckles cynically. "You might scare others with your badge and your brittle words, but they don't scare me."

Jim takes a picture of the dead bodies still left unzipped in their body bags. "Whatever makes you sleep at night, Wayne. Nobody reads your paper anyways."

Wayne glances at the mirror camera. "And what type of law enforcement gadget is that? Can't possibly be legal."

Jim retorts back. "It's a standard 360-degree lens camera. It has the ability to see all images in any given room provided that they can reflect off clear surfaces within 100% visibility. It's legal."

Wayne shakes his head in disbelief, as he shifts gears to another topic. "And what about the tenant, Ms. Maxine Baker? What happened to her?"

Jim runs a finger over a liquid spilled on the countertop, and he gives it a quick sniff. Some acidic substance, he realizes. He looks back at the journalist with contempt. "There was no Maxine Baker. We have concluded that the house was run by freelance arsonists of some kind."

Wayne's voice trembles. "Freelance Arsonists?" The head DEO Coroner Examiner, who eavesdrops in the conversation, butts in, "you see, sir, freelance arsonists are people who are paid to put up a false name to register out a certain living quarter. Whenever the grim task they are paid to do is accomplished, they usually burn all the evidence. This includes the residence they operated from. The residence and the false name registration are merely a front to gigs involved with crime. They ultimately burn all evidence linked to their operation and drop out of sight."

Wayne's face swirls up with confusion. "Who would pay to do such a thing?"

Jim snaps off his gloves and returns the camera to his pocket. "Cold-blooded criminals that are now under investigation. Are you satisfied now, Wayne?"

Wayne snorts with skepticism. "You don't honestly expect me to believe that's what happened? What about the young men you brutally murdered, those poor souls who lay with their guts out on the floor? Don't you have any sympathy?"

Jim stiffly responds, "Those men initiated contact after I knocked on the door. I gave them the three principles of probable cause. They refused arrest and got dealt their fate." Wayne lifts his eyebrow as he takes notes. "And how do I know you followed the three principles correctly? All you can give me is your word."

Jim snaps right back. "That's right. You have my word to follow and nothing else. I am the authority here, and the rest of you are civilians. Understand the laws in place. You don't comply, things end up very badly for you."

The head DEO Coroner Examiner turns his attention to the sink, as he leaves the conversation.

Wayne closes his notebook. "What if the DEO takes the so-called laws into his own hands, and doesn't wait for others to initiate contact? What if he acts first and answers questions later? Nobody can dare question him, right? What if you kill someone by mistake? Or not by mistake, but by a hidden agenda?"

Jim decides not to engage the rude journalist's behavior into a grudge match. He glances down at his watch. It blinks in bright red letters: New message from Ike: Criminal got away, heading back home, see you tomorrow. The detective types in a random code, and the message disappears.

He scrutinizes the cold news journalist with a distasteful look. "You live in a fantasy land, newspaperman. You keep asking the wrong questions and alleging the wrong things. Someone's going to find you in a dumpster if you're not too careful. Hope it's not me."

Without another word, Jim strides away from the kitchen and towards the front door.

Wayne stands in place, red in the face. He beams back to the departing officer. "You act like we live with hell on Earth! This isn't some playground for your laid-out destruction. It's peoples' livelihoods at stake! The laws of today's world won't last! Someday you'll slip up and slip up bad! I hope I can witness your fall! That's what's called inevitability, detective!"

Jim ignores the reporter's ravings and leaves the scene quietly.

***

Jim slouches back in a sturdy booth inside Tony's Bar, a couple blocks away from the Stone Block district. It is a darkly lit bar with patchy blue paint that covers the walls. An open patio with orange tent umbrellas lay right outside. The detective inspects the letter left in one of the perpetrator's pockets as he waits for his drink. It reads: Revolution is among us, meeting next at collapsing house of green, regular time, don't be late.

He squints and rereads the passage. What in the hell does collapsing house of green even mean? It didn't help either that he couldn't narrow down the regular time when the thugs were supposed to meet. Could the house of green be code for a warehouse? What revolution was about to take place? With a sigh, the detective realizes that the trail led to a dead end. He is back to square one.

A drink coaster lands on the table by Jim's side. A slender woman with long strawberry hair and stork-like legs appears in front of him. Her green dress shirt with rolled-up sleeves showcases her lovely tanned arms. She chucks down a glass of Black Angus, a dark port beer that happened to be Jim's favorite. He looks up to her cheerful face, made up mostly of a vibrant smile and a flare of vivacious bright green eyes.

"One Gentleman's Black Angus slider with a twist of lemon," the waitress announces.

Jim glances back at the foam that slowly flattens at the top, before he swipes the beer. "Thank you miss."

The waitress, instead of rushing back to her other orders, glares back at the detective's facial features with some sort of odd familiarity. "Wait, I've seen you before, haven't I? You're a DEO, aren't you?"

Jim crumbles the letter into his breast pocket, with a soft smile. "What makes you think that?"

The waitress firmly replies, "You and your partner were here yesterday arresting that jerk, some sort of thug."

Jim takes a gulp of beer and wipes away the soapy suds off the rough edges of his mouth. Sour and dark, just the way he likes it. "You mean Bryme? The smaller round gentleman with long sideburns?"

She nods in recognition. "Yes that's him! Thank you for getting rid of that pest. He has been causing problems with several other customers. I'm just glad that he's gone for now."

Jim chuckles softly. "Well you probably won't have to worry about that loser for a while."

The waitress leans her body into his table, intrigued. Her hands glisten off the surface of the wooden table. "What makes you say that?"

The detective takes another sip before he responds. "Let's just say Bryme is laying low right now. With all his problems going on, I don't blame him. You won't have to worry about him. The last thing he wants to do is repeat the same episode here in your establishment."

The waitress smiles as she sticks out her hand, "So you are a detective! I'm Eva!" Jim takes a good look down at the woman's hand drawn towards his chest before he reluctantly shakes it. "Nice to meet you, Eva."

"What's your name?" she asks right back with a savory taste of curiosity. Her bubbly personality seems to give him remote interest, yet he convinces himself not to act hasty towards a welcoming host.

The detective chugs half the glass pint. He holds in a belch before he answers. "You can call me Jim. Jim Cazco."

Eva places her elbow on the table and rests her hand under her chin with glowing interest. "Cool name! Tell me, Jim, do you enjoy your work?"

He replies, "Sometimes, but it depends on the day." Her eyes wander down to the detective's folded-up pistol that sticks out of his side. "I always wondered what it would be like to live that kind of life. It has always fascinated me."

He shakes his head warily, then tries to change the subject, "Trust me, it's far too dull and disappointing. How long have you been a waitress here?"

Eva's expression quickly changes. "I...I'm actually not too sure."

"Not sure?" Well, what were you doing before waiting tables?"

Eva leans back, arm off the table. She starts to draw herself out of the conversation. "I...I'm not sure of that either."

Jim's eyebrow contorts unfashionably, somewhat confused, but also not caring fully to ask further questions. He drinks his glass empty. Vibrant sensations lead to the satisfaction of his taste buds. Eva reluctantly pushes her hair up and shows the detective the back of her neck. Jim's eyes grow large, as two red dots reveal themselves at the top of her neck. "You didn't actually get that procedure done. Did you?"

She slowly nods her in regret, as her eyes divert away from the detective in shame. He leans back in his chair, unsure of what to say. "You, poor kid. You must have gotten your memory wiped. I have dealt with cases where patients erase parts of their memory, to forget terrible things that they might have done or witnessed. It's a long process of brain surgery and mind manipulation. I think they call it memory intrusion."

Eva's eyes started to water, and her voice started to tremor. "Or have all of their memory erased completely. I don't know why I would do this procedure to myself, but apparently, the operation was done months ago. I just can't go back now. You must think I'm a bad person."

Jim looks deep into her eyes, and sees her spirit slowly break. "No, I don't blame you. That's a tough life to live. I see lines of people all the time, waiting outside those dark clinics that operate those controversial surgeries. Clinics that pose themselves as random convenient stores. Most of their clients are druggies, criminals, or people that just can't live with their own life decisions anymore. You really shouldn't have done that."

A tear trickles down Eva's cheek as she reveals a tattoo on her left wrist. It reads: 10/04/2057. "I got it done 3 and a half months ago. I don't remember anything before that. The clinic set me up with this job and a small rental house to stay in. That's about it."

The detective blinks, wide-eyed. "I'm so very sorry. I can't possibly imagine not remembering who I am."

She wipes away her tears. "Maybe someday I'll recover at least some parts of who I was. Now I mainly put all my focus into the present and the new people that I meet."

Jim sees a smile return to her face. "That's good. I'm glad you're shifting gears to that." With a slight brush of his hand, he accidentally knocks over his empty glass down to the floor. "Oh...I'm terribly sorry."

Eva picks a towel out of her thin-pressed apron and wipes off the table. "No, it's perfectly alright." She drops to her knees and picks up the empty broken glass.

Jim jumps to his feet, feeling awkward. "I'm sorry that I broke you're mug. Here, I'll place a couple extra dollars for you." The detective places a couple dollar bills on the table. "Um, thanks for the drink. Keep the change."

Eva watches the detective glide toward the front door. She throws the towel on the floor by the cup, and stares at him as he strolls out of the bar. She sighs gently and heads back to the register.

4

A pair of dark clouds can be seen outside of a 12th story window of Chief Brahm's office, which overlooks the rest of the agency's headquarters. Inside the office, Jim and Ike sit patiently, as they wait for the chief to start the briefing. Ike taps around a manila envelope on top of his lap.

Fred Brahm, a tall stocky man, pounds through the door with a cigar in his mouth. His dark brown dress shirt begins to untuck itself from a pair of tan-colored dress pants. Sweat stains cover in large clumps on his back. Brahm saunters his way over to his chair and takes his seat across from his two employees. He shuffles through some papers on his desk. "What do you got for me gentlemen?" he roars.

Ike hands the chief a picture from his envelope. "Bryme is dead. Two bullets to the temple. He was found behind a paint encoding factory near the north side of the city."

The chief examines a picture of Bryme's lifeless body that leans against a brick wall. "That's unfortunate for him. Any lead on possible suspects?"

Ike shakes his head. "Nothing yet. No sign of footprints or fingerprints at the crime scene. Whoever did Bryme in was awfully quiet about it."

The chief shifts his attention to Jim. "What do you have for me, hot shot?"

Jim slopes back into his seat. "The metal bracelet from one of the suspects is still being analyzed in our basement lab. So far, tests have come back negative for radioactivity. No trace of drugs. The metal bracelet looks like it was brand-new or hardly used."

Brahm's voice booms back, "We'll see what else comes back in the ongoing tests. There might be traces of chemical compounds that will help us catch the culprits."

Jim wisecracks, "If only the criminals would use chemical compounds that are out of date. Then we'll be able to find the culprits before next month's bonuses." The chief, unamused, throws a semi-burnt paper onto the table. Both partners give a quick glance to each other in silence.

Ike picks up the tattered paper delicately, and studies its contents. "What's this?"

Brahm takes a large puff of his cigar before he answers, "A paper that was found taped to the front door of this building. I want you both to inspect its message. It mentions someone's name." Jim asks, "Who's name?" The chief empties the remains of his cigar butt into a nearby ashtray. "It reads: Remember Nathan Duggle."

"Who is Nathan Duggle?" Ike asks in bewilderment.

Jim's ears perk up slightly, as he reads the message for himself. The chief grumbles on, "I don't have the slightest idea. Something is about to go down, gentleman. Something big. We have to be on top of it. I can't have more lives lost to this criminal, this Nevo character. We still have no idea who Nevo really is or what part he plays in the big picture. Look up any known files of this Nathan Duggle, and inspect the same locations for any resurfacing evidence. Hopefully, some vital information will pop up in your next submitted reports. That will be all, gentleman."

Jim staggers out to the sidewalk with Ike, as more threatening clouds loom overhead. The detective stops abruptly a couple feet from his car.

Ike turns around with a concerned look on his face. "What's wrong?"

Jim smirks as his eyes wander in the distance. "I think I have an idea where the location is for the thug's Saturday meeting."

Ike replies, "Really? Where is that?"

Jim answers, "There is this specific warehouse I have in mind on the other side of town. We should go now to investigate."

Ike jerks his head back in befuddlement, "How do you know it's a warehouse?"

Jim follows with his properly diagnosed analytics, "Most warehouses in town are brand new or at least made in the last 5 to 10 years. The silver nitride I recently discovered on the bracelet would be found in a facility that is a lot older than 5 to 10 years old. Nobody new in the textile or machinery business would make metallic silver in large quantities. It's too expensive."

Ike nods his head slowly and tries to follow the logic. "I'm surprised you didn't mention silver nitride to the chief. Ok, so it might be a warehouse. Which specific spot do you have in mind?"

Jim grins. "You should look up my history sometime. My first big case was cracked at a run-down warehouse. An investigation from 15 years ago."

Ike nods his head nonchalantly. "I think I was already told a shortened version of that story. Didn't that make you famous?"

Jim winces at the mention of his illustrious status. "The rest is history. Just get in the car." The two partners jump into the vivacious Bentley and storm away. A thick coating of clouds take over the sky as the atmosphere becomes chilly and damp.

***

A three-story warehouse lies dormant beside an elegant flowing river on the east side of town. Window fragments scatter in millions of pieces over the cracked concrete. A foul stink of burning rubber and charcoal fills the liquefying air. Puddles of newly formed raindrops trail down a long descending driveway into the entrance of the basement.

Jim and Ike emerge at the bottom of the grade, towards the empty warehouse ground floor, with their guns drawn. Oil drips like sewage from the high ceiling above. Half-disintegrated cars with gardening tools lay gathered together in the center of the large room like a giant junk yard. A stairwell on the far side lies close to a dark storage hangar. A dock resides on the opposite side and leads to a lively river, with currents that flow off in the distance.

A lone table sits by a secluded corner office on the opposite side wall. A handful of chairs sit around the table close together. Ike smoothly glides over to the opposite wall and slides open a long line of blinds by the shattered windows. A beautiful view of the river lay vastly beyond the dimensions of the two huge broken window frames. An unsettling chill grabs hold of Jim.

"I'll check upstairs, and you can check the basement partner," Ike exclaims.

Jim nods his head as the younger detective runs over to the stairwell, then disappears upstairs. Jim reaches out his hand onto the table. He feels the rough texture as he closes his eyes.

Jim imagines a group of young men who wear leather jackets with sunglasses. The men lounge about the table. They laugh and smoke cigarettes, without a care in the world. He visualizes them all playing cards, as they rest their feet on top of the table. All of a sudden, Jim sees a younger version of himself seated at the same table, next to another young man with blue eyes. A tall man with a pointed beard walks over to the table and shakes the hand of the younger version of Jim.

Leaky tears trickle down his pale face as he stands there motionless. Jim opens his eyes, disappointed, to see the table empty and lifeless again.

A breeze sweeps by the blinds. The detective turns briskly around to gaze at the dark hangar across the basement: a place he dares not venture.

Ike returns back to the basement floor. "There's not much upstairs on the second floor. I haven't checked the third floor yet. Find anything down here?" Jim shakes his head wildly while Ike continues, "I think we should go. There might not be much here after all."

Jim interjects, "You continue searching the top floor, and I can have a squad car pick you up once you're done."

Ike replies, "What will you do?"

Jim hides his tears. "I need to do some research myself. Over at the personal records, they might help me with more information."

Ike sees the tears on his partner's face. "Are you ok?"

Jim gasps loudly, "Yes, I'm fine."

Ike pauses momentarily while he ponders how to place his next question. "Did you know Nathan Duggle?"

A chill runs down Jim's spine.

He replies weepily, "Nathan Duggle...is a dead man, Ike. Yes, I knew him long ago. He had so much promise and affection for life. I was there when it happened. When it was inhumanely taken away from him. He's gone now."

Ike shakes his head. "Oh, I'm so sorry. I understand why you didn't want to mention him back at headquarters."

Jim brushes it off. "It's ok, Ike. Let me know what you find on your end. I'll do likewise."

Without another word, Jim paces his way over to the bottom of the grade in silence, unable to bottle his trembling emotions. Ike watches him fade out of sight. "Good luck!" he beams back.

Jim walks out of the building while fear hangs over his head. This new case will have to be treated with care, he reasons. He can't allow this new plot to be anything like his first case. If things get out of hand like before, history will repeat itself, and chaos will destroy everything in its path.

***

Jim steers down the road while his wiper blades spin swiftly across his windshield. He stops at a crosswalk as a young woman with mucky hair and shabby overalls darts across the street. She stops around the corner behind a huge line of people who wait outside a memory wipe clinic.

The detective sees a long line of lonely, demoralized people that extends down the block. Jim remains in his car, helpless in response to the crowd of broken hearts and discouraged spirits that lay out before him.

A bright yellow sign displayed out the front entrance reads: Memory Forgiveness. Jim's internal voice echoes a dismal tone in his head. "More and more, they come out in droves. The dejects, we like to call them. These people were hit hard with a painful situation in their life, and were unable to cope through the haunting memories that linger from it. Here they come to eliminate those mental scars and hold onto hope in starting over."

"The so-called brain surgeons, or vision creators, hide somewhere deep within the clinics. To stay anonymous, the vision creators dress up in exotic clothing. Those monsters conceal their faces as they operate on these poor people. Wow, what a sleazy crap hole." He wonders if this is the same building where that poor waitress sold her past too.

Jim shakes his head as he proceeds further down the street. What was her name again? She had a beautiful smile and a stunning demeanor. Her interest in him puzzles him. He knows that he is not a shabby looking man, but a beautiful girl like that? Love and affection left his heart long ago. He struggles to tell the difference between simple interest and true electricity when two special people meet.

Suddenly, the detective stomps on the brakes. The Bentley comes to a quaking halt as he suddenly remembers her name. That is right, he realizes. Her name is Eva.

5

Heavy downpour bombards Dr. Mack Gordon, a young aspiring scientist, as he zips past a food truck with a folded newspaper over his head. His white dress shirt soaked down to his torn khakis. Gordon's glasses dance around violently on top of his feeble nose, as he rockets by a deserted greenhouse, with a sign that reads: Protect Your Most Prized Possession, Mother Earth. He then crosses through a vacant lot with several sets of wooden benches that appear on the sidewalk.

One of the benches is occupied by Varra, a young notorious con artist, who takes long puffs on her cigarette. She is a young petite woman, with her hair dyed pink. Her low-cut T-shirt stops short at her belly button. She has torn jean shorts that droop halfway down her thighs, showing off her pale legs. Soft hints of glitter scatter along her upper cheek bones by her eyes. Varra crosses her legs and reveals her red dress shoes. Her cigarette begins to thin out of its gold-encased holder, which indicates that she has been perched on the seat for quite some time. Varra holds up a raggedy old umbrella as she waits impatiently for the scientist.

Gordon stops just short of her. He heaves out his lungs in exhaustion, while Varra exhales a large cloud of smoke into his face. "You're late," she says. Gordon coughs rapidly, while he waves the putrid fumes away. "I'm sorry. I just got caught up with work. Is he still here?"

Varra elevates her eyebrow mockingly and turns her attention to a large dark figure who lurks behind the scientist. A huge, bionic arm rests down on Gordon's soggy shoulder. A silver coating shines brightly on the metallic arm while a giant hand grips the scientist's flesh like a ragdoll.

Gordon's face twitches in trepidation, as a sharp pain pulsates through his back. "Night and rain go hand in hand, but you and deadlines refuse to cooperate," the dark figure bellows. Hairs on the back of Gordon's neck prickle upward, as he faces forward. "Forgive me sir. I was just checking last minute data. Otherwise, I would have been here on time."

The massive beast releases his grip. "Do you have those diagrams with estimates?" The young scientist grabs a crease-folded paper from his pocket and raises it above his head. The huge claw-like prosthetic, where a human arm once existed, quickly snatches away the paper. The huge hulk takes a few moments to study the diagrams of three large canisters, then says, "How does the carbon monoxide stay dormant?"

Gordon shakes his head, "It doesn't, but carbon monoxide can be fertilized with a mixer of soil and other compostable compounds. Its chemical reaction can be delayed, at least for a short while. You can only prolong the inevitable."

Gordon turns around slowly to see his boss, who stands behind him. The goliath looks over the estimates on the paper. He stands 6 feet and 6 inches tall, which dwarfs the rest of his crew in the background. His messy black hair slicks off to the side, while his long chin protrudes outward. Menacing bright grey eyes make the villain seem unnervingly charismatic. Muscles bulk out of his arms and legs like a champion wrestler.

Behind the tall figure stands three other thugs that Gordon has never seen before: a short man with a beard, a tall slender man who wears a fedora hat, and a medium-sized man with blonde hair tied up in a bun. The three men eye Gordon, as Varra trots over to the tall brute, and stops abruptly by his side. She continues to puff out smoke as the parking lot rests momentarily in silence. Gordon gulps in fear.

"We have liftoff, folks," the goliath grins with a devious smile. He folds the paper and hands it to Varra, who drops the paper in her circular purple purse. She then produces three small manila envelopes and distributes each envelope: one to the short man with the beard, one to the man with the fedora hat, and one to the blonde hair man with his hair tied-up.

The large brute clasps his hands in excitement, "Ladies and gentlemen! Tonight, marks the beginning of a brand-new era. One where we can take back society. The courts and law enforcement will be stripped of their humbling powers and handed to those who actually need it. Power belongs to the people, and power is what we'll have. And also, yes, you can open your envelopes now."

His eyes wander curiously at the others, as they open up the envelopes one-by-one and read their documents. After a quick chuckle, he continues, "Inside, you will find an assignment that fits your specific skill set. All assignments must be done individually without failure. Each one of you will have an equal hand in shaping this new revolution. With your help, we can expose the flawed structure of this society and crumble it down to its weak knees. It will be reshaped to the way we see fit, without judgement. Nothing will get in our way. We will finally have order!"

The small crowd's attention draws quickly away as a law enforcement car dashes down the street in the distance. Blaring sirens and flickering lights swiftly fade out of view. Frustration and anger weigh heavily on the leader's face. He clenches his fist tightly as veins pulsate down his engorged neck.

"No mercy. No more corrupted law enforcement. No more flawed regulations. We will make sure that, in the end, there will be no more." The tall man with the fedora steps forward. "How do we know when it's all done?"

The villain's face eases its tension. "I have a nice hideout for all of us to rendezvous nearby, a house of green. Report to me when the job is finished. Let me know if there are any problems. You will know that the revolution is completed once the newspapers have reported the destruction of the so-called law and order. When this city cries out on its knees for a new leader, then you'll know it's over."

The man who wears the fedora nods his head comprehensively, as he pulls a picture out of his envelope. The behemoth continues, "There are five stages in our operation for insurrection. We are in the middle of the first stage, as we speak: the initiation stage. Not enough people know who we are yet, so now is the time to properly introduce ourselves. Communication will be minimized to keep the element of surprise, but reach out or stay at the hideout if absolutely necessary. Your assignments start right now. Good luck."

Varra pulls out her extinguished cigarette from its long-encasing holder and flicks the dying flame on the concrete. Gordon, the short man, and the blonde man disperse into darkness as the storm rages on. The man who wears the fedora totters up to the leader. He holds up his picture. "Are you sure you want me to carry out this special assignment? I know he means a lot to you."

The boss shakes his head. "No, my friend, it has to be you. I have chosen you for this specific assignment, because you are the best man for that job. It has to be done swiftly, without failure."

The man tips up his fedora and bows his head in compliance. "Yes sir, Mr. Nevo. It will be done." He places the black and white picture, that reveals Detective Jim Cazco, back into the envelope. He walks away in silence.

Varra and Nevo stare at each other, as the only two who remain on the abandoned lot. Nevo places his hand below her chin and feels out her jawline curves. Varra smiles as she glares right back into his big nefarious eyes. "So begins your path of vengeance."

He kisses her forehead gently as the rain soaks them down to the bone. "Justice," he corrects her. She clings to him tightly, which highlights her misplaced affection for the giant in full display.

***

Eva wipes the sweat off her brow as she finishes cleaning the remaining glasses by the register at Tony's Bar. The onslaught of rain has scared away the rest of her potential customers for the evening. She stops to take a thorough glance around the empty bar, which resembles a ghost town. The waitress polishes and places the rest of the glasses away into a small, neat cabinet behind the bar. As she ponders whether she should close-up early, the waitress briskly turns to the clock on the side wall. A black cat with small slits for enigmatic eyes, which slide back and forth on the clock, reads 9:47pm. That leaves only 13 minutes before closing time.

After she contemplates for a brief moment, Eva makes up her mind and heads straight over to the closed sign that hangs on the opposite side of the front door. Just as she slides the open card around to closed, a drenched arm emerges onto the door handle. She glances up in surprise, as he watches a weary man drip heavily on a previously well-kept doormat.

Raindrops slide off Jim's cheeks. "Are you still open...Eva?" The detective cannot believe that he almost forgot her name again. His eyes are red from the tears that disheveled his face.

After a moment of hesitation, the waitress eventually smiles. "Sure Jim, what can I get for you?"

Jim takes a seat next to the first table that catches his gaze. "I'll take the Black Angus again, please."

She nods. "Sure."

Eva turns around to the cabinet behind the register. She removes one glass and fills up the cup. The beer glass lands smoothly on a coaster on top of Jim's table.

The detective grasps wildly through the air, unable to cusp the glass, as his eyes remain fixated out into empty space beyond the foggy windows of the bar. The wind blows boisterously out on the quiet street, whisking away thick trails of rainwater down the roadway to a nearby overflowing gutter. On the fourth try, Jim's stony hand clutches the glass cup. He sighs unenthusiastically.

Eva finally catches onto his somber expression. "Is there something wrong?"

The detective's glassy eyes struggle to fight back his raw emotions. He says bluntly, "It must be a gift not to remember the past. Even if there is a possibility of something coming back to haunt you."

Eva grabs another chilled beverage from behind the bar. She plants herself on a seat across from Jim. "What do you mean?" He questions himself if he should trust her, if he should open up to her. It had been so long since he had confided in a civilian. He had only met her less than 24 hours ago.

His eyes slide discreetly over in her direction. He takes a giant gulp of beer and wipes off foam from the rusty corners of his mouth. "A new case I'm working on, I shouldn't be saying this...but I believe there is a connection to my past." Eva eyes him cautiously. She observes how his body tightens. "What kind of connection?" His mouth trembles as it opens, unable to form words. His gaze ventures to the floor as he sighs more feebly this time.

Eva, who melts at the sight of the heartbroken detective, touches his fingertips. "I can't imagine the overbearing stress from a job like that. I'm sure, because of the nature of your work, you would rather keep things confidential. But it never gets better if you hold it all in. That's just not living life. Everything happens for a reason."

Jim detects the sincerity on Eva's face. Her soft cheeks complement her beautiful smile and mawkish expression. She continues, "We got the drinks. The whole place is to ourselves. Why don't you tell me a story?" He slowly picks up his cup and nods reluctantly. The two raise their drinks and clink them together.

After another luscious sip of beer, Jim decides to humor her. "Which story do you want to hear?"

Eva smiles gently. "A story from your childhood." He leans back in his seat in disbelief. Why would she want to know that?

"My childhood?" he asks delicately.

"Yeah," she beams back. "What's your family like?"

The detective's anxious fingers slide down the glass, as an angst-ridden expression covers his face. A realization shudders through his mind. Jim does not remember the last person he had discussed his family with.

The detective folds both arms and tries not to be too forth-coming. His eyes wander around the room. "Well, I mainly grew up with a mother, father, sister, and brother." Fantastical imagery suddenly flashes back through his tender brain, as his childhood self sits at a lavish kitchen table with an aproned woman, a large stocky man, a young girl with sandy-blonde hair, and the blue-eyed boy. The aproned woman, who adopted Jim after the house fire, passes him a bowl of juicy potatoes. Jim smiles and nods his head in gratitude as the tall, stocky man slices through a long chunk of baked ham.

Eva's voice snaps Jim back to reality. "What are they like?"

Jim pauses as his head sways a bit side-to-side. "Well, my mother, she went by the name of Gladys, you see. She was a very lovely lady who previously worked at an extravagant bakery. My younger sister, Chloe, was a straight-A student who was very passionate about the environment. Later on, she became a nurse."

Eva watches his body language shift as his arms fall to the side. "What about the other two?"

Jim nods his head as he tries to focus his attention back on her face. "My older brother — everyone called him Pretty Boy, due to his rugged good looks. Growing up, Pretty Boy was known as a street guy with a great sense of humor. He didn't have the good grades, but he always came through for you when you really needed him." She grins enthusiastically. "But what was his real name?"

The detective hesitates for a moment as he takes another sip to delay his response. "His real name?" His eyes glisten as he formulates an answer. "Dennis. Yeah...my kid brother Dennis."

Eva nods as she looks the detective up and down. "Did you have a nickname?"

Jim pauses as he tries to hold in a chuckle. "Unfortunately, yes. But it isn't very flattering."

She giggles. "Like what? Tell me."

"Cottontail," Jim replies.

"Why Cottontail?" Eva asks back.

Jim shakes his head, "In my neighborhood, I was seen as the soft one. I wasn't a tough guy like my brother. Kids thought I was soft like a bunny rabbit. Hence," Jim threw up his arms sarcastically, "the Cottontail nickname was born."

Eva cracks up at the thought, with her hand trying to cover her mouth. "I would never have thought you as a soft Cottontail." Jim shrugs. "That's my neighborhood for ya. Kids can be harsh. Luckily nobody calls me Cottontail anymore."

The waitress watches his composure change slightly. "And what about your father?"

His long hands curl back around the beer glass tightly. "My father," Jim sighs as he pictures his father, who skims through a newspaper and fixes the shine of one of the many rings on his bulky hand. "My father was an interesting man. We called him Big Daddy. He always wanted what was best for me."

Captivated, Eva asks, "What did he do for work?"

Jim replies, "Big Daddy was a construction worker. He was a muscular, heavy-set man. Not so much the humorous type."

She giggles at his description, “I wish I knew my father. Was yours a good man?”

Jim’s eyes revert back to the floor, as unwanted imagery fills his mind. He pictures his younger self jumping out the back seat of a BMW parked on a ransacked street. He walks behind a barbershop and slowly creeks through the back doors. An old Hispanic gentleman bleeds profusely as he gasps for air on the floor, as two men stand over him menacingly. Jim looks up at the man who holds a bloody, wooden bat. The man is his adoptive father. Big Daddy grinds his unkept yellow teeth at the sight of the child’s presence. A lit cigar dangles on the corner of Big Daddy’s mouth. The smell of ash and smoke fills the room like hazardous waste. This is the reason Jim chose to stay away from tobacco altogether.

Adult Jim nods his head reluctantly, back in the bar. “He was a fair...just man. Always did the right thing.” He quickly finishes off his beer to escape the quizzical look he expects in response to his lie. Luckily, she had none.

Eva finishes her drink as well, then gulps the last drops before she slams the cup back down again. “See, that wasn’t so bad, was it? A nice family story. I would like to hear the end of it sometime.”

Jim grins as he slides his index finger over the ring of his glass, “What about you? What’s your story?”

Eva gazes back at him, confused. “What do you mean? I’ve already told you. I can’t remember my family. With my memory wipe, everything about my past is a giant blur. I mean, sometimes my dreams are filled with the smells of an elaborate garden and the sounds of horses running off in some race track nearby. But all the images are a blur.”

Jim asks softly, “Then tell me what you do now. How do you spend your time?”

The waitress leans back in her chair and thinks about the detective’s inquiry. Nobody had asked her that. She answers, “I spend most of the week working during the day. A couple nights, I go out and party. Try to make some friends.”

Jim says whimsically, “Sounds like a fun night out. You have probably made a lot of good friends by now.” To the detective’s surprise, Eva shakes her head, then looks to the floor. “It’s actually a complete disappointment. You see a whole mixture of people here and there. But the crowd stays isolated and disengaged. I don’t know how it was before my procedure, but everyone seems distant. They act like they’re struggling to stay alive. It’s as if the times have worn people down, and they refuse to interact with each other. I just don’t understand it.”

Jim sighs as he glances down at the gleam that comes off her fresh, red nail polish. “Sorry, I don’t know either. We might never be able to understand that one. That’s just life.”

6

An unidentified man sits in the driver's seat of a small white van parked on the side of the street. Distinguishable fur trim brown leather gloves, with cut-out knuckle holes, are worn around his hands. A blue velvet jacket covers his skinny arms. The mysterious man grips around the edges of the shredded steering wheel intensely. He slumps down the driver's seat and out of view. The man jots down notes on a thin notebook and glances up to the back end of a Bentley LX50, parked a couple cars ahead of him.

Eva and Jim emerge from Tony's bar a couple feet away, which forces the dark figure in the van to duck his head. His wandering eyes gravitate back to Eva as she locks up the bar.

"That doesn't sound too bad, if you ask me," Eva says as she locks up the front doors. "Life is just hard sometimes. It's best not to leave with any regrets," Jim answers. The unrelenting rain causes Eva's mascara to run down her cheeks, as she tries unsuccessfully to shield her face. She shakes her head in disbelief. "You got to be kidding me! The one day I forget my umbrella, is the same day I get completely drenched."

Jim holds back a smirk, then quickly produces his own umbrella from his coat pocket to help her out. Overhead flaps spring open as the two figures stand closer together. She bows her head gracefully. "Thank you, detective." Jim stops for a moment and gives her face a good look over. She has high cheekbones, smooth fair skin, and soft gentle eyes. He senses a beautiful glow about her, more than just a bubbly personality, but a soothing aura and strong drive. He must find out more. "You live far?"

Eva shakes her head. "Not too far — just a mile down the road here."

The detective straightens out his coat. "A mile in the rain at night is farther than you think. How about a ride?" Eva looks at the Bentley behind him. "You won't be arrested, I promise," he adds.

Eva grins as she walks over to the car. "Sure. I can finally cross something off my bucket list — riding in a law enforcement car in the middle of the night."

Jim snickers at her remark. "With a memory like yours, I'm surprised you have a bucket list at all."

***

The streets remain desolate and quieter than a church mouse. That is, until a peppy Bentley comes into view and roars down the misty road.

Eva can't keep her eyes off the Drexwell control box near the stereo of the vehicle. "What is this for?" she asks.

Jim takes a quick glance at her item of interest. He replies calmly, "Law enforcement used to rely on human operators to answer distress calls, locate vital information, and even help assist arrests. But that seemed to be too costly. Some cases were even lost to human error. Unfortunately, humans can't be held as completely reliable. That was the old system of the defunct police department, which is now extinct like the dinosaurs."

Eva leans in closer to the circular sphere at the voice box. "So this is their answer to that problem? A machine that can do all of those tasks at the same time?"

Jim sneers sarcastically. "Drexwell is more than a machine. It's an independent database that can look up files, voice activate on command, and analyze data through its own processing scanner. It's a separate security system connected to the digital net."

Eva glances over to the machine with amazement. "Wow, talk about cutting edge technology."

Jim lowers his head toward the Drexwell box. "Drexwell, I would like you to meet Ms. Eva." Two light pitch beeps resonate from the box before a female voice returns back, "Good evening, Ms. Eva. How are you today?"

Eva's mouth opens in utter amazement. She did not figure that the contraption would function in such a realistic way. Eva pictured something similar to a robotic simulation, but nothing like this. Jim gives out a chuckle.

"I'm fine, Drexwell. Thanks for asking," Eva says playfully, "how about you?" Drexwell replies simply, "I am doing well, thanks." Eva gives Jim a dirty look as he continues to laugh.

Halfway down the block, Jim sees Eva peer into the rear-view mirror. "What's wrong?" he asks.

A concerned look appears on her face. "How long has that white van been following us?" Jim looks back to see a white van approach from about 100 feet away. They slow down and halt at the oncoming red light, while staying perfectly quiet. Unable to make out the person in the van behind them, the detective presses a couple buttons on his Drexwell device. "Hold on. We got ourselves a bumpy ride."

As soon as the light turns green, the Bentley zooms off into the far-left lane to make a U-turn. The white van follows close behind. The Bentley screeches loudly as it immediately breaks its path on the U-turn and speeds off in a left turn down the perpendicular street. A siren blares, and red lights shine onto the Bentley's roof. The white van stops abruptly at the intersection, unsure of which course of action to take. The Bentley disappears off into the distance.

***

Wind picks up on a sleepy street in the old part of town with old-fashioned houses lined up in succession. Cracks run along the sidewalk, and rows of concrete lay unevenly down the block. The Bentley leisurely glides into a spot on the side of the street. A small house with a fresh coat of blue paint, gated by a newly constructed wooden fence, lies in the background.

The energy inside the car soon fades away as a request flows out of Eva's lips. Jim sighs in a disgruntled fashion. "I don't know if I can do you that favor," Jim replies in a pessimistic tone.

"Why not?" Eva asks earnestly.

"Personal records are the master file documents that identify everybody. Lawmakers don't like documents taken out of their facility, even if it's for a short period of time. You need to be a government essential worker to be able to access those master files in the first place. It usually is a lot easier to ask for a copy on the digital net."

She asks back cheekily, "An essential worker like you?" A long, uneasy silence ensues.

Jim sighs. "Look, I get that you want to recover your past. Most likely, there is a master file with your information on it. But there is a big risk. If you or I get caught holding such documents without proper notification, then we can face serious jail time. The government wants everything reported. It's not that I don't want to help you; it's just not possible."

Eva looks down weepily. "I already tried applying on the digital net for a copy. The government board refused my request. They say it's due to my connections with vision creators. You know, those brain surgeons? Anyway, getting grants from the digital net is not something that happens for me often. Many databases and programs are protected for those...proper citizens...that they are willing to protect."

Another long silence occurs, and Jim nods his head. "Yeah, I see what you mean."

Eva firmly grasps her hands around both arms. "A big mess; that's what it truly is. Please. It would mean a lot to me if you could do this one favor, Jim. I just have to know...I could come from a wealthy family. I could be a veterinarian. I could be a first-grade school teacher. Maybe my family is looking for me somewhere out there right now. So, please...don't worry. I won't tell a soul. I just need the truth." She fastens her long fingers around his arm.

The detective shakes his head. "Truth, no one needs it. Truth can destroy a man. That's enough pain to corrupt anybody, and it's far too disappointing. Trust me, you don't need the truth." Her voice tremors, "Please." Jim groans glumly, understanding her point. He hated using the digital net himself. When it comes to accessing personal records, he would rather go to the facility in person. Eva continues desperately, "Don't we all make mistakes? Don't we all get a chance for redemption?"

Jim stares right back into her eyes, as if he knows exactly what she means. She slowly releases her grip as he itches his head. "I'll see if a facility visit fits into my busy schedule. No promises, but I'll have to finish the big case that I'm presently working on first."

Eva nods her head accordingly, then smiles fondly, as she searches for a good non sequitur. "Thank you for driving me back."

Jim smiles back. "Thanks for keeping me company." The detective pauses as he gazes back at her lips. "You want me to walk you over to your front door? Just for safety?"

Eva nods her head and steps out of the vehicle. "Sure officer. Follow me."

She scopes through her purse as they approach the porch. "I know my keys got to be somewhere in here."

Jim looks around nervously at both sides of the street as they arrive at the front door. Stacks of cars sit quietly on both sides of the street. It is too quiet for comfort.

"Aha," she exclaims as she pulls out a black computer-like chip out of her purse. She slips the chip into the key scanning detector beside the door. Within a brief instant, the door unlocks. The waitress extends out her hand towards the detective in gratitude. "Well I guess this is goodbye for now, Jim."

Jim thinks fast on his feet and blurts out, "Is it alright if I get your contact info? You know, so I can get in touch with you if I can obtain your personal record."

Her eyes widen with delight. "Sure, you can have my number. Wait here. I have a pen and paper inside. I'll be right back." She vanishes into the house as Jim's attention ventures back to the sidewalk.

He waits patiently outside the door and hopes to see the waitress' head to quickly pop out again. The rain picks up faster and pushes a thick chill over Jim's spine. He looks up to a lamp post that flickers sporadically. An unsettling feeling creeps in. The detective senses that he is not alone.

After a couple minutes, Jim knocks on the front door. No one answers. He projects his voice, "On second thought, I can just come back at a better time! Is there a day coming up that you're free?" Still no response. Now the detective gets a little worried. Jim slowly opens the door and quietly enters.

Inside the house, Jim gazes at Eva's new wallpaper. Images of fluffy Corgis cover the left side of the wall. He passes by a messy kitchen with a cluster of plates that fill up the sink. On the other side of the kitchen lies the living room. A screen door at the backend of the house reveals a giant backyard. A huge maze of tall bush hedges can be seen out back. Eva must share the backyard space with a couple neighbors, the detective reckons.

With a distaste for the eerie silence, Jim reaches around for his gun. "Eva! Are you here?" He hears footsteps that come from the other room.

Eva suddenly appears around the corner. "Sorry to make you wait. It feels like everything is deeply hidden in this house."

Jim sighs in relief and hides his revolver behind his back. Eva smirks as she hands him a piece of paper. "Here you go. So, what do you think of my place?" The detective glances around the room and pretends to be enthusiastic. "Looks like a nice cozy pad."

Eva frowns as she takes a closer look at his shoulder. "Did you get red paint on yourself?"

Jim looks at her quizzically. "Red paint?"

Eva picks up a rag on the countertop and reaches out towards his shoulder. "Yeah, there's a smudge at the base of your neck. Here, I'll wipe it off."

A dark chill flows through Jim's body as his eyes travel to a red dot down by his clavicle. Jim's eyes widen as he clutches her arm. "Get down!"

A bullet enters through the back window and hurls right above Jim's shoulder, but it misses him by inches. He pulls her straight down with him to the floor. Four more bullets ricochet off the refrigerator. Glass shatters upon impact from the bullets at the back-sliding door.

"What the hell is going on?" she screams out in fear.

He picks up one of dead bullets. "There appears to be a sniper out back. Keep your head down."

She clings onto his coat in panic. "A sniper? What do we do?"

Jim has the same question. Once he finds the answer, he slowly crouches up to his knees. He gives her a sobering look. "I have an idea. Do exactly what I say, and we'll live. Where is the nearest bedroom?" She points down the hallway. The detective raises his watch to his mouth. "Ike. Come in, Ike. I need your help, buddy. Get down to 412 Maple Street fast. It's a matter of life and death."

A dark figure hides in the wind-brushing hedges in the backyard and pulls out the silencer knob attached to his rifle. He takes off his fedora and wipes the sweat off his ears. He briskly slides back on the fedora and makes a beeline to the shattered back-sliding door.

He steps through quietly and tries to pick up any trace of sound. A woman's shriek suddenly rings out in a nearby room. The man with the fedora rushes over to the door. He opens fire at the door without warning. A whole clip of bullets ravage the door to fragmented bits. The remaining foundation of the door slumps off the hinges awkwardly, to reveal a small bedroom.

The intruder drops the empty clip and quickly fills his rifle with a new one from his pocket. Deep breaths escape his windpipes as the man with the fedora enters the bedroom. He waves his gun around in astonishment, since there is no one else in the room. Cactus wallpaper covers the walls, with a small window that lies parallel to a compact bed.

Another woman's shriek erupts from under the bed. He quickly opens fire and dismantles the bedpost and mattress. A few seconds of silence fill the room as the perpetrator waits for movement. With a closer look under the bed, the man with the fedora sees a red light that flashes on Jim's DEO wristwatch. His eyes widen. "What in the hell?"

Jim jumps from behind the living room couch and quickly unleashes a full round of bullets into the bedroom. The man with the fedora rolls over on the floor to dodge the gunshots. The detective reloads his gun as he makes a break for the sliding door. The unknown assailant opens fire at Jim but makes no contact. The detective quickly escapes out to the backyard. The intruder then reloads his clip once more, as he rushes over to the shattered back door, and heads into the maze-like backyard in hot pursuit.

As the perpetrator disappears from view, Eva comes out from behind a tall vase near the front of the house. She crawls her way into the bedroom as discreetly as possible. She peers into the mess that used to be her bedroom. A red light flashes and catches the corner of her eye: Jim's wristwatch. Eva picks up the watch and heads over to the wrecked bedroom window. She carefully peeks through the backyard, being cautious of the cunning gunman. Eva spots Jim, as he hides behind a hedge a couple yards away.

Bullets ring off down the slope of the backyard. From the back window, Jim sees his wristwatch fly through the air and land a couple feet away from him. The detective grits his teeth, thankful that Eva has a strong throwing arm. He slides his stomach onto the mossy ground and crawls over to his wristwatch. A couple more bullets ring out down the hill side as the detective dives on top of the watch. Jim swiftly rolls his body back to safety behind another bush. "Drexwell, attack user," he whispers into the watch.

The Bentley, which sits patiently outside Eva's house, blinks its lights on, as the engine springs to life. The dashboard inside makes a couple of loud pitch beeps until the vehicle suddenly takes off. Gas pedal on full throttle, the car spins around the curb and crashes through the side wooden fence of the neighbor's house. Mud flops over the sidewalk, as the Bentley speeds its way out of sight.

The rain pours down even harder, which makes the assassin's visibility extremely blurry. He stomps through the largest brush of hedges, but he is unable to locate any sign of the detective. The man with the fedora reaches the end of the hedges when, out of thin air, a pair of hands grab his gun from behind.

Jim does his best to restrain the gunman as he slips an object onto the assailant himself. The intruder elbows the detective in the stomach and pushes him straight to the ground. Jim's revolver flies out of his pocket and onto the wet mud.

The gunman reaches for an extra clip in his pocket but realizes that he has run out. He throws the rifle to the ground in disgust. Jim returns to his feet and punches his adversary in the face. The gunman, who is much taller and better built, takes a couple steps back. He lashes out right back, with a powerful blow, straight to the detective's jaw.

Jim falls on top of one of the hedges and wipes the blood from his chin. Swelling forms below his mouth. With one last effort, he takes two more swings at the assassin's rib cage. The gunman dodges the attack and catches Jim's tight fist. He karate-chops the detective in the throat, which spawns temporary neck paralysis. Choking on his own vocal chords, Jim flies backward onto the ground once more, as he twitches uncontrollably.

The assailant picks up Jim's revolver with an unnerving smile on his face. Jim gasps in desperation as he struggles to breathe. The detective looks up to see his own gun pointed between his eyes.

The gunman laughs at the detective's defeat. "Pity. All your credentials precede you, DEO. I was expecting more of a challenge." Once Jim catches his breath, he blurts out, "Appearances can be deceiving."

The gunman continues mockingly, "For you, I wouldn't say so. To be honest, you don't strike me as an officer. You don't act the type or walk the walk. Maybe you'll have better luck in the next life." He cocks the revolver back and aims at the detective.

Suddenly, the assassin's wrist lights up with red flashes. The detective's wristwatch reveals to be strapped to the assailant, and indicates the handful of seconds before impact. Jim takes notice and immediately ducks to the ground, with his arms over his head.

Bright blue lights of the Bentley fly through the air, from behind the hill of the tall hedges. The man screams out in terror, as the car crashes into him with full force, and pins his mangled body against the side fence that lies a couple yards away. Blood squirts out of the assassin's chest as he drops Jim's gun. He lowers his head and lies motionless, trapped between the car's front bumper and the fence.

DEO agents storm the backyard through the newly-created hole on the other side of the wooden fence. Eva shakes her legs nervously, as she cautiously avoids walking over the shards of glass piled up by the backsliding door. An officer wraps a jacket around her as another officer walks over to the dead intruder.

Blood paints the side wall with a haunting shade of red. The Bentley's hood is bent in half with gas that steams out of the engine. The officer takes off the wristwatch from the dead man. He then tosses the fedora on top of the victim's head to hide his pale face. "What a terrible way to go," the officer mutters under his breath.

Jim lies on the ground, as he holds his neck in pain. Blood continues to drip from his chin. He feels the swelling of his neck soften, which makes it easier to breathe. A long hand extends out to him. Jim looks up to see Ike grab his arm. The younger counterpart hoists him to his feet.

"You decided to have all this fun without me," Ike says sarcastically.

Jim grins as he slowly becomes upright. He holds one hand firmly on the side of his neck. "Yeah, lucky me. Next time, the fun is all yours. I won't intrude."

7

The next day, Jim lies back in his bed with bandages on his face. The pain still swells heavily in his throat and stings his discolored chin. Even with Jim's most recent close call, the detective feels that he certainly dug himself out of worst situations.

Eva walks over to his bedside. "More water?"

He nods his head gently. "The more the merrier. Thanks, Eva."

Ike enters the bedroom with a newspaper in his hand and waves at Eva before addressing his partner. His face fills with more concern than usual. "You never seen that man before? The man with the fedora hat?" Jim shakes his head. The young sleuth hands his partner the newspaper. "I wonder what else that assassin was involved with?" Jim opens up the newspaper. "Beats me."

A booming voice enters the room, "We still don't know!" Chief Brahm makes his presence felt as he strides over to the bed. Ike gives his boss a short, quick salute. Brahm continues, "No identity card, no wallet, no proof of personal records."

Jim rubs his eyes. "Is his body still in the lab?"

The chief replies, "For the time being, yes. But I don't like this Jim. I don't like it one bit. This nameless man stalked you like wild prey, like a trained professional. He knew where you would be, who you are, and what you represent. We still don't know if the assassin was working alone or if he was in cahoots with someone else." The chief anxiously eyes the bruises decorating the detective's head.

Jim throws down the newspaper with the date reading in green digital characters: January 18th, 2058. The title news bulletin reads in huge green digital letters: Unknown Assailant Found Dead in Shootout. "I have no doubt that it's connected to something much bigger. Someone that well-informed couldn't possibly have worked alone. Don't worry, sir. We'll find the culprits."

The chief shakes his head and points at the detective. "You are not doing anything for the next couple days! Not in that condition! Stay in bed! That's an order!"

Jim nods his head grudgingly. His chief was right, even though he did not want to believe it.

The chief takes out a cigar from his breast pocket and smells the butt end, as the wheels spin in his unsettled mind. First, the death of Bryme, and now, the death of this John Doe. Could they be connected?

Brahm turns to the younger detective. "Looks like you're up, kid. Go back to see what's left of this young lady's house, and make sure you do a clean sweep. Report back if any evidence shows up."

Ike snaps his head forward. "Yes sir."

"Good. We'll catch these hooligans before they strike next. Best be on your guard from here on out. That goes for the whole lot of you." Jim, Ike, and Eva nod in unison.

"We'll start from there and see where we end up. Hopefully you will feel better after a couple days, Jim. I'm counting on it. And without any further ado, goodbye folks, and good luck," the chief bellows as he strolls out of the room.

Ike paces over to his partner. "Hope to see you on your feet soon." Jim raises a finger to pause their conversation, as he grabs a fat envelope from the night stand. He stuffs the packet filled with heaps of cash into Ike's hand. Initially perplexed, the younger officer starts to shake his head with discontent. "No Jim, not again."

Jim closes Ike's fist around the envelope. "Please take this to the same location, Ike. You're one of the few people I can trust."

Ike sighs with displeasure. "Well, fine, I'll do it this time. Someday, I'll become the most well-known DEO, and it will be you, who will hand out my mail."

Jim smiles, "Thanks pal."

Ike departs from the room, leaving Jim and Eva alone. She gazes out of the beautiful balcony attached to the bedroom. Her eyes become mesmerized by the beautiful hilltops and futuristic homes scattered in the distance. The sun slowly towers over the hill tops and brightens the small crescent valley behind Jim's home. It is a beautiful view that Eva could get used to.

"How's the view?" Jim asks her.

Eva walks back to Jim's side and places a wet towel over the detective's bloody chin. "I hope I'm one of those few people you can trust," she says keenly.

Jim hands her an empty water cup. "I guess I have no other option but to trust you for now, being a witness and all." She fills the water cup in another room.

Eva hands the full cup back to the detective, as he sits up in the bed. "Thank you. Now, since the utter destruction of your house does not permit for you to return home, I'll have to provide you a temporary lodging where you can stay protected. A watered-down version of a safe house, if you will."

Eva retorts back, "And where would that be?"

Jim takes a sip. "I don't know yet. Preferably somewhere close to headquarters."

She takes a full glance around the room. "How about here?"

Jim spits out some water onto the bed sheets. It donned on him earlier, but how would it feel to have a stranger move in now?

"Here? I don't think that's a good idea. It's —"

She interrupts, "Of course it's a good idea. You need someone to protect you while you recover. I need someone to protect me from whatever else is still out there. Plus, this place could really use a woman's touch; a little sprucing up here and there. It's a win-win."

Jim takes a deep breath. "Eva, I don't need protection. I just need 24 hours to rest. I'll be back, good as new."

She laughs mockingly. "Great, then we can protect each other. Who else better than you?"

He rewards her faith with a blank stare. No way out of it now. Jim picks up one of the pillows behind his back and throws the fluff case in her face. She catches the pillow, while Jim halfheartedly points to the door. "Your bed will be in the room next door. It's your room, for now, until this whole situation blows over."

Eva bows sarcastically. "Thank you, good sir. I'll be the best roommate you ever had."

Jim shoos her away, and the happy waitress leaves the room to rearrange her new living quarters.

The detective leans back onto the bed. God, what has this woman gotten him into now? Jim rubs his eyes, as a dizzy spell invades his mind. The physicality from the fight still lay vivid in his thoughts. An ongoing headache fades in and out.

The idea of possibly getting to know Eva intrigues him, but everything seems to be happening all too soon. How much worse can things get, he wonders. The detective slumps back and falls asleep instantly. His mind wanders helplessly through time and space, back into the past.

***

Big Daddy, the detective's tall and stalky adoptive father, bursts open the back door of the house to a spacious backyard. A fresh coat of bright brown paint decorates the fence. Thorn bushes and a small flower garden can be seen in the foreground. Big Daddy's nice leather jacket sways side-to-side, as his mustard yellow and red bowtie stays fixed in place. His moustache curls up in anger as he drags out young Pretty Boy by the collar. The young detective and young Chloe follow close behind.

Pretty Boy lands firmly on top of a destroyed mound of dirt in the middle of the backyard. Muddy seeds are displaced outside of the dirt mound in small meshes of clumped soil.

"You little punk!" the angry father boils with rage. Gladys swiftly opens the back door. "Honey, stop! He's just a boy," she begs.

"A boy full of trouble," Big Daddy beams back. He kicks over a couple of the dirty seeds laying by the waste side. "What do you call these, you little twerp?"

Pretty Boy quietly eyes the discarded seeds with no reaction. Big Daddy rambles on, "This family is trying to grow an apple tree. Why did you have to destroy the mound we filled yesterday?"

Pretty Boy pouts with his arms crossed, unwilling to look back at his enraged father. "I didn't mess up your precious tree, dad."

Big Daddy lights a cigarette and takes a couple puffs.

Then, he slaps his son in the face. "Don't lie to me! It's always you, child! Why do you always have to destroy everything?"

Gladys nervously twiddles her fingers around by her knees. "That's enough! We can always replant the apple tree. There's no harm done."

Big Daddy regains his grip on the child's collar. "No! That's not it! I want this little punk to own up to his actions! A little punk who thinks he's a bad boy! Take responsibility for once in your life!" Pretty Boy squirms timidly.

Big Daddy makes a fist. "You still think you're so tough, huh?" Puffs of smoke pervade the child's face, but, Pretty Boy refuses to cough. He is used to this type of interrogation by his father.

The young detective raises his hand abruptly and waves it around wildly in the air, to politely gain the attention of Big Daddy. "Hey, wait! Stop!"

His adoptive father stops in his tracks, full of confusion at the child's weird gesture. After a couple moments of silence, Big Daddy squints. "Yes, what is it, Cottontail?"

Cottontail looks straight into the large man's menacing eyes, "I want to apologize, Big Daddy. I was the one who messed up your seed patch. It was me."

The ogre-like man lets go of Pretty Boy and marches over to Cottontail. "Oh really? You did this?"

Cottontail takes a big gulp and nods his head. "Yes, it was me. I'm very sorry, sir. It was an accident. I'll make up for it."

Big Daddy cocks an eyebrow. The shriveled cigarette almost falls out of his mouth in disbelief. He is unconvinced, yet he cannot prove the child wrong. He thought his new foster child was not capable of doing something so reckless. He realizes he must let it go.

"Well, if it was you, just make sure it doesn't happen again. Growing apples will help give us a healthy diet. This family needs an apple tree to make fresh food. Sooner or later, we will grow one that stretches high above the fence. Fresh apple juice with apple cider to match a delicious apple pie. We won't have to waste precious money at the grocery store. Is that understood?"

Cottontail's gaze fixates on the lit cigarette that dangles on the side of Big Daddy's mouth. The sight of the burning tobacco and the smell of toxic smoke freezes the poor child in his tracks. Overwhelming fear floods Cottontail's mind, as the smoke reminds himself of the house fire from not long before. "Yes sir." Big Daddy flicks the dead cigarette on the ground beside the destroyed mound and stomps it into the earth violently.

Gladys clasps her hands together. "Alright, everybody inside. Get ready for supper."

"Yes Momma," the three children respond in unison. The young detective's inner voice resonates loudly in his head, as he reminisces about his past, "It's hard to believe, but it's all true. These people shaped the very well-being of who I would become. The biggest lesson that I learned from these people is that life is full of losses. The outside world can be harsh and unforgiving. But even after the outside world removes the most enjoyable things in life, in the end, there will always be family."

Cottontail reaches out his hand to Pretty Boy. His adopted brother gazes back and reluctantly accepts the helping hand to bring him up to his feet.

Sometime later, Cottontail creates a new circular mound with clay around a divot. The new mound is closer to the backyard garden, which he hopes will be a better fit for the new tree. Chloe buries five seeds inside the divot and sprinkles water on top from a full cup. Pretty Boy walks up from behind Cottontail. He eyes the cast-off child suspiciously. "Why did you take that heat for me?"

Cottontail looks up at the sun as it sets in the hills in the distance. An orange gleam beckons beyond the horizon. He shrugs. "Because you're my brother now. I have to take care of what's most important in my life."

Pretty Boy contemplates this notion, then nods accordingly. A new growing appreciation causes him to grin. He sticks his hand out wearily. "I have a couple more seeds for you guys to plant."

Chloe smiles and plants the seeds deep under the soil. She pours more water on the dirt. "You know why trees are the most important food source in the world?"

Both brothers look at each other with complete mystification and shake their heads. She chuckles. "Trees are the most important food source because their roots go deep underground. The farther down you go, the fresher the soil will be."

Cottontail looks down at the dirt on his hands in amazement. "Wow, that's a lot of food."

She continues, "Enjoy the soil while it lasts, boys. If we continue to trash the soil and the environment, then there will be no more clean food or water."

Pretty Boy interjects, "Have you seen how much soil there is in the ground, Einstein? Tons."

She snaps back, "Not if we continue to trash the environment. My teacher says if we don't act now, the world will become more trash than natural resources."

Pretty Boy rolls his eyes in utter annoyance, as Cottontail scoops out a couple broken twigs from the ground. He plants three twigs in front of the clay mound. "When this tree becomes big and strong, we'll be able to take all the apples we want. My hope is that Momma will make a lot of apple pies." He wipes off his hands.

Chloe smiles as the three kids stare at the ground. Pretty Boy grabs a big stick and scrapes out three letters in the wet clay in front of the twigs. He writes the letters D, N, and C. Chloe looks into the soft eyes of her new brother, Cottontail. "By the time we're adults, we can have all the apple pies we want. This will be our little Duggle Tree." All three kids stare at their mound in wonder, excited to consider all the tasty apple pies coming their way.

***

Night falls back to the present day, as an unidentified man, with the same distinguishable brown gloves, strolls street block after street block around the main street of downtown. Rundown buildings line up in succession. Pockets of trash piles stack up on every corner. The stretch of rundown buildings soon flourish into skyscrapers that tower high up in the sky. Millions of lights cover different compartment levels for each establishment.

The man strides through the entrance of the tallest skyscraper building, with big vertical letters that form the words: Personal Records. He stops abruptly by the elevator to see Detective Jim Cazco, who waits for his turn to hop on the elevator. The detective waits patiently, with a few others, as the elevator doors slowly open. The dark figure continues to walk on by and down the hallway in silence.

The elevator ascends a couple stories into the air before it shifts horizontally across the massive building. Occupants in the elevator stand quietly, as the elevator climbs up several more stories, before it shifts horizontally once more. Jim glances through the clear glass window. He sees the rows of columns that glow in dark fluorescent blue lights around him, like illuminated catacombs. Hundreds of workers and law enforcement staff swarm the bottom floor down below like army ants at a picnic.

The elevator suddenly stops, and a woman's voice echoes from the loudspeaker, "Sector 705A: Restricted Zone. Watch your step, please."

The mirror doors quickly open, and Jim walks out. He paces down a dark corridor, until he stops short of a pair of large glowing doors. The same woman's voice projects from an eye scan screen, beside the door handle, "Identification please."

The detective leans into the monitor, and a green light scans the pupil of his eye. "Detective Jim Cazco. DEO Class 1A." Two beeps answer in a dignified response.

The doors open to reveal huge bookcases stacked on opposite walls of a large room inside the control tower. A woman in her mid-fifties, Molly Fishburne, sits behind a desk as the main control operator. Molly has pixie cut grey hair and unwrinkled cheekbones, which identifies her as a model citizen of a finely aged section of society. An ocean-like fragrance emanates from her slim figure. She gazes at a giant screen that is mounted on the wall, which maps out the entire building.

Plastic encoding protectors cover her fingertips so that she can manipulate and move around digital files in the empty space in front her. Digital illustrations are created through the heat sensors from the plastic encoding protectors, which are controlled by mere guidance from Molly's fingertips. Millions of digital files fly off the giant screen and stream out in long flows of traffic. Molly picks up those files and places them in different locations above her desk. She sends left-over files back onto the giant screen.

"Doesn't look like you get out much, Molly," Jim jokes as he approaches her desk. She smiles softly. "It's been a while, Mr. Cazco. How is everything?"

He scratches his head. "As good as it gets."

"What brings you to the personal records?" she asks inquisitively.

"Nathan Duggle," he answers.

Molly hesitates for a brief moment. "Is there a middle name?"

He shakes his head. "Not that I know of. Born sometime in 2019."

Molly gazes around her giant screen and presses the encoding protectors on her forefinger and middle finger together. "Just a moment."

Jim notices the plastic coverings glow on her fingertips. She skims through an endless sea of files that flow out of her screen in a sporadic fashion. She wiggles her fingers in the air, as if to type words on an invisible keyboard in the empty space in front of her. A few seconds later, she springs up to her feet. "I got it. Follow me, detective."

Jim follows Molly to a small circular platform at the far end of the room. They both hop on as the transport comes to life. The platform levitates high up in the air away from the confines of the control tower. With no roof to the control tower, the detective and the operator ascend into low lit space, higher up in the building.

The master files, also known as the original personal record documents, fly in a luminous glow in coordinated air traffic paths around them. Jim watches in awe as thousands, maybe millions, of files shuttle their way through the air waves, and travel from one side of the building to the other. Civilians probably request digital copies all the time, Jim reckons. That would explain the frequent flow of the physical, master files. The rhythm of file circulation reminds Jim of more orderly traffic to some random highway. If only real life was like that.

The platform stops beside a dark pillar that sticks out sideways. Molly types a couple of imprinted characters with her plastic encoded fingers onto the side of the pillar. Within a brief moment, a blue light emits from the side pillar. A lone envelope file covered with plastic encasing slides out of a tiny slit from the structure. She hands him the document.

"Much appreciated," he replies.

"Anything else I could do for you today, officer?" Jim shakes his head, as the platform descends back down to the control tower. Regardless of how many times the detective made his way through file circulation, he always came out fascinated by the otherworldly experience.

***

A couple of minutes later, Jim walks out of the Personal Records building. He walks down the block and cautiously eyes the sea of people around him. He sees a white-bearded man that stares back at him. Another woman with her hair tied back in a knot glares at him too. He keeps cool, as he focuses his attention away from the wild street walkers that shift around him.

The detective turns down an alleyway. He opens up the plastic encasing and starts to read papers from the Nathan Duggle File. He skims through each page. The man with distinguishable brown gloves follows within a close proximity behind him. The detective stops abruptly beside a half-deteriorated trash bin that sits close to a rusty side gate. The unidentified man hides behind a corner and watches closely as Jim reaches into his pocket.

Jim pulls out all the paper contents from the envelope. He lights the stack of papers on fire with a small lighter he keeps in his pocket. He slides the empty folder back into his coat. After a brief pause, he pulls out an empty cylindrical container of where his anxiety stress-free pills once lay. With a sigh, he discards the container into the flaming trash bin.

Ashes drip off the documents like grease tar from an ashtray, while the container melts away within seconds. Jim watches as the items disintegrate fully. The remaining burnt ashes scatter into tiny bits. The detective wipes his hands off and walks away.

The unidentified man scurries over to the trash bin, only to be disappointed. He finds the unsalvageable, ash-like remnants of the documents that lay inside.

8

Chaos ensues in the trustee council's chamber at the Earth's Last Chance Corporate Headquarters. Earth's Last Chance is the biggest waste management and environmental restoration company in the world. The company's initiative is to combat the war against growing trash, as well as to protect city streets and disappearing suburban neighborhoods across the nation.

One carefully monitored dump exists at the back lot of the corporate building, with different types of trash grouped in different compartments on a large platform. Machine processors separate trash into different piles in the landfill sector, which gradually moves to isolated clumps at the far end. Eventually, the trash is pushed to a hot furnace at the edge of the platform for disintegration. Toxic waste becomes ash that dissolves into the Earth's atmosphere.

To restore the natural environment, one must deplete a junk pile before resources diminish. Despite progress, trash continues to mount. Earth's Last Chance still has a long way to go.

All the board members bicker at each other at an incredible pace. The trustee council, composed of twenty of the smartest environmental minds on the planet, are called together for an important meeting. Scattered stool chairs and desks descend down a circular chamber, deep within the center of the large room. The members wear bright yellow robes, with rosy red sashes, and a small green tree insignia displayed on their chest.

One of the members, who has blonde hair tied-up in a bun, holds onto a pair of metallic spheres, with an attached string between the two. He secretly rotates the spheres around his palm under his desk. A stand-up card sits beside his elbow with the name Dr. Verner. He perches warily on a higher-level section of the chamber, as he surveys the others quietly.

A slamming gavel disrupts the side discussions and finally brings silence into the room. The chattering disappears as Vice President Larker, an elderly man with a long white beard, lowers his gavel with conviction. "We will have order today, gentleman! We must resolve the new situation at hand."

One of the youngest members, Dr. Henders, stands up in protest. "We must appeal the dead president's decision to disband! It is not right to end all operations that we struggled so hard to attain!"

A man with a curled-up moustache, Dr. Rayland, smacks his hand on his desk. "The late president controls 51% of all decisions for the company! We can't fight a signed confession, affidavit, and declaration of disbandment! As strange as the timing is, we must honor the dead man's wishes!"

Larker dusts off his glasses with a rag. His wrinkly face drains of energy. The past 24 hours have not been kind to him since the late president's demise. He slides his spectacles back up his long, stout nose. "We can search for a motive with the time we have left, before the court orders for this building to be condemned. Everything's not lost. We must find evidence to suggest the confessions were not something planned by the president, at least not consciously. As tragic as his death may be, we still have a job to do. The clock is ticking, gentleman. I suggest we question our entire staff to see if they know any big leads."

Dr. Rayland shakes his head. "How can we prove that the former president didn't sign all three documents? The crew under my branch had nothing to do with this mess. There must be some outside source at work." Dr. Verner, who sits above Dr. Rayland, eyes him cautiously.

Larker smirks back. "That's what law enforcement will be here to find out. I have already reached out to the authorities, regarding this morning's unfortunate incident with the late President Malcolm Polingo. We have already agreed that the council will give full cooperation with their investigation. No one will be accused, without proper evidence from the DEO agents themselves."

Dr. Henders replies, "Do you think notifying the DEO agents is wise? They might bring a whole new mess, versus a more organized investigation on our part. We are allowed to self-regulate after all. It's our own facility, for goodness sake."

Vice President Larker wags his gavel. "When it comes to suicides and homicides, it's best to leave that work to the professionals. We will wait for the conclusion of the investigation, but at the same time, we will need to pack our equipment, per Polingo's written confession. Report anything suspicious or unusual activity going on around the facility. That is all I have for you today. Meeting adjourned, gentlemen."

Members rise to their feet and disperse from the chamber. Dr. Verner follows the crowd but abruptly turns a corner from out of the room, when someone catches his attention. He watches as Detective Jim Cazco and Detective Ike Brooks wander into the council chamber, after the rest of the members have filed out.

The two detectives stride up to the vice president's desk and reveal their badges. "Glad to see you've made it," Larker expresses gracefully, as he shakes Jim's hand.

"Thank you for seeing us on short notice. Where is the crime scene?" Jim asks.

Larker shakes Ike's hand before he ushers the two detectives to a hallway at the backend of the room. "Follow me."

Dr. Verner, who eavesdrops from the front entrance of the room, leans up close to the door. As the chamber becomes completely empty, he disappears down a flight of ascending stairs that lead out of the building.

***

The two detectives and the vice president enter a giant office down the stretch of a long hallway. Books have been thrown out of their shelves, clusters of torn papers pile up all over the floor, and broken chairs lean against the side walls. Jim peers out of the broken, oval-shaped window frames that appear behind the office desk. A trail of blood spills over the ledge.

Both detectives slide on pairs of gloves as they move about the room. Jim glances back at Vice President Larker. "He went through the window and landed onto the street below?"

Larker nods in regret. "Mr. Polingo was found at 6am this morning, right outside on the street corner. None of my workers were present to watch his fall."

Jim flips through the papers that lay on the dead man's desk. "Did he write these papers?"

A group of DEO Coroners enter the room to take pictures of the crime scene. "To my approximation, yes. I recognize Polingo's signatures and cursive penmanship," Larker confirms.

Jim swipes up another crumpled document. "You were close to the president, I take it. Was he a depressed man?"

Larker replies, "For the last 25 years, Malcolm has been a great friend and mentor to me. The man started this company to protect the world from pandemics, natural disasters, and insufferable diseases. He was a very outgoing man with a lot to live for. I doubt that an optimistic person can be depressed enough to take his own life."

Ike adds, "Sounds like a great man."

Jim shoos the DEO coroners away from the desk. "Depression is one thing. Did the president ever appear suicidal?"

Larker shakes his head dismissively. "I never suspected anything of that nature, sir. Nobody has. The man was very much about life. A suicide is the last thing I would predict."

Jim produces a plastic bag from his pocket and slides the crumpled document inside. He points at the office door. "As you can probably tell, there are no scratches or marks on that door. As messy as this room is, I'm surprised to see no forced points of entry or aggression taken out on the wooden frame."

Ike gazes at the door intently. His partner was right; no scratches.

Jim continues, "However, this latch here from the broken window behind me remains locked. It would make more sense for a suicidal man to first unlock the window and fall to his demise, rather than to simply burst through the glass. It's easier that way."

He pulls the gloves off his hands. "Do you have any idea why the president wanted to disband this whole organization? His suicide note doesn't give much of a motive to me."

Ike analyzes more loose papers on the desk, which include order forms and signed petitions.

Larker scratches his head. "To be honest, none of it makes sense. Two days ago, he spoke about developing a program to open more public junk yards. This morning, he confesses in a signed document that the company's main directive will never be accomplished. He then demands, without discussing with anyone else, that all public service must shut down immediately. Sounds fishy. It just doesn't add up."

Jim snatches up the declaration of disbandment document from the desk and reads it thoroughly. "I am with you, vice president. I don't believe a man has a sudden change of heart without discussing his intentions to those closest around him. This crime scene doesn't make full sense either, yet most of the evidence here does point to suicide. Something tells me at first glance that this crime scene was all carefully staged."

Larker nods his head in agreement.

Jim adds, "However, it's still a hunch. We obviously have more work to do. Is it alright if we look around the establishment?"

Vice President Larker smiles enthusiastically. "Please do. I expect your very best, sir."

Jim unlocks the window latch and steps onto the ledge. He crouches low and gazes out to the street down below. About five stories beneath the office window lies the remains of the president, splattered on top of a parked Silver Escalade V40. Jim rubs his fingers over a blue liquid caught on the glass shard fragments next to his foot. Larker walks up to the broken window frame and waits for the detective's next move.

Jim turns his attention back to the Vice President. "We will have to question your entire work force. I will ask you to give my partner Ike the name of all the individuals that work here in this building. Let them all know that they are subjected to testing." Larker responds eloquently, "As you wish, detective."

Jim jumps back into the room. "How much time can you buy before operations are fully shut down?"

Larker glances down at the revolver that sticks out of the detective's pocket. "If we're lucky, a couple weeks. The courts are already processing copies of the suicide note and declaration of disbandment that were submitted earlier today."

Jim replies, "It will probably be shorter than that."

Larker adds, "We can appeal those documents, which can delay the process of dissolution. But without proving a reasonable doubt that this wasn't suicide, we're only prolonging the inevitable."

Jim nods his head. "That will have to do for now."

After a closer inspection of the detective's face, Larker stumbles over his next couple words, "Say, have I...met you before, officer?"

Jim stops for a second, then smiles back. "I believe so. A long time ago, I had the honor of shaking your hand and President Polingo's hand. I applied for a job here." Larker squints in disbelief. "Really? In what department?"

The detective answers tenderly, "Genetic Microfiber Plant Restoration."

The vice president's eyes widen, while he grins in recognition. "Sounds a lot different from detective work. Anyways, I thought you looked familiar. What was your name again?"

Jim chuckles, then shakes Larker's hand once more. "Lead Detective Enforcement Officer Jim Cazco. That's some pretty good memory you got, vice president."

As Larker lets go of Jim's hand, he gives a sour look. "Oddly enough, that's not a name I remember. But then again, with my old age, it's hard to remember most people I run into."

Jim pats the vice president on the back. "All good, sir. Remember, don't let any of your employees leave town. I will have testing available for tomorrow."

Larker asks, "You think the murderer is still in our midst?"

The detective leads Larker out of the room. He lowers his voice and leans in closer. "This might take some time, but realize that justice is always our top priority. Due to protocol, we must assume that everyone is a suspect. Show me the body, and we'll go from there."

Larker nods his head, "Yes sir, Mr. Cazco. This way please." Ike follows close behind.

***

Wayne Smothers muscles through a crowd of DEO Coroners at the street corner, as he tries to photograph the dead body on top of the parked Escalade. The president's body lay stretched out on top of the hood, with both headlights cracked, and the windshield fully burst. Blood gushes from Polingo's neck as his open eyes gape out into empty space.

Wayne comes within inches of the pale face of the deceased man. The journalist quickly takes a couple pictures with his portable camera. Jim comes over to the side of the wreckage and pushes the reporter back. Jim points at Wayne with disgust. "Someone get this man out of here! This is a crime scene, after all!"

Two DEO Coroners pull Wayne aside and detain him over to the curve.

"Hey! I have rights too, you know! Get off me!" Smothers yells back.

Ike leans down and picks up an object that shines out of President Polingo's hand. He eyes it before he hands it to his partner. "Looks like a broken electrical sphere charger. These are not easy to find."

Jim eyes the sphere and feels around a dent to one of the edges. "Looks like it was used as a weapon. The same blue liquid on the ledge is still leftover onto this electrical sphere."

Ike smirks. "I smell foul play."

Jim says, "See if you can find a second one, they're usually more powerful with a polar opposite sphere." Ike nods as he places the evidence in a small plastic bag.

Jim pats his partner on the back. "You can take it from here, Ike. Let me know what else turns up." Jim gives a little parting salute before he slowly walks away.

Ike stands there flabbergasted. "Are you going somewhere?"

Jim smiles as he briefly turns around. "I'm going to head over to my favorite bar. My car is still in the shop for repairs, so I'll get some exercise by walking. Let me know if you find anything else here. I need to sit and think about this over a nice pint of beer."

His younger partner puts his hands on his hips skeptically. Jim raises his watch up to his mouth. "DEO Cazco ID Number 2091670. Request for Lie Detecting Fingerprints Board. Send to my address on file. ASAP. Thanks."

The detective takes off down the street. He walks by a condemned building that exudes a cloud of white smoke. The building sits in eerie silence with a sign that reads: Bolt Incorporated. A factory plant, that once mass-produced cyborgs, now lay deserted among outdated models of machinery. Robots and machines in the present day, however, are far more sophisticated than they once seemed.

***

The man with the blonde hair tied-up in a bun, who uses the name Dr. Verner, enters a phone booth a couple blocks away from Earth's Last Chance. He wipes water droplets from his forehead, as he glances around cautiously outside the window, to ensure he is alone. The man types a couple buttons on a small control panel that lay under a giant master computer screen. Lights flash, while the computer screen reads: Accessing incoming call. Lights on the ceiling grow dark.

A moment of silence fills the phone booth as static takes over the screen. Suddenly, the screen dissolves into an image of Nevo, as he grins back at the doctor. A dark voice takes over the booth, "Is the assignment completed?"

The blonde man takes a deep breath before he says, "The subject has been disposed of, master. However, the assignment hasn't reached completion."

The booming voice counters, "And why not?"

The blonde man gulps. "Detective Jim Cazco is here, investigating the suicide report."

The dark voice pauses briefly before it answers, "Yes, I know. Another assignment has already failed. But we can't control that. Your new task is to get rid of Jim and his partner. Make sure you see to it through the end. I will not tolerate failure."

The blonde man's head lowers. "He will be taken care of, master. I guarantee the new subject's termination."

His boss thunders back, "Good! After the DEO agents are dead, I want you to break into the Department of Personal Records and steal a document for me. A copy of the name on file will print out momentarily."

A scanning noise beeps below the screen. A long document spits out a few seconds later. The blonde man studies the document, before he returns his attention back to the screen. "It will be done, master."

Nevo gives a devious smile. "Good. We will start phase 2 of our operation, after both detectives have been properly disposed of. We'll call it: government solicitation. It's about time we wake up those wigs in the big chairs. And I know exactly how we will draw them out. Prepare yourself. I'll see you again soon."

A yellow tint inside the blonde man's pupil twinkles as he bows. "Very good, my master." The lights flash back on in the booth, while the image of Nevo dissolves from the screen.

Varra puffs on a cigarette from the same long gold-encasement in the corner of an abandoned lot at the other side of town. She watches as an unidentified man, with distinguishable brown gloves, parks a white van beside the stop.

She observes the man as he slowly steps out of the car. "You're late," she complains. The man pulls a chunky envelope out of his blue velvet jacket. He walks up to her and hands over the envelope discreetly. She slightly opens up the envelope, then smiles as she sees huge clumps of rolled-up dollar bills inside. Varra nods her head as she hides the envelope in her purple purse. "Take a walk with me."

The unidentified man follows her down the sidewalk as a couple kids dash by. Varra waits until the kids are out of earshot before she looks back at the man.

"Looks like your time is cut in half," she smiles. She flicks off the dying ash onto the concrete and continues, "The bomb isn't completed yet. A specific date hasn't been set in stone, but a target deadline should be coming within the next couple days."

She eyes him closely as the unidentified man stays quiet, close by her side. "You don't talk much. I like that." The man nods his head in agreement as he keeps his focus straight ahead of him.

Varra says firmly, "The incriminating files are now in our possession. Our plan is now officially at stage two. But all is subject to change. We will need access to your operating headquarters at some point. Just to check up on what you're doing now and then."

The man nods once more. She stops in her tracks and smirks at the man, "That's all I have for you today. See you next time. But don't forget to bring more cash."

The unidentified man nods for a final time and shakes her hand. He then turns to the opposite corner of the block and paces out of view.

9

An outdoor orange umbrella fills up with pockets of water above Jim's head. The detective crosses his legs at a patio table outside of Tony's Bar. He unfolds a blank newspaper from his lap. The date reads on the top right corner in green digital characters: January 24th, 2058. He stares at the empty space in the newspaper and says, "Natural Preserve Home Listings, please." A series of green letters materialize out of nowhere, and crawl their way down vertically like binary code. The digital words form a series of house listings, which include individual prices that rotate into the center of the page. Each housing entry circles back to the top of the page in an endless cycle.

Eva walks up to the doorway of the patio with a beer glass and a small water dish on a small black tray. She stops by a skinny pole right outside, where a dog with a collar sits chained to the post. The dog's soft eyes glance up to the waitress as she places the water dish next to his snout. She pets his head as he wags his tail energetically. "There you go, little guy. Hope that holds you over until your owner comes back." The dog graciously accepts the water from the dish and drinks down a few quick gulps.

Eva watches Jim closely as she enters the patio and stops by his table. She slides a coaster on the table and places a full glass of beer on top. "On the house, Mr. Roommate." She chuckles.

He raises the glass to thank her. "What are you looking at there?" she asks inquisitively. Jim smiles, while he tries to keep the paper close to his chest for privacy. "The life of a DEO can be a strenuous one. It's good to have a change of pace once in a while."

She smirks. "So something like entertainment pages of lovely attractive women?"

Jim answers, "Good thought, but no. That kind of time I don't have. My pleasure is more in a good taste variety."

Eva giggles as she glances down at the detective's digital newspaper incredulously. "Forest insulated homes? I thought those homes were for the rich. Never thought you were the type."

The detective grins right back. "Anyone who wants to transition to a more peaceful lifestyle is the type."

She nods her head in agreement. "Fair enough. But why look up those listings? Don't tell me they are for entertainment purposes?"

The detective takes a big sip of his beverage. His taste buds pulsate with satisfaction. "Like I said before, a DEO likes a good change of pace. Looking at different listings of forest insulated homes is soothing for me. It helps ease my stress. And for now, I'll stick with that."

Eva shakes her head in disbelief. "Suit yourself. Hope you get back to work at some point."

Jim jokingly straightens out his digitally-enhanced newspaper. "Don't count on it." Eva swiftly returns inside the bar, to take shelter from the cold air and rain outside.

Jim eyes the materializing images of each furnished house next to their respective listing. He runs his finger over the image of a beautiful house with a grandeur garden and sunflower patches stacked in several rows by the front porch. That would be a great place to escape to, he reckons.

Jim considered the idea of moving out to one of those green energy homes up north for quite some time now. It would give him the ability to live in tranquility, up in the rainforest. He could leave the blaring noises of the busy city life behind. The idea that he could savor the clean air, chirping birds, flourishing wildlife, and beautiful trees simply intrigued him. No more chasing bad guys, no more crime, and no more sleepless nights. There might even be a botany lab he could work at near the preserve.

He finishes off his Black Angus. Unbeknownst to Jim, his watch blinks with flashing red lights and reads: Lie Detecting Fingerprint Board Delivered. He produces a small notebook from his coat pocket, old and ripped through the many years of use. Jim writes down a couple words as he continues to read an article that catches his attention: a large dome-like house with a beautiful yard. Encompassing a large garden, the high-priced dome is seen pictured above a steep canyon in the countryside.

That would be a perfect fit for him. The detective jots down the contact information for inquiry.

Eva watches Jim discreetly behind the register, as she smirks at the sight of the detective at work. She allows her imagination to wander, as her sight becomes fixed on the detective. Something about his charisma had captivates her, but she does not know why. He has an intense presence, she reflects, but deep inside that crusty shell, lies something more soft and gentle. Eva sighs quietly to herself, as she contemplates if she will ever see that softer side of Jim.

***

As a new day beckons, the Earth's Last Chance corporate building sits in uncomfortable silence. Dark clouds form outside, with the threat of rainfall in pursuit. A line of corporate workers stand single file as they approach a dark room. The workers, who all wear the company's robe attire, look annoyed as they slowly inch up to a pair of dark yellow doors. Dr. Verner waits near the back of the line, unsure what lies beyond those doors. He twirls the small spheres in his hand once more, hidden under his sleeve. His eyes dart around intermittently, nerves creep in.

In the corner of his eye, Dr. Verner sees a figure lean against the wall, right outside the door. As he moves up in line, the blurry figure that focuses into view is Detective Ike Brooks. The young detective raises his wristwatch close to his mouth and mutters something quietly. The cunning doctor squints at the low beeps that resonate from the detective's wristwatch. Ike and Dr. Verner lock eyes with each other. Awkward tension brews between the two, as the doctor walks up to the doorway. Dr. Verner realizes that he will have to dispose of the young detective soon. If not, death will be the only welcoming vice to come his way. A moment later, the doctor vanishes inside the dark room, as he keeps the spheres tightly wound in his palm.

The dark room remains silent except for the vociferous footsteps of Verner's leather boots. A projected light can be seen farther down on the left side, as he enters a large room. A small group of DEO Coroners in their usual attire stand against the wall beside a large wooden table. On the table sits a large generator, which emits light, and a typewriter-looking device, with wires that spew out. Detective Jim Cazco sits by the table, as he writes notes in his ripped notebook. At the tip of the wires are adhesive, plastic covered sensors, similar to the ones Molly Fishburne wore at the Personal Records Control Tower.

Dr. Verner hides the spheres in his pocket, and places his hand on top of a chair across from the detective. "Why am I here?"

Jim glances up before he points at the chair with his pen. "Take a seat."

Two DEO Coroners pace over and pick up the long wires. They clamp the plastic covers to the doctor's fingers on each hand. They carefully stick each sensor around his fingertips so they won't fall off.

"What is this?" he asks nervously.

Jim opens up his notebook to a new page. "Standard procedure, doctor. I'm Detective Cazco. Please understand, we are just doing a routine polygraph test for all the employees. Just a couple questions. It won't take too long."

Dr. Verner nods his head reluctantly, while his eyes wander to the fingertip covers.

Jim starts his line of inquiry, "Identify your name, specific branch, and company ID code."

The doctor notices that the light on the generator centers its white iris around his pupils. "Dr. Lucius Verner. Waste dismissal branch. Code 2Q1ZD4."

Jim nods his head. "How long have you been with the company?"

Verner replies, "About two months now." The detective looks down at the lie-detecting fingerprint board. A lone steady needle shifts side-to-side, without much deviation. The needle has ink at the pointed end, that marks a line onto the polygraph paper. The paper rotates ever so slightly after certain intervals have passed. An empathy gauge below the graph reads neutral.

"There's not a lot of data of where you worked before," Jim replies.

Verner butts in, "Beforehand, I worked for a nonprofit company. Stow's Waste Prevention. You might not see a lot of information about my prior workplace experience, due to the fact that it isn't a government regulated program. They're out of business now."

Jim nods his head again. "And what do you specifically deal with in waste dismissal? Do you press a couple buttons, or do you simply just take out the trash by hand?"

Verner sardonically grins at the detective's condescending question. "Waste dismissal is a very important part of this facility. I create the online programs that troubleshoot sensors all throughout different trash compactors. Paper, plastic, aluminum, and glass must be sent to the correct canisters, before becoming compact and disintegrated. Leftover dust particles dissolve into the Earth's atmosphere, and that's the last we see of it."

The detective looks up to the doctor's face. "So all of these duties fill up your job?"

The doctor refutes back, "Of course, sir. Waste organization is my specialty."

Jim continues, "What was your working relationship with the late President Polingo like?"

Verner pauses as he glares at the DEO Coroners behind the detective. All of them hold blasters in their hands, as they judge the doctor intently. The doctor's smile remains unbroken. "The relationship was very solid. I always saw the former president as a mentor figure, even though we only worked together for a short time. He was a true visionary who will be greatly missed." The light generator begins to intensify its brightness around the doctor's eyes. A small yellow ring forms around his pupils. "Can we lower the lights? It's getting too heavy on my face."

Jim nods in compliance as he presses a button down on the generator. The iris on the table light lowers its beams just a touch. The detective resumes, "Tell me in a couple sentences what it was like growing up?"

Verner shrugs indifferently to the question. "It was kind of like most childhoods, I guess. Caring mother and father. I played sports and excelled at school."

Jim straightens out one of the wires that sticks out of the lie detector. "What does your family think of your work?"

Verner answers, "My family is all dead, sir." A moment of silence fills the room. Jim watches the pendulum on the needle stay at the same pace. The empathy gauge fails to deviate. "All of them?" Verner says nonchalantly, "My family's work was seen as obsolete in a demanding and ever-changing world. They lived prosperous for a while, but eventually, their luck ran out. That's the result of social progress, sir."

One of the DEO Coroners walks up to the detective and whispers something into his ear. The doctor squints his eyes, as the light generator sharpens its focus once more on his eyeballs. The intensity builds up fatigue and anxiety on Verner's face. "The light still feels a bit hot. Can you please dim it again?"

Jim nods his head as the DEO Coroner walks back to the wall. The detective presses a different button on the generator. "What is your goal at Earth's Last Chance?"

Verner's eyelids become heavy as his forehead sweats. "Goal? I strive to work."

Jim shakes his head. "Striving to work isn't a goal. What personal quota would you like to fulfill long term at this facility?"

Dr. Verner's hands fidget nervously. "The light is too bright! It's not easing up! I can't see properly!" The level of contempt boils wildly within the disgruntled man. If only he could kill the detective now. As Dr. Verner glances at the DEO Coroners across the room, he realizes his mission would be impossible to carry out at the present time. There would be too many witnesses.

Jim adjusts the iris to the light generator by a side knob to the bulb. He tightens the screws to make the iris almost completely shut. "My apologies, doctor. That should make it better. Just two more questions."

Dr. Verner grits his teeth. "And what would that be?" The detective catches a glimpse of the yellow glow in the doctor's eyes. Jim stares at the yellow ring with wonder. "Do you live for accomplishments? Or do you live simply to be happy?"

Dr. Verner chuckles in disbelief. Those were his last questions? The detective's face remains adamant, unmoving. Verner bites his lip back, as he tries hard to disguise his newfound distaste for the detective. "I live to tolerate, Mr. Lawman."

Jim nods his head slowly and closes his notebook. "That will be enough for today. Thank you for your cooperation." He gestures his hand toward the exit. "You can go now."

DEO Coroners peel off the plastic covers from the doctor's fingertips. Verner smirks. "Good bye." The doctor jumps to his feet and proceeds out of the room. Jim eyes the doctor as he disappears out the door.

Verner turns a corner of the building while Detective Brooks comes out of a different corner, and walks down the opposite side of the hallway. Ike raises his watch up to his mouth. "Equipment received for the blaster. Walking to the operating room now." He lowers his hand and strides down the length of the hallway.

***

Dr. Verner nervously paces back and forth in a back alleyway on the other side of the block. Rain starts to trickle down as he kicks a couple rocks by a nearby gate under an overpass freeway. He twiddles the electronic spheres endlessly around his palm. A run-down Volkswagen THX38 parks itself on the side of the road behind an overflowing gutter. Lights gleam off Verner's eyes as the vehicle's headlights fade.

A short, fat bearded man with a chain necklace walks out. He adjusts his leather jacket as Verner stands in the mud impatiently. "You're late," Verner mutters to the man.

The short, bearded man smirks. "Plans have changed. Boss is adding onto my assignment."

Verner shakes his head. "DEO's are now investigating the death of the president. They have been interrogating all of the workers."

The short, bearded man scratches his chin. "Crap, that puts a damper on things."

Verner holds up a memory card in his hand. "You'll have to take my data. I won't be able to finish the rest of my assignment alone. There is nothing else I can do right now, but sit and wait until the investigation is over."

The short, fat bearded man shakes his head wildly. "I'm not finishing your assignment. I've got a lot of work to do as it is. Do you know how much running around and bribing I had to do in the last couple days?"

The doctor tosses over the memory card. "The authorities can't find that data on me. If I leave my assignment now, the courts will eventually rule in favor of law enforcement for a homicide case. If a homicide case is proven, then the closing of the Earth's Last Chance doesn't happen. That means my whole operation for the last couple months was all for not!" The short, bearded man spits in the dirt. "I can't just wait in the shadows forever. There is no time left to waste. Muscle is supposed to be your expertise."

He throws back the memory card to the doctor. Verner's hand twitches uncontrollably with irritation. "The courts will make a decision by the end of the week, with overpowering evidence of a suicide. The president's office was left exactly in the state that it should be. I did everything right, with no slip-ups. Workers are already packing equipment out of the building as we speak. I just need a little more time. For now, keep the files. Add it to your own footage."

Verner throws the memory card back at the short, bearded man who chuckles. "You're all alike. I don't believe your story. You're just a lazy piece of trash. You can wipe out those detectives with your bare fists, yet you refuse to do so. It was wrong to trust you in the first place. You can't even handle two overrated agents."

Verner quickly turns around and snatches the short, bearded man. The doctor pins him to the gate. He squirms as Dr. Verner lifts him off the ground. "Stupid, insufficient man! Once my orders are complete, and the job ends, you will be rendered as useless. There will be no need to keep you around. Your end will come sooner than later."

Verner face plants the man into a pile of mud. The tubby thug struggles to wipe away gunk from his face. A revolver falls out of his jacket pocket. Verner picks up the gun and gazes up at the freeway overpass. He watches a pair of cars zip on by. The rain begins to fall down harder around them. "Fine! I'll take your stupid files," the short, bearded man submits. "Your time will come too, jerk!"

Verner snickers. "And by the hands of whom? Something tells me you might already know the answer to that question."

The short, bearded man lies in the mud, and stays silent for a brief moment. He gazes up to the doctor quizzically, "What are you talking about?"

Verner gazes up to the misty sky with an unworldly grin. "After our operation is over, I don't see much use for my expertise either. In my original assignment, I was supposed to terminate the man donning that beautiful fedora hat once his own assignment ended. I assume our master will probably honor me with the same fate. I don't know how your assignment is supposed to end, but I have a certain inclination."

The short, bearded man is eerily reticent and says nothing.

Verner smiles as he tosses the gun back to the short, bearded man. "I'll be ready if you do decide to come after me. But now is not the time for that." The short, bearded man glimpses at his colleague's rugged demeanor.

Verner's face curls into a cunning snarl. "Wait and see what I'll have in store for you, little man. Wait and see." Without another word, the doctor departs down the alley and back towards the Earth's Last Chance Corporate Building. The short, bearded man climbs upright, as he feels around the crease of the memory card in his hand. He clutches the chip and regrettably trudges away.

10

Several hours later, Doctor Verner wanders down the hallway of the Earth's Last Chance Corporate Building with a tattered envelope in his hand. He cautiously looks around the empty hallway and sees no sign of life. The doctor shuffles his footsteps quietly down the corridor. Raindrops fall expeditiously on the long window sills. Verner comes to an abrupt stop at the dead president's office. After he puts on two gloves, he pulls the door open. The crime scene appears unchanged, as blood and turned-over chairs paint the room. The doctor slowly slides a sharp object out of the envelope.

A dark voice beckons behind him, "Just couldn't stay away, huh?" Verner whips around to see a dark figure approach from the far side of the corridor.

Detective Jim Cazco hugs the lie detector fingerprints board close to his chest, as he meanders by a side pillar on his way to the office.

"Excuse me?" the doctor asks quizzically.

Jim grins back. "There was a broadcast by your boss that the building will be shut down until further notice. Didn't you hear the announcement?"

Verner smirks sardonically. "My mistake, officer. I guess I'll be leaving then." Dr. Verner slides the sharp object back in the envelope and folds the casing into his pocket.

Jim steps closer. "It's too bad that the president had to kick the bucket. With his absence, it appears that the whole company will fall in shambles."

Verner sighs unenthusiastically. "Yeah, it's too bad."

Jim interjects, "Say, there has been something bugging me."

Verner asks back, "And what would that be?"

Jim replies, "You don't look much like a doctor. In fact, you don't act the same way the others do at all. I notice your reactions are more sporadic and irregular, as if you were cut from a different line of cloth. Tell me, which factory made you?"

The doctor freezes. "I beg your pardon?"

The detective replies, "The cut-up job was very professional. Not much there to draw on, as far as a homicide is concerned. Having him personally sign a written confession and an affidavit was the true icing on the cake. The signatures register as positive matches to other written works analyzed from the deceased. I can only guess those signatures happened before the cut-up job took place. Polingo probably signed them out of fear for his own life, as if someone threatened him to do so. A suicidal man would be more likely to unlock his window before jumping off the ledge to his death. The dead man has cuts on his face, which doesn't match the material from the Escalade that he fell on top of."

Verner keeps still. "Cuts don't mean anything. How can you assign logic to a suicidal man?"

Jim answers, "That could be true. But the blue liquid found on the ledge and on the dead man's forehead had the same form of machinery grease. That type of grease will only be found in an artificial life form. It wouldn't make sense for a nature preservationist to hold onto machinery grease anyway."

Dr. Verner smirks. "Think you've found something important, have you?"

Jim adds, "It gives me a real kick when I see a crime scene drawn out so vividly. Unfortunately, minor slip-ups gave you away."

Verner lowers his hand deeper into his jacket pocket. "You got a colorful imagination, detective. You make so many deductions without concrete evidence."

Jim moves a couple steps closer. "You look like a new fluid model. I can almost not tell the difference anymore. Every detail is so well drawn out."

The doctor barks back, "I will not be belittled by mere accusations that will never stand in a court of law!"

The detective says gently, "Luckily for me, you gave yourself away when you took the lie detector test. When I asked other suspects questions, their emotions graph fluctuated unevenly during their tests. Everyone's graph should fluctuate to a whole range of emotions – that was the point of the test. This particular lie detector can not only detect moments of rage, but also mood swing patterns, anxiety levels, and apathy. This test is essentially done through reflexes of the hand and tonal shifts. Your emotional response flowed exactly the same and never fluctuated. Plus, the personal record I obtained yesterday for a Dr. Verner was never notarized, which means it's probably a fake. You're coming with me, whoever you are. Handcuffed to me or in a body bag. Your choice."

Verner clicks the two spheres together in his pocket. The long piece of string that connects the two orbs begins to glow. Suddenly, Verner pitches his leg out to the side. He leans forward, ready to pounce. "No detective, I don't think so. I can finally say this without worry. Eat dirt and die!"

The doctor pulls out the glowing electrical spheres, with the string attached, to reveal an electrically-charged sling bola. With a great thrust forward, Verner chucks the bola straight into the detective's path. The sling bola spins wildly in the air, as Jim raises the lie detector over his head. He uses the device as a shield.

The sling bola wraps tightly around the lie detector, as the impact of the electrical charges rip the device in half. Jim falls to the ground with the broken pieces of machinery scattered by his side. He guides his revolver out of his side holster and aims at the doctor. Bullets fly down the corridor. To dodge the gunfire, Verner jumps behind a nearby pillar.

Jim jumps up to his feet and runs over to a pair of double rotating doors in the testing center behind him. A sign above the room says: Botany Laboratory. He disappears behind the doors as Verner snaps his fingers. The sling bola flies smoothly, as if remote-controlled, back to the doctor's hand. After Verner combines all the strength that he can muster, he flings the electric sling through the barrier of the rotating doors. The electrical weapon travels past the doors and continues deep inside the testing center.

Doors fly off their hinges as the sling bola boomerangs its way down another strip hallway, which reveals a series of separate plant lab stations. The electric sling comes to a stop as it collides with a drawer somewhere near the far end of the hallway. He snaps his fingers again, to bring the weapon back to his hand.

Verner creeps down the lab stations with a mesmerized look on his face. The thick glass wall structure of the facility is lined with lab station after lab station down a long passageway. Bright green light bulbs are suspended from the ceiling, which illuminates every lab station. A broken pipe spews sewage on the far side next to a decontamination station. Petite desks with small computer screens occupy each station.

As Verner walks slowly down the aisle, he kicks out chairs and smaller plants that lie in his path. He searches endlessly through empty spaces between the lab stations, to hunt down the whereabouts of the resourceful detective.

Suddenly, the fire sprinklers activate above the lab stations. The doctor looks around nervously. He proceeds further down the alleyway quietly, while he tries to detect any sort of movement. Verner gets to the end of the hallway and reaches another pair of double doors. A sign reads above the doors: Magnetic Field Testing Room. The doctor takes a deep breath as he steps into the next room.

The doors reveal a processing room with a long conveyor belt that connects to a small assembly line. White tiles surround the sound-proof walls. A dark red circle is painted on the far back wall. Verner stands in place for a brief moment, unable to identify the detective's whereabouts. He groans impatiently. Without warning, a hefty metal plate detaches from the ceiling, then falls down at an impeccable speed, above the unsuspecting doctor. The plate lands with a loud bang upon impact, as it flattens the doctor to the floor. Jim lands awkwardly above the plate, then rolls off.

Once the detective catches his breath, he notices the metal plate bends in half. With insurmountable force, the metal plate launches over to a side wall, then crumples tiles by the wayside. Jim glances up in shock as he sees half of the doctor's face torn off from the plate's impact. A metallic cheek and a robotic red eye shines menacingly back at the detective. It is a cyborg, the detective confirms. Jim raises his gun and fires two shots at the android, with one of them grazing off the robot's shoulder. Unharmed, Dr. Verner swipes the gun out of Jim's hand. The robot then strikes a strong blow across Jim's face.

The detective flies backward and lands beside the small conveyor belt near the center of the room. He picks himself back up again, only to find the tenacious android glare right back in front of his face. The android reaches over the belt and picks up the bruised detective by the neck. He slams Jim's head on top of the belt. As blood gushes off his lips, the detective yelps out in pain. His vision becomes blurry. He kicks the androids legs out from under him, after which Verner falls hard onto the floor.

Jim clutches onto the cyborg's clothing, to take advantage by slugging him twice over the head. Upon impact with the metal physique of the android, the detective's knuckles bruise. Jim holds his right hand in pain as his adversary turns back around, unharmed.

The android spits out machine grease with a demented smile. "You'll have to do better than that!" Weaving together the last ounces of his energy, Jim prepares for one final strike. As he screams out brashly, the detective lunges into the cyborg. They both land onto the floor tiles. Jim slams the robot's metal head on the cracked tiles to slow him down.

This proves to be unsuccessful. Verner twists Jim's wrist around, which forces the detective to break his hold. As the cyborg whips around, it strikes Jim above the left eye. A black eye forms instantly. Verner hops back upward and grabs hold of the detective's neck. "Don't you see, detective? Your species isn't cut out for the new age. Now is the time for a being far more superior." Jim launches a swing but does not connect. The android jabs into the detective's gut and then clunks the officer right in the nose. Jim falls back onto the tile floor. Blood squirts from his nose.

The relentless android clasps his hands together with satisfaction. "Ha-ha! You might as well give up, DEO. You can't win."

Jim spits out blood and slowly crawls over to the big red circle to the back wall. Verner follows him mockingly and says, "Where are you going? Face your executioner like a man!"

Jim raises his watch up to his bloody lip. "Now...Ike," he utters softly. Verner raises his arms. "I'm going to enjoy killing you, detective."

The cyborg grabs the exhausted detective by the collar. Jim lies on his knees, motionless, as the android hovers over him. "Look at you," Verner taunts. "You couldn't even put up half a decent fight."

Jim wheezes out wildly as his watch flashes a red light. Verner adds, "As much as I enjoy administering torture, my orders were to end your misery. So, that means goodbye!"

Jim swings his neck forward toward his wristwatch. "Do it now, Ike!" he howls in one last gasp.

Suddenly, a magnetic force picks up the android off his feet and pins him against the dark red button on the back wall. Jim rolls away on the ground for safety. He stops behind the conveyor belt and protects his face with his arms in a fetal position. Verner tries to pull his body off the wall, but the force is too strong.

"What is...happening to me?!" the android cries out. He acts as if he is frozen into place on the wall.

With an unwelcoming surprise, the android gazes across the room to a pair of glass doors that slide open on the opposite side of the room. To his amazement, the doctor spots Detective Brooks with a blaster machine gun. A long crane-like apparatus with a long narrow nozzle wriggles its way out of the opening in the wall. Ike maneuvers the blaster's movement with a control panel tablet in his hands. He aims right at the cyborg, and zeroes in on the target.

Ike pulls down a pair of thrusters from the tablet as a ball of electrical charge mounds on the tip of the blaster. With one final blow, Ike smacks on an orange blinking button on the device and beckons, "Eat cement and die!"

Verner grits its metallic teeth together, "Eat what?" It was too late.

A huge electrical ray emanates from the blaster, which reduces the entire back wall to mere rubble. The force of the blast sends the android backward and slowly caves in parts of his protective barrier on his chest. Verner catapults through the crumbling wall and falls to the depths of the corporate dump down below. He lands outside in the toxic waste platform behind the Earth's Last Chance building, as layers of tiles pile around him. A large thump ripples the waste heap upon impact. Cement cinder blocks fall on top of the cyborg's ripped torso and on a pair of short stubs where his legs used to be.

Rain pours relentlessly down on the dump with mud and trash bags that lay close together around the implosion. The dump is quiet for a couple moments before a robotic hand shoots outward from the rubble. The android gasps as it attempts to heave its remains through the mush in a last-ditch effort to escape. The cyborg struggles to climb over the vast mountains of trash to evade capture.

All of a sudden, a gunshot rings out from behind him, and the robot abruptly halts. He gazes down at the ink that starts to spray out of his chest and into his robotic hands. Smoke puffs out of a large hole in his chest. He slowly slithers down on his back in pain.

Ike reloads his gun as he approaches the dying creature.

"Who are you working for?!" the young detective barks loudly.

The android's eyelids flutter as more ink spatters out. "Are you working for Nevo? Tell me! While you're still alive!" The robot's mouth moves, but no audible words come out.

Ike watches the red light on the robotic eye vanish as the cyborg's head slowly rolls backward. He watches in silence as rainwater washes away the ink that disgorges out of the android's chest. Verner's body lies motionless.

Thunderbolts dance along the dark sky. A group of DEO Coroners bolt pass the short, bearded man at a gate on the corner of the dump zone. He flares his nostrils. Being somewhat conflicted, the man feels anguish at the sight of the robot's demise.

The young detective walks back through the jungle of trash, as his head hangs low. He passes by the short, bearded man, and gives no notice. Gritting his teeth with contempt, his adversary stares out into empty space. Menacing eyes slowly rotate up to the threatening clouds in the sky. Rain pelts down unmercifully as the DEO Coroners recover the wreckage of the fallen android.

11

Half a week later, Ike scurries through the unrelenting rain and makes his way over to his BMW parked below an abandoned hangar. Car lights shine down the secluded roadway, amidst paper trash that mounts along the sidewalk. He climbs into the driver's seat, cautious not to spill the coffee cups he grasps tightly with both hands. Ike passes one of the coffee cups to Jim, who takes a quick sip in the passenger seat. The young detective pulls his door closed before more raindrops moisten the fabric of his nice suede seats.

His older partner sits calmly, as he converses with an image of a large bulky man who appears on Ike's Drexwell screen. The heavy-set man is well-groomed. He wears a dark suit, with a lavish golden ring on his pinky finger. A well-brushed goatee complements his roundish face. State Governor Rink Dermott sits calmly at his Japanese Garden, which is located deep within his marvelous estate. He sits on a wooden bench beside a series of bonsai trees that trail behind him, towards a small pond filled with elegant lily pads.

Jim reaches a couple fingers through his coat buttons and underneath his shirt, while he waits for the briefing. He painfully pulls off a bandage that sticks from his gut. A bruise still lingers on his stomach below his rib cage. It is a leftover parting gift from the gruesome fight with the android, only days before. His left eye remains slightly swollen with a black contusion. The knuckles on his right hand are held tightly wound with a protective wrap.

Ike takes out his notebook and a pen from a small cubby-hole inside the car door and places it on his lap. He takes small sips of his hot coffee, so as not to burn his tongue.

Dermott clasps his hands together with a deep breath. "Well, now that you're all here, we can finally get down to business. I will try to make this quick."

Jim nods his head. "Sure, what can you give us?"

The governor continues, "Last Tuesday, a defense grid had shut down at our naval base by the capital. The system was down for almost twenty minutes. Surprisingly, the backup system never went on. A report was later sent out to us for explanation. It states that the power plant, which wires the defense grid, was broken into sometime earlier in the morning."

After a sip, Jim replies, "Sounds pretty heavy duty."

Governor Rink adds, "The connector for the wrapping cables, which locks into the different servers of the grid, was sprayed with some yellow substance. Some flaccid sticky material. We still can't determine exactly what it is yet. An electronic timer was placed on the circuit breaker panel. A trip wire attached to the circuit breaker panel duped our online database into thinking that the power failure never occurred and that the break-in never transpired. The break-in was only discovered after the alarm signal from the timer was detected by a check-up frequency responder. That would be our boys up in the control tower."

Ike interrupts, "What kind of outside source could time a power outage before the authorities begin to notice?"

Dermott clears his throat. "We deduced that an experienced hacker got into the system. The same person must have physically broken into the control panel at the plant. They must have rewired all the data message sender cables and activated a small watch timer that can calculate enough time before detection. The new frequencies look almost identical to the originals, which makes it hard to recognize a switch had ever occurred."

Jim drinks the rest of his coffee before he answers. "Are you sure it's all one person? Wouldn't it be more plausible that an entire team of people orchestrated this whole thing?" The governor shakes his head. "We don't think so. A small hole in the gate with only one pair of footprints was discovered at the plant. Graffiti was sprayed on the side of the control panel with a name written in huge, murky letters."

"What was the name?" Jim asks.

The governor stammers, "A criminal that our department had unfortunate run-ins with before. He goes by the name Cullers."

Ike looks back in bewilderment. "Who's Cullers?"

Dermott replies, "Cullers is a notorious cyber-net hacker who has been on our most wanted list for quite some time now. His true identity has not been properly identified." An eerie silence falls inside the BMW. Both detective's look at each other with amazement.

Jim asks, "Beside power failure, was anything stolen?"

Dermott says grimly, "In deep regret, yes. Six classified files from my own computer went missing after the power went back on. There is no trace as to where the files ended up, but they are very important documents nonetheless. If they end up in the wrong hands, complete chaos could ensue."

Jim nods his head. "I understand. We will investigate this matter."

Dermott fiddles with his goatee before he answers, "Don't underestimate this criminal, detectives. He is both highly intelligent and awfully dangerous. I will print out a picture copy of the graffiti for your records as well as the images of the sticky substance. A pair of copies have already been sent to your employer."

"Perfect," Ike remarks. Two documents slide out of the Drexwell scanner below the video screen. "Thanks a lot, governor. We'll report what we can find as soon as we have it."

Dermott nods his head, "Best of luck, gentleman. Time will not be on your side. The hacker might leak out those files sooner than later. Best be on your toes."

"We will." Ike salutes. The video screen turns to static. Ike mutters, "Not a lot to go off of."

Jim eyes both documents. One document shows the yellow, plasma-like goo that covers the metallic clipping and the bundle of five different cables. Jim's mouth slowly creeks open, as he eyes the cables intently.

Ike leans in to take a peek himself. "What do you see?"

Jim points to the picture. "All these cables are not the same. Look here, one cable has metallic clipping independently versus the other four bound together. The other four look thicker."

Ike squints as he peers in closer. "So what does that mean?"

Jim leans back and folds the documents into his coat pocket. He rubs the itchy bruise on his eyelid gently. "It means someone left the wrong cable after they completed the job. They must have used different cables to trip the panel box." Jim points down the road. "I might know somebody that can help us. Take us over to Hanover Street and 3rd Ave."

Ike nods his head as he fastens his seat belt. "You got it." The BMW engine roars alive and zips off down the street.

***

Ike's BMW lands beside the curb a couple blocks away. A nearby electronic store with a lit-up sign reads: Eugene's Mainframe & Parts Shop. Computer monitors fill up the window displays for the outside public. A lit-up connecting arrow on the ground leads the detectives to the glass front door. Inside, a dwarf man sits on a lanky chair, as he connects different cables together by the register.

"Business looks slow for a change, Eugene," Jim says casually. He leans against a tall glass table, as Ike takes a seat on a smaller chair, opposite the store owner.

"Detective." The man's face tenses up in fear. "What a...pleasant surprise." Jim gazes down at the cables on the table, and realizes that they do not match the cables from the picture. "I'm here on official business."

The tiny man hops off the chair with a chuckle, then returns a finished wrapped internet cable to the table behind the register. "Always official business with you guys. What's the story this time?"

Jim butts in, "A top of the line hacker. Goes by the name of Cullers. I'm not really in the business, but your name came first to mind."

Eugene's eyes shift around cautiously, with his back turned to the two detectives. "I do not know that name."

Jim takes out a picture of the yellow goo that encompasses the bundle of cables. "But you do know someone who uses old hacking tactics."

Eugene twirls around and analyzes the picture. His fingers ripple onto the glass, contemplating nervously. He smirks. "What makes you think this is an old hacking job?"

Jim pulls out the other picture of the graffiti and hands it to the store owner. "Because most modern hackers don't physically visit the site of where the job will go down. Most of today's bunch like to use the comfort of their own home, without close proximity to link them to the crime. They either download a virus to attack the online system, or, for more reassurance, they can transfer their conscious mind into the digital net matrix and hack directly inside the mainframe."

The dwarf smiles as he hops back into his chair. “You mean a net diver. Those don’t pop-up a lot.”

Jim leans in closer. “Our culprit could very well be a net diver. As long as he has a head reader modifier connecting to a power source strong enough to transfer mind matter into virtual reality, it would work. But we don’t know that yet. What we do know is that the criminal showed up in the flesh on purpose.”

Eugene scratches his head lightly. “So this hacker is some sort of Neanderthal. Why would he show up there?”

Jim interjects, “He might be trying to make a statement. Maybe to ensure the grid shuts down longer without notice. Or maybe he wanted to permanently ruin those connecters on the cables to weaken the connection for a longer period of time.”

Ike smirks as he butts in, “Maybe he wants us to think that he’s a Neanderthal, while in reality, he is a net diver.”

The dwarf man grins as he squints up at Jim. “Who did you say was the employer?” Jim stares right back into Eugene’s eyes. “I didn’t.”

Eugene chuckles, impressed with the detective’s deductions. “Smart as a whip. You’ve haven’t changed one bit. Tell you what, I know a contact. He knows everything to do with power cables, especially older models that you would be interested in. He’ll be able to give you more answers.”

Jim replies, “Tell him I want to meet. Give me a number to contact.”

Eugene nods, “As you wish, detective.”

As the store owner scribbles on a notecard, Ike's eyes examine the various computer parts scattered along the walls: power cables, power strips, 10V batteries, memory cards, computer chips, and so on. Platforms along the wall list the variations in different price tags. It makes sense to him that this hacker used old tactics to obtain classified government files. But for what purpose? What were in the files themselves? Ike contemplates the possibilities as his face becomes lethargic. He gazes out at the rain droplets that glisten off the bright yellow store sign that hangs outside in the gloomy weather.

***

Hours later, Jim sits patiently alone with a newspaper in his lap at an outdoor food court. Rain pours outside the protective overhead that covers the picnic tables on the second floor of a lavish mall. The detective finishes off his scrumptious hot dog, then licks his fingers to clean off the condiment residue. He peels off the leftover bandage wrap around his knuckles and throws it out by a nearby trash bin. He stares at the small bumps on his knuckles, which look mostly healed. The unbearable stinging sensation finally leaves his hand.

The detective opens the newspaper with the date: February 1st, 2058. "Reveal headlines," Jim commands at the paper. Suggestions soon scroll onto the paper in a similar binary code format. He scans through different headlines in green digital letters but is unable to select a specific one. A person who wears torn Converse sneakers brings a fruity fragrance over to his table.

A high pitch voice bubbles in front of him. "You got a light, cutie pie?"

Jim turns over his paper to see Varra, filled with red face paint and pink hair tied back in two lengthy pigtails. He stares at her as if she was some sort of wild animal. "What did you say miss?"

She leans her face in closer towards him. "You got a light don't ya?"

Jim shakes his head. "Sorry kid, I don't."

He raises his newspaper back towards his face.

Varra giggles. "You got anything going on Friday night, cowboy?"

Jim exhales grudgingly, then ditches the newspaper back onto his lap. "Nope. I guess I'm just a boring person." She smiles sarcastically. "Well if you don't have plans, cowboy, you should come with me. There is a great club I know you'll love."

Jim sighs as he tries to guess the girl's age. It could range anywhere from a high schooler to a young adult. "A club's not the best place for me, kid. Maybe not for you either. Are you some kind of student or something like that?"

Her deceiving smile opens wider to reveal all her perfectly aligned teeth. "I'm a palm reader."

Jim leans in, half-interested. "Really?"

Varra nods her head. "That's right, cowboy. How about I read your palm? C'mon it will be fun."

Jim shakes his head. "Sorry kid, I'm not big on palm reading. No offense."

She sticks her hand out anyways. "No offense taken. I'm Melanie."

The detective looks down at her hand, hesitating for a couple moments, then looks right back at her playful expression. Unaware that she gave him a false name, Jim stands up to his feet and shakes her hand. "I'm Clay."

Varra smiles as she turns over the detective's hand, "Well, cowboy. Let's see what kind of man you are."

She feels the rough creases that mark the flesh of his right hand. She then glosses over the X-shape scar by his thumb before she turns his hand over to reveal his palm. Varra eyes his palm intently. "Interesting. You have the strength of a builder's hands. And with this formation here, you have the make-up of a genuine soul, a man who looks to do good."

She feels out the bumps and lines on his palm. "Intentions are good, but origins are an uncertain mystery. Jumbled, intertwined, and dark." Her eyes widen as she looks back into his eyes. "You have already lived the life of two men, both impulsive and mischievous."

He gives her a quizzical look as she points to the right side of his palm. She continues, "Look here! Wow, there is a third man!"

Jim asks back," Wait, what's a third man?"

Varra responds after a brief pause, "You have a vital choice to make. If you continue to choose the troubled combination of the first two lives, that is where you will remain. That will define your soul until the end of time."

The detective glares down at his hand, mystified. "What happens in the third life?"

She grins sweetly. "In the third life, you are a completely different man. New, youthful, and full of life. He chooses to be everything the other two were not. He learns to forget about his past and decides to focus on his future. Unfortunately, you can't be all three."

His eyes widen. "Can the third man be truly happy?"

Varra glimpses covertly at the gun in the detective's holster. "It all comes back down to choices, cowboy. Your third life has endless possibilities. However, you will have to fixate on a path that will presume your fate. Be open to all new ideas and new beginnings."

He grabs hold of her wrist tightly. "Does this third man work in law enforcement?"

Slight annoyance brushes by her face. "Let go of me please. You're hurting my arm."

He quickly releases her arm, not realizing his strength. "Sorry."

A twinkle shimmers in Varra's eye. "I can't tell you what your exact path is, but you will see it when the time comes. The crossroads of spiritual manifestation will leave you with nowhere left to hide. You do know what spiritual manifestation is, don't you, cowboy?"

Jim nods slowly as she massages out the rough tension brought onto her wrist. Her smile remains, despite the detective's persistence. She glosses over him suggestively. "You are cute...you look like you could be a lot of fun."

The detective grins. "Are you a real palm reader?" Varra nods instantly.

Jim chuckles. "That's an intriguing reading, miss. Do I owe you money for reading my palm?"

Varra's smile disappears. "This time I'll give you a discount, cowboy. You can go buy me a drink, and I know the best spot for it. How about you come with me?"

Jim hesitates as he looks at the young woman up and down. She looked stunning. However, he remembers what his mom once told him about meeting strange women like this. Dream deferred. He smirks. "I'll have to say no. Sorry, you seem like an interesting kid. Thanks for the advice."

She raises her eyebrows. "Not even one drink?"

Jim grows serious. She was tempting him; he knew it. Oh, how cruel and seductive women can be. "You got tenacity kid, I'll give you that. Unfortunately, I can't leave here. I'm supposed to be meeting someone at this very spot."

Varra asks unassumingly, "Who?"

Jim shrugs. "Just...a person. Doesn't really matter."

She jokes, "You are way too uptight, cowboy. There's a big party not far from here. Why don't you hang out there for a bit with me and come back later to find your friend? It will be a lot more fun than just waiting in the rain."

She winks at him as she runs a finger down the lining of his coat buttons. Jim gets an uneasy chill down his spine. She's trying really hard now. He grabs her hand and extends it away from his body. "I'm sure it would be fun. But my answer will still be no. Better luck next time." She shakes her head and laughs. "You are something else, cowboy. That's for sure."

The short, bearded man strides up to the table, pretending not to recognize Varra. He stares straight at the detective's face. "You the man I'm supposed to meet?" Jim glances over to the new addition to the table. "Are you Gable?" he asks swiftly. The man nods. "That is I. Sorry that I'm late. Hope that I'm not interrupting anything." The short, bearded man takes a glimpse of Varra from the other side of the table, giving her very little notice. Jim shakes his head. "No. Please take a seat. This young lady here was just leaving."

The detective shakes Varra's hand one last time. "Maybe next time kiddo. Go have a fun night without me."

She smiles. "You'll be missing out. See you around, cowboy."

Varra trots off down the walkway with a crowd to the stairs. Her smile evaporates in the cold, misty night. She snaps her head back and takes a glimpse of the two men before disappearing out of sight.

Jim shakes the hand of the man who calls himself Gable, before they both take a seat at the table. The detective reaches back into his coat pocket. "My contact says you're the man to see about hacking and identifying cables."

Gable nods his head. "That's what they tell me. Do you have something of interest?"

Jim pulls out a small envelope of cash and carefully slips it into the tubby man's hand. Gable takes a quick glance at the dollar bills before he hides the envelope in his own pocket.

The detective then slips over a picture of the graffiti art of Culler's name, as it glistens over the side of the government wiring panel. He hands him a picture of the goo substance around the power cables. "The hacker goes by the name of Cullers. Broke into a top-secret facility and stole classified information from my client. He's an expert in rewiring F2 extensions. I need your help to catch him."

Gable nods his head. "Cullers, huh? Sounds like a legit incriminator. It won't be easy to find this kind of scumbag."

Jim asks, "Where do you suggest I start?"

Gable hands the detective back both of the pictures. "Your man must be old school. The picture shows the rewiring of the power cables was done by bare hands. You can see fingerprints over all the wires. Most criminals either use pliers or administer gloves to hide their prints."

Jim eyes the picture thoroughly. "You're right. I do see handprints. Not very visible, I'm afraid."

Gable continues, "A lot of older hackers reroute extensions at the local library on Eighth Street. They usually work on the weekends."

Jim nods his head slowly. "You think Cullers works there?"

The short, bearded man simply shrugs. "That would be the first place I would go to in order to find out. The earliest I see them there would usually be around 8a.m. Saturday morning."

Jim slips the pictures back into his pocket. "I'll scope him out tomorrow then. Thanks for the tip. I might come back to you again if I need any more help."

Gable replies casually, "Whatever you need, my friend. Pleasure doing business with you."

Jim immediately checks his watch, as his eyebrows raise slightly, "I'll have to go. Supposed to meet up with someone at the train station."

Gable nods his head. "Union Station?"

The detective smiles as he stands up. He straightens out his coat. "Yeah pal, have to be there in the next twenty minutes. Hey, thanks again. So long."

Jim covers his head with the newspaper as he surges out of the safety of the food court overhead and into the boisterous rainstorm. Gable gives a little mocking salute as the detective disappears in the distance. His uneasy grin surfaces. "Good luck, cowboy."

12

Out on the hillside, a double-decker leveling platform decorates multiple layers of bricks on both sides of Union Station. Jim peeks around anxiously at platform number 4, as he waits for Eva's train to show up. He sees an old lady and a young boy pass by him on the platform, but otherwise, the platform lies deserted. Most of the trains that pass are empty. People just do not like to ride the train as much as they used to.

He stands under a golden sign, which specifies the heading of platform number 4, to avoid more abuse from the heavy rainfall. Jim sighs and kicks the side of a nearby trash can in annoyance. Why did he ask her out for a drink? Jim ends up on a dry bench in the middle of the platform. As he bundles up in his heavy wool coat, a slow shiver reverberates down his spine.

He peers slowly up at the unforgiving rain, as it cascades down into large puddles at the base of the muddy stairs, which lead to the platform's exit. Eva is definitely late. The train should have arrived ten minutes ago and she did not phone. Should he just leave?

Recently, the detective regretted becoming roommates with the waitress. He is happy that Eva is alive and well from the attack at her house. The assailant with the fedora hat has yet to be identified, even after that whole episode. Strangely, the last couple weeks were filled with mixed emotions. At times with her, he becomes distant. In other moments, he's enamored by her beauty.

He shakes his head vigorously at the thought of her slim figure, her long eyebrows, and her bright smile. Eva is a witness, he convinces himself. Jim should not have feelings for a woman already troubled with memory problems and strongly linked to this whole case. Next time she comes close to his face, he should pull back and act more professional. The detective should have set her up at a different lodging the same day that her house was torn apart. Oh well, Jim reflects. Here we are.

He accidentally drops the picture with Cullers' graffiti onto the wet concrete. Crap, there goes the evidence. To his surprise, a large hand reaches under the bench, scoops up the picture, and hands the document to the detective. "I think you dropped your picture, sir," a dark voice bellows. Jim graciously takes back the picture. The large man sits on a parallel bench behind the detective with his back hunched over.

Jim folds the moist picture back into the breast pocket. "Thanks pal."

The dark figure conceals his long arms inside a black trench coat, with his eyes on the platform stairwell. “What brings you to Union Station?”

Jim itches his head as he gives out a yawn. “I’m just like everybody else, man. Looking for a way out of this rain.”

The man in the trench coat smirks as he glances up at the murky sky. “I know exactly what you mean. So much rain takes over now. There’s hardly a stint of clear sunshine.” The detective nods his head slowly. “It comes down to people messing with the environment. The ozone layer collapses. Things like that happen.”

The stranger places a Trilby hat on his head. “Those same people can make this world a crummy place.”

Jim nods his head in agreement, with his eyes fixed on the empty platform. “All it takes is one bad apple. Unfortunately, they can be found just about everywhere.” An uneasy silence comes over the two men.

The man in the trench coat sighs gently in discontent. “All this...trash. People I see occupy every street corner and discreetly walk among the rest of us like unsuspecting parasites. Someday, the perfect storm will come, with all its glory. Hopefully, it will be enough rain to wipe out the disease and plague on every block. A rain to wash away machine waste, senseless crime, and the disgraceful stink that stains upon the roadways. Let the chaos wash down the drain to the steamy gutters with the rest of the darkness, to wipe away the putrid stench of disorder and corruption. Enough rain to engorge into a huge flood, to prepare this good Earth for cleansing. One can only hope that when the flood eventually dries up, sunshine and purity will make this place flourish once again."

Jim tilts his head slightly, somewhat surprised by such a descriptive response. He gets a glimpse of the stranger. "That's an interesting ideology."

The man in the trench coat stands up. He walks over to the trash can and throws out a piece of paper. "Sir, do you know if this train takes me to Maple Street?" The detective raises his eyebrows at the sight of the behemoth of a man, as he reveals his full size. Jim shakes his head in apprehension. "No pal. Maple Street is actually up the steps on platform number 1. It's just on the other side." He points at the nearby steps to the exit, as his queasy stomach rumbles. He notices a tattoo around the man's clavicle. It is an eye inside a pyramid insignia.

The stranger hides his face behind his hat. "Must've gotten bad directions then. Can you point it out to me directly? I'm afraid I respond poorly to most directions."

A nervous vibration comes from Jim's hands. He realizes the entire platform is empty, except for the two men. The detective stands up. "Yeah, follow me." Jim leads the tall brute off the platform and down the stairs. He steadily keeps one eye on the stranger.

Jim cautiously holds a hand by his belt as the two men stagger down the steps to the ground level. The detective stops by a lamp post and gazes up at the giant figure. The overhead lamp illuminates the sweat on the goliath's brow. The man pulls in his trench coat and tucks in his hat to hide his sinister face. Jim points to another pair of stairs. "Go up those stairs until you hit platform number 1. It's about a 20-minute ride to Maple Street."

A shine reflects off the huge man's teeth. "Much obliged, sir. It's good to run into people that actually know where they're going for a change." Jim squints at the man. "Have we met before?" The hulk's bright grey eyes reveal themselves in the dim light. "Maybe in the past lifetime, yes. Unfortunately, most of my memories fade after a while."

The detective slowly reaches for his gun. "Anything else I can do for you, mister?"

The big man grins. "Perhaps one more thing. Maybe you can tell me why a DEO agent waits around random train stops in the middle of the night." A lightning bolt dances over the dark sky. The detective grips onto the holster of his revolver. Both men stand in complete silence, as they stare at each other.

In one fell swoop, Jim whips out his revolver and points it at the behemoth. A giant metal hand clamps around the pistol's barrel. The detective's eyes widen as he looks up at the man in the trench coat. "Go ahead. Pull the trigger," the beast says daringly.

A litany of bullets burst out of the gun, and disappears into the assailant's large bionic palm. Jim gathers his strength to try and pry the gun free, but to no avail. With ease, the large man snatches the gun away and throws the weapon back up on the platform behind them.

A horn sounds off from an oncoming train that arrives at the platform, while the revolver skids by the bench. The revolver glides its way through the platform, until its stopped by a red dress shoe. A firm hand reaches for the gun and clutches around the handle.

Jim takes a swing at the giant but fails to connect. The big bully slaps the detective in both ears at the same time, which pierces his eardrum instantly. Jim falls straight to the ground in overwhelming pain. The ringing sensation almost paralyzes Jim. Blood drips from both ear canals. His head aches and throbs heavily. He squeals in agony.

The man in the trench coat picks up the detective by the collar and hoists him up to his feet. Jim struggles to stay conscious. "What...in the hell...are you?"

The giant figure chuckles. "I'm your worst nightmare. Mostly I'm built like a man, except for the arm. This prosthetic here is a result of necessary sacrifices. You probably know what I'm talking about. After all, I have you to thank."

Jim grits his teeth. "I have no idea what you're talking about!" He flings a fist out toward the hulking figure. The same claw-like hand catches Jim's punch with ease.

"On the contrary, Jim. I think you do know. We're not so different, you and I."

The detective glares at the man's sinister face with astonishment. "You know who I am?"

The big man grins. "I know much more than that." He lobs a blow firmly onto Jim's chin, which forces the detective to fall over to the wall beside to the stairs.

The hero bumps his head on a concrete cinder block, as the tall menace closes in. The large brute snatches Jim's tie. "We are wasting time." A gigantic metal fist surges through the air by Jim's head. The detective ducks the blow at the last second. The blow crushes a full cinder block from the wall into crumpled bits. The swelling grates Jim's ears, which makes his legs feel woozy and unable to operate fluidly.

He firmly clutches his earlobes as more blood seeps out. "What did you do to me?" As uncontrollable nausea takes over his system, his hands shake.

The giant folds both arms impatiently. "Beforehand, you served no use to me. However, as certain news comes to light, I might have a use for you before you die. Unfortunately, I'm running out of time. I have questions that need answers. You will give me the answers right now. Or else this is the end." Jim inches to the sidewalk like a helpless slug that waits for a large muddy foot to stomp it. Awkwardly, he moves a couple feet before a tight grip grabs his shoulder.

The detective screams out in distress. "Look pal! You got the wrong guy! I have no answers to give you." A firm hand suddenly grips the detective's ankle. With one hand, the giant hoists Jim's whole body upside down. The brute dangles him in the air like a helpless ragdoll. "Truth does not come from your mouth, detective. Whatever happened to the silver nitride fusion bomb?"

Jim forces his head up to get a clear view of his captor's face. "How do you know about that?"

The man in the trench coat shakes his head. "Jim, you're still not getting the game we're playing. You do not ask the questions! All I want to hear is answers! If you don't give me answers, then you hold no future use to me!"

Jim pauses while he shifts his body weight side to side in the air, in the hopes the giant will lose his grip. However, it proves unsuccessful.

The detective's body turns numb. Blood rushes to his troubled brain. "They are gone. Destroyed," Jim answers reluctantly. The large man peers into the detective's eyes. "How is that possible? Where did this happen?"

Jim's panting grows louder and louder. "They were buried. All of them. You won't be able to get to them now." A sharp grip constricts tightly around the detective's ankle. "I need full answers to every question! I'm through playing around! Give me the full details now! Or you die right here on the pavement."

At the end of his rope, Jim wheezes sluggishly. Life feels as if it leaves his body, as his vision blurs. Fate, it seems, does not come without a sense of irony.

A lone bullet rings off into the night as Jim falls straight onto his head. He lies motionless on the sidewalk, freed, as the large menace holds onto his bleeding hand. Jim's adversary roars with pain. A woman's scream follows, which echoes loudly into Jim's ears. The detective coughs blood out of his mouth as a large hazy figure runs off out of view. The sensation of piercing vibrations shift from Jim's ear canal and down to his feet. His whole body shakes out of control.

A smaller figure comes into Jim's view but remains fuzzy. He gazes at a pair of red dress shoes that come towards him. A shine from an object in the figure's hand catches his eye. After a few seconds, the blurriness of the object magnifies clearly into his vision and reveals the detective's revolver. He blinks his eyes repeatedly to clear his vision. The figure with smooth, manicured hands, grabs onto both sides of his face.

Jim squints his eyes to see a foggy image of Eva, which is a true blessing. She has come to rescue him, he realizes.

Jim attempts to smile in relief, but his face refuses to budge. He is glad to see her. Her mouth moves quite rapidly, but no sound leaves her lips. Law enforcement lights flicker in the distance, yet no sirens ring. His eyelids start to flutter and fall closed. He blacks out. The ringing fades from his ears, and all other sounds stop.

13

A slow and painful week later, Jim washes out the rest of the dried blood left over from the crevices of his tattered ears in the kitchen sink. The leftover swelling from a discolored contusion remains on his chin, while a gash lingers above his left eye. He gently caresses the circular bump on his chin, which puffs up like an inflated red balloon. Jim sighs as he reaches out his hand. "Towel, please."

Eva observes him with a concerned expression on her face, then places a new towel in his hand. She watches the troubled man cough out loudly, while also worrying about the after effects that wear severely on the poor detective's body. Eva feels strong sympathy for Jim. The brutal appearance of his battered face ruined the image of what she once thought was a prosperous job. For her, this new perspective placed law enforcement in a different light.

"I think you should see somebody about your ears," Eva remarks. As Jim pats his face, he takes little notice of her.

"What I need is somebody to get rid of this headache. It's been a week now, but it simply won't go away."

Eva's eyes turn glassy. "I hate to see you like this, Jim. The trauma has given you permanent damage." The detective lifts his head out of the sink. Now drying his soaked hair. "What do you think I should do? Stay cooped up in my home for the rest of my life?"

Eva folds her arms together in disapproval. "I don't think you should be in law enforcement. Look at you, the madness of it all is tearing you apart."

Jim drops the towel in a scrunched wet ball in the sink. "And give up on a career? In the middle of the investigation?"

Eva's eyes meet the floor. "It's hard to watch you get beaten to a pulp. Nothing is worth that. How many more fights do you think your body can take?"

Jim smacks his hand on the countertop. "I don't think you understand! This is my life! Picking fights and chasing down criminals is what I do! I don't know more than that!"

Eva chastises him, "So what happens when it destroys you? You are looking at cerebral brain damage and much worse. What good are you after that? That's all worth a small shiny medal you can keep locked up in some box in your room?"

He glares right back at her with contempt. "Not everything lasts, Eva. As you can tell, I'm not much of anything else. Just an officer that's abused by the system. That's how it always has been. I need to put all my efforts into apprehending that man, to take him off the streets before he inflicts more damage."

She stares deep into his eyes, as her mouth trembles. Eva inches closer to Jim's face. "No, I think you're made for something more. I don't see you as a vicious person. I believe there is a soft, caring person underneath that tough skin of yours. This doesn't have to be you. You always have a choice for a better life." His face hides his internal anger, which grows deep inside him. "More like what?"

She peers down to his beaten lips and touches the curves of his bruised chin. Tears build up in her eyes as she moves closer to his face. She could not hold back her feelings anymore. He was a simple law man that arrived at her bar out of all places. Originally, she did not care about him much. But as she learned more about Jim, he piqued her curiosity and compelled her in a way she had never felt before. There was no person like him. So much of his personality, resourcefulness, and essence gone to waste. She wanted the chaos to end.

The detective, stunned by her luring movements, remembers the conversation he had with himself at the Union Station platform: act professional, not sensual. He backs away from her advances. Emotionally invested to a fault, he decides that his job demands higher standards. "Once this case is over, you can find a new place. And I can finally be left alone. From there, you can go back to your happy little fantasy land. I choose to be with the action."

He slams his worn-out fist on the countertop. She backs away in fear, as she witnesses the detective's dark side. Without another word, Jim strides over to a long green couch in the living room and throws himself between the cushions. A tear trickles down Eva's face. She darts to her room and slams the door. He looks back at her door in immediate regret.

Silence takes over the living room as Jim sits by himself, lonely. He gazes around the spacious room. Portraits hang on the white walls of himself and other co-workers from the DEO branch. There is even a picture of himself and Chief Brahm, as they shook hands. He sighs and taps his fingers on a pillow on his lap.

Why did he have to do that? This is the same woman that risked her life to save him. She overcame her own fear of the large brute at the train stop and opened fire on his assailant. It was Eva who put forth all her efforts to the release of the poor detective from the villain's ferocious grip. Has she developed feelings for him? He delves deep within himself to find the answer. How could that be? He only knew her for a couple weeks. He worked most of the time. It seemed illogical that she swiftly became attached to him.

"Voice Power Control TV on. Channel 438," he commands to his large television set that sits a couple feet away. Through voice activation, blue lights turn on the flat screen, as it opens to a news channel.

A middle-aged woman, who wears a black business suit, smiles gracefully as she charms the television viewers. She rests two blue pills in the center of her palm, while she reads a cue card from behind the camera. "Take two capsules a day, and your sinus pain will fade away! It's that simple! If you order now, you will also receive a brochure that goes through a full breakdown of nutrients. Never take before swimming, and always, always, always, drink plenty of water. You won't regret it." The fakeness in her voice makes the detective's eye twitch.

Jim rubs his eyes. "TV, turn to channel 439." The television set turns the station to a commercial of a man in a gold suit with a long pink tie. The man points back to the screen with a big smile. "You too can get your memories processed the way you always wanted! Regardless, if you want to start over fresh or remove certain sections from memory, this is an opportunity for you! We do it all! Come on down to Memories Unlimited on 726 Bohr St. Our vision creators will get the job done, or your money back, guaranteed!"

Jim's eyes are glued to the image of the salesman. He sure hoped that the money is guaranteed back, or a lot of suckers will hit double whammies.

The eccentric man continues. "We have a special offer for you this month. Our magic telekinetic powder not only helps get rid of painful memories, it also offers a powerful stimulation to help clear stress that bottles up in your troubled consciousness. Trust me, there's nothing like a soothing frame of mind."

Jim ponders the thought. A clear head — maybe that is exactly what he needs. It could be worth a try. At the very least, he could treat an office visit like a therapeutic vacation from his own stress.

After a couple moments, he says, "Voice Power Control TV off." Voice activation forces the television set to immediately shut off. Jim grabs his wool coat from the top of the couch. "Voice Power Control, living room lights off," he orders. The room falls to darkness as he strolls pass the kitchen and down the narrow hallway to the front door.

***

Two terribly dressed men bicker amongst themselves, next to an abandoned store on a rainy street. The white paint from the wall has slowly deteriorated over time, which has led to the reddish sour appearance of worn-out bricks. They laugh with each other, unconcerned with the dismal environment around them. One man stops his prattling, as a dark figure slowly paces behind the two. He points out the figure to his friend, and the two split in different directions as the detective's silky boots stomp down the street in dejection. Jim roves down the cracked sidewalk, as he sulks deep within his thoughts.

The inner voice in his head comes back to haunt him. "Even though I walk through the darkest valley alone, I will fear no evil. My thoughts, my gun, and my persistent need to stay alive give me comfort. The pits of purgatory are dark and cold, which make it seem to go on forever. The stink that starts to grow more and more into the air makes me believe there is something more sinister that waits in the shadows. Eternal pain is at the end of the tunnel, with what I can guess is the hottest furnace I would ever encounter. Whatever Grim Reaper waits for my demise, I can only welcome him with open arms. This is the only world left for me now. But it will be great to have a better piece of mind before my whole world ends."

A pair of flashing lights gleam off the wet cement. Jim stops abruptly as he sees giant purple letters that spell out: Memories

Unlimited. A pair of large wooden doors stay open, as they lead to suffocating darkness inside. The detective saunters over to a nearby trashcan. He slips his revolver with the holster inside, then buries them under a torn newspaper he found in the mud. Jim stops behind the only two people in line. It is surprising to see such a short line, even at this time of night, he reckons. His heart rate climbs as nerves creep in. Is it a mistake? Will his visit do more bad than good?

The two strangers in line disappear through the wooden doors before him. Jim raises his arms as a security guard, dressed in an orange vest, checks his person for weapons. The security guard gives him a nod a moment later. The detective recedes into the darkness without the protection of his gun or his peace of mind. Dark green arrows emerge on the carpet floor, as they zigzag Jim down the pathway of the dimly lit building. Like a mouse trapped in a maze, Jim travels deep down a winding passageway, with no end in sight. Butterflies flow out from his stomach.

A pair of green arrows direct Jim into a large dark room. He stops briefly at the doorway before he enters. Dark portraits of pyramids and eyes fill up the walls with a fluorescent glow. A sturdy brown chair sits in the middle of the room with a series of short descending steps around it. "Welcome, sir. Please take a seat," a booming voice bellows. Jim staggers his way to the chair, and tries to locate the sound of the voice. "What is your full name?" the booming voice continues. Jim gulps and thinks up a quick lie as he takes a seat. "Jerry Gumble."

A tall figure with a dark cloak wrapped over his body creeps in from the far corner of the room. A mask with a long, curved wooden nose covers his face. A dark robe gives the greeter some sort of theatrical look. "What can I do for you, Jerry?" Jim stares at the wall while his head starts to feel heavy. He becomes suddenly mesmerized by a single portrait on the wall: a sailboat out at sea with a large eye on its sail. "Are you a vision creator?" he asks.

The man with the dark cloak claps on plastic encoding protectors over his fingertips and reflexes the sensors on each finger in the air. He glides over behind the detective, then looks him thoroughly up and down. "With the nature of the job, my real name will stay anonymous. But yes, I'm a vision creator. You may call me Vision if that makes you feel comfortable."

Jim nods his head delicately. "I need your help, Vision. I need you to change a memory."

Vision takes a closer look at Jim's stylish coat. "Are you law enforcement?"

The detective's palms become doused with sweat. "Of course not." The vision creator circles around and stops in front of the detective. "Are we doing a portion of your memory or a full memory sweep today?"

Jim shakes his head. "No, just one specific memory." Vision picks up a small stool off the ground, which blends in perfectly in the dark room. He pops a seat beside Jim. "One isolated memory change might be a tad more difficult. How vivid is the memory?"

Jim struggles to keep his head upright. "Too vivid to naturally forget."

Vision gleams right back with dark, beady eyes. He feels like the brain surgeon is looking straight into his soul. "You want the single incident buried deep in your subconscious?"

Jim beams back. "I want the whole memory gone forever. Deleted completely."

Vision sits quiet for a couple moments. "You better not be law enforcement. I don't work with those."

Jim immediately shakes his head. "I told you I'm not law enforcement. I'm a construction worker," he lies once more. Jim holds out a credit card, which Vision quickly swipes away to process for payment.

The vision creator points at a rag in front of Jim's chair. "Kneel." Jim rests down on both knees, hunched forward on the carpet. Vision guides Jim's head with his rubber glove, until he has the detective's eyes stop dead center to the wall. "Look at the sailboat picture in front of you, Jerry. Listen to every word I say as I walk you through a dream state of mind."

Jim nods slowly as his head feels like it will fall straight to the floor. The vision creator grabs the detective's hands, then shakes them until they go limp.

"Unfortunately, I won't be able to delete the individual memory permanently. Too risky, and it might take out other memories in the process, if it's done incorrectly. However, I can have your mind focus on a new memory that we will create together. How does that sound, Jerry?"

"Ok," Jim mutters, as he hears his voice ripple all the way down his throat. For some reason, he actually felt like everything would turn out okay.

The vision creator gets up from his stool, and paces over to a bowl of a blue sand material that lay against the back wall. He scoops up a handful of the substance and sprinkles it above the detective's face. The powder clouds around the detective's forehead and cheek bones. The vision creator then clumps a ball of the remaining powdery material and blows it all over the detective's face.

With gentle guidance, Vision arcs the detective's head slightly to the left. At a click of his fingers, the plastic encoding protectors start to glow. He lays a lone finger on the detective's temple. A chill spreads through Jim's body. Vision points once more to the picture of the sailboat. "Focus on the eye of the sailboat. It will take us on an amazing adventure to a distant land."

Jim's eyes gawk with fascination at the image. Vision continues, "The adventure we will focus on is a childhood memory. Something that brings you joy. You are now walking out of the harsh confines of this room and right into this new memory."

In a dream-like state of mind, Jim feels the walls of the room opens up to another dimension. The room turns completely dark. The persuasive vision creator closes Jim's eyelids. Jim notices sensor tabs on the fingers of Vision's left hand vibrate loudly. His body starts to loosen and feel like Jell-O. Vision's mouth leans close to Jim's ear. "You are walking through nothingness, until you stop short of an object on the ground. Tell me, what is the object?" A dark landscape enters into the detective's view.

Jim smiles. "I see a large tree."

Vision's voice continues. "Describe it to me in complete detail. What do you see on the tree?"

Jim pictures the dark landscape dissolving into a hillside, as he totters up to a large oak tree. "A large oak tree stands on top of a small hill. The leaves are missing, but the roots go deep underground. It is a huge tree...about 30 feet tall, I'd say. Wind blows tall grass around the hillside."

Vision asks, "What is the tree doing?"

Roots fly out of the ground and tie around Jim's feet. Jim answers, "The tree binds itself onto me with roots coming out of the ground. The tree is pulling me closer and closer to the base. White dandelions seeds float in the air all around me."

Vision's voice proceeds further, "Is anyone else there?"

Footsteps creep up the hill slowly behind the detective. They suddenly stop as Jim turns around. A woman smiles gently. "Hello, my son."

Tears form in Jim's eyes. "Momma is here."

Vision's voice asks back, "What is she doing, Jerry?"

Jim's smile widens. "She is kneeling a couple feet away. She's smiling at me."

Vision pauses abruptly before he continues, "Your mother is happy to see you. She is glad to receive your love and affection. Is anybody else there?"

Jim looks around to see his sister, Chloe, materialize. She kneels beside their mother, while she grabs her hand. His brother, Pretty Boy, follows suit as he appears on the other side of their mother. He takes hold of her other hand and kneels beside her. Big Daddy is the last one to appear and grabs onto Chloe's free hand. He walks behind the tree and kneels. Big Daddy grabs the other hand of Pretty Boy to complete a circular chain around the detective.

"My whole family is here. Kneeling and praying at the foot of the tree. They circle around me and the tree peacefully. My heart feels like a glowing star." The roots pull Jim closer to the tree. A bright yellow glow flashes in his chest. Jim's tears flow like a coursing river. He reaches out with all his might over to Momma, in fear that she will fade away. Momma nods her head and glides closer to the detective. The family firmly locks arms as they bind closer together around the tree.

"Momma, please don't go away! I'm sorry. Please bring me back. I take back all I've done. I didn't mean to hurt you. Bring me back to what everything was like before. And I swear, I won't let you down this time." Momma breaks the chain and caresses Jim's chin with her soft hands. She wipes the tears off his eyelashes, then takes a look at his face. "Before you go to the light, you must travel through darkness," she whispers.

In emotional euphoria, Jim feels his chest ache and his body tremble. Suddenly the roots pull Jim under the base of the tree, through layers and layers of endless dirt. Underground turns completely dark as the detective's body becomes numb. All he can see now are bubbles that float by his face, as the ground suddenly changes formation into liquid. It is as if he materialized in the depths of the ocean. He holds his breath, unsure where the dark abyss will take him. He feels dazed and confused, but at the same time, he feels complete.

Jim's eyes suddenly bolt open after their long sleep. A large grin freezes on his face, which seems to remain in place forever. Gaping endlessly at empty space, Jim gingerly stands to his feet. He feels weightless, as if he has no cares in the world.

"Hope for a better turnout," Vision exclaims as he appears beside the detective. He hands Jim back his credit card. The detective glides gracefully out of the room. How long had he been there? He had no idea. It felt like several days or weeks went by.

Next thing he knows, Jim walks outside on the sidewalk over to the trashcan. Remembering to retrieve his gun, Jim reaches inside the crumpled newspaper from within and pulls the gun and holster out from the muddy covering. He guides the revolver and holster back around his waist. In ecstasy, Jim feels like he walks steadily on soft clouds, and not a sound can be heard around him. His feet stroll down the path, with solid effort to stay upright. The rain stops suddenly. He commences the long adventure home with his mind stuck in a drug-like state of nirvana.

***

Feeling as if three lifetimes had passed by, Jim meanders slowly inside the kitchen of his own home. Yellow brick tiling encompasses the walls by the sink, with the slim, shut blinds above the faucet. The detective's big smile refuses to leave. His previous headache and the ringing from his ears cease. He glances over to Eva's room. No lights appear underneath.

Tomorrow he will make it up to her, Jim promises. She deserves to feel special and appreciated. He can give her that and more, if she allows him to do so. Eva's soul is tender. If only she understood how he had felt about her. He cannot sugarcoat it any longer. His life needs to include her, despite his rigorous work schedule. The waitress is his guardian angel now. He had to give her his faith and compassion, something that he neglected for years. It will happen. Tomorrow is a new day.

He staggers into his room and miraculously shuts the door. Kicking his wet shoes off through different parts of the room, he feels sleepy and ready for bed. He peels his shirt off like a banana peel, while he rests his gun holster on the rug beside the mattress. Then, finally, Jim lands ever so gently on his smooth sheets.

14

A sunny morning lights up a promising weekend as Eva emerges from her room. She rubs her eyes and yawns, groggy from a late night of partying. It was an adequate night of drinking, but alas, it did Eva little good. After she slipped out in the middle of the night, the waitress decided to have some fun at a nearby bar. Her happiness was short-lived. She did her best to feel alive while sadness and loneliness continued to eat her up inside.

The flagrant demeanor displayed by Jim the night before was not something Eva wasn't already accustomed to. In her late-night escapades, she had been looking for romance in all the wrong places. Too many abusive partners for her to count. One thing that worries her is the present living situation. Maybe if Eva could find her own place through the local home listings, then she could leave Jim and his wild behavior.

But obtaining the record file still weighed heavy on her mind. If she can stick it out a little while longer, then hopefully Jim can recover her file.

Jim sits at the kitchen table and sips a cup of coffee patiently. He reads an article in the daily newspaper. The date reads: February 9th, 2058. Eva jumps at the sight of the detective, as he quietly enjoys a nice cup of Joe. "You're here?" she asks, astonished. Usually, the detective would quickly grab breakfast and dash out the front door before she could even speak. That was his daily routine. Today seemed different.

"You look like you've seen a ghost. How about some coffee?" he replies lightheartedly. Eva sluggishly glides into a chair on the other side of the table. Slight tension fills the room, yet the negative energy quickly begins to change. He pours coffee in an empty cup in front of Eva.

She reluctantly picks up the mug and takes a sip. "Thank you...I thought you were pretty much always at work."

Jim keeps his eyes on the newspaper, as he reads a new article about a furniture sale. "Usually, yes."

She looks stunned. They both rest for a moment in silence.

"So what's new?" she says with a raised eyebrow.

Jim finishes the rest of his coffee as he focuses his attention back on Eva. "Earlier this morning, I got a message from the chief. He wants me to take the weekend off due to post-traumatic stress. He's worried about my wellbeing. You were right. It all went to my head."

She stares at him in disbelief. "But you're not off the case?"

Jim folds his paper and places it down on his lap gently. "No. After the case, I don't know what I'll do." Eva gazes at his calm demeanor. It does not add up.

Jim smiles earnestly as he makes direct eye contact with her. "I want to apologize for yelling at you last night. I was wrong. I should have never turned my aggression out on you. Instead, I should have thanked you for saving my life. I want to make it up to you."

She looks at him quizzically. "Make it up to me?"

Jim nods his head. "It depends on your plans for the rest of the weekend. Do you work?"

Eva pushes her bangs away from her face in surprise. "Well, um...I work tomorrow night. I might have plans for later today."

Jim nods his head gently. "That's all fine with me. What're your plans for the afternoon?"

Eva hesitates, "Sorry, what plans did you have in mind?"

The detective's smile widens, unlike what Eva has seen before. "I was wondering if you wanted to go with me to the fair today. It's supposed to be clear skies this weekend. So, I thought we might as well enjoy a rare sunny weekend outside before the rain returns."

Eva chuckles. "Like some kind of date?"

Jim shakes his head. "Heaven forbid. The last couple weeks have been quite stressful for the both of us. I think we could both use a paid visit to the fair and hangout for a while."

Eva slowly nods her head in agreement. "Fair enough. How would we get there? I thought your vehicle was still in the shop?"

Jim takes a silver key out of his pocket. "I picked up the car about an hour ago. The Bentley is as good as new."

She laughs. "Sounds like you pieced a plan together."

Jim sets down the keys on the table. "So, what do you say?"

Eva looks up into empty space in deep thought. After a brief moment, she locks her eyes back down to Jim. "Let's give it a whirl," she says wistfully.

***

Meanwhile, trouble brews in a dark housing complex on the other side of town. The short, bearded man leans over the kitchen table of a crap-infested apartment. A tattered couch emits a horrendous odor, and a broken television set lays scattered in pieces beside the front door. Four dead bodies, which belong to a handful of young thugs, decorate the landscape by the kitchen table. Blood flows from these corpses as the short, bearded man twists around the key of a mechanical device in the center of the table.

A loud knocking sound comes from the front door. The short, bearded man ignores the disturbance. Suddenly more knocks follow in rapid succession. Detective Brooks' voice booms on the other side of the front door. "Open up! Law enforcement!"

The series of non-stop knocking evolves into loud, persistent kicking. Sweat drenches the short, bearded man's face as he realizes that he is pressed for time. A beep rings on the device, as he changes the clock setting on a small attached monitor to three minutes. The short, bearded man carefully places the monitor into a small silver box, then tucks the wires under the monitor. He cautiously plants in two screws on both sides to hold the whole box in place. The short, bearded man then slides a pair of old batteries into the toaster next to the electric stove and firmly thrusts down the toasting knobs.

Broken wood bursts into the apartment as the front door collapses off its hinges. Detective Brooks raises his gun as he slides through the shattered doorway. "DEO! Don't move!"

The short, bearded man darts off into the bathroom in fear. Ike runs over to the kitchen table and stops abruptly at the ticking sound from the silver box. His eyes widen as he realizes a bomb has been planted for detonation.

"Oh no," his voice quivers as he drops the gun on the table. He raises his wristwatch to his mouth. "Activate Phillips head screwdriver." A long screwdriver shank and Phillip's head slides out of the side of his wristwatch. With the Phillip's head, Ike unscrews the bolts from the bomb and peers into the sea of wires that spew out from under the monitor. Among the sea of wires is a series of six different colored wires entangled around each other. Seconds later, the bathroom window shatters.

The short, bearded man climbs out onto the ledge of the window sill, about six stories from the ground. The ledge itself lies narrowly close to a semi-enclosed metal-slit elevator shaft. In the pocket opening, small cracks of sunlight seep in.

With little time to react, he pulls out a small metal contraption and aims up near the dark rooftop of the building. With a click of a button, a cable flies out of the device and sticks with a long mechanical claw to the metal rooftop six stories above. He squeezes firmly onto the metal handle as the device slowly pulls him up to the top floor. The contraption would move faster if it did not have to carry all that dead weight.

***

Instantaneously, kids scream and adults clamor in the grassy knoll over at the entrance of the fairgrounds. A young Pilipino lady who wears a grey suit hands Jim two ticket stubs. "Here are your tickets, sir. I hope you two have a magical day."

Jim smiles. "Thanks, you too."

Eva and the detective stroll into the park and see numerous rides around them. Kids shout at a merry-go-round a couple feet away. Behind the merry-go-round lies a rollercoaster with an outer space theme. A huge line from the rollercoaster winds its way close to a small petting zoo. One colossal Ferris wheel lies in the background.

Jim and Eva stroll up to a games booth. She turns to him slowly. "Funny...I thought you were all work and no play?"

"I hardly think I do any concrete work at all actually. Ask my partner. He'll vouch for me," he jokes right back.

Eva snickers as they stride up to a ball throwing booth. A vendor waves a straw hat around. "Good day to you, folks! One dollar for three balls. Knock the bottles off the table to receive a prize! You interested?"

Jim smiles as he hands the merchant a dollar bill. "I just have to knock down the pyramid of bottles to get a prize?"

The merchant's fake smile glistens brightly. "That's right, sir. Remember, you only get three chances."

Eva smirks. "You got an arm?" Jim licks the roof of his mouth. "You kidding me? I was a baseball player at the academy." He throws his first pitch, but his aim flies off over to the left.

She laughs. "I guess the academy was running short of players."

Jim gives her a sarcastic look as he throws his second pitch. This time his throw flies too high, which misses the bottles by a good couple feet.

Eva glances back at the detective. "Oh, so close. I'm sure you make a great detective. But probably a lousy pitcher."

He stretches his arms all the way back. "Guess again." He rockets a ball right onto the table and knocks the bottles clean off.

The merchant claps enthusiastically. He hands Jim a little stuffed panda as a reward. "Congrats sir! Here is your prize."

The cunning detective smirks and hands the stuffed panda to Eva. "There's a lot that you don't know about me. But now you know I can throw."

Eva points to an object behind Jim. "I actually want that one." Jim whips around to see the object. His eyes grow big.

A couple of minutes later, Jim pulls a little wagon with a huge stuffed lion toy on top of it. "Let's put this in the car and come back," he says as he struggles to guide the gigantic stuffed animal through the long stretch of grass.

"Okay," she giggles.

Back at the broken-down apartment, Ike waves a fluorescent light from his watch into the bomb device. He gazes at a blue wire, then focuses onto a green wire, and then glances over to a purple wire. With the help of the fluorescent light, Ike sees a glow flow from both ends of the purple wire. That must be it, he reasons. With one quick yank, Ike pulls out the wire cautiously. The clock on the device stops at 1:04.

The young detective sighs. He then bolts over to the bathroom and peers out the window. He hears the cable retract above him. It appears that the culprit entered the top floor near the elevator shaft. He sees the short, bearded man rush over to a control box next to the shaft.

Ike climbs out to the ledge and watches the elevator pass by him all the way to the top. The fugitive takes out a flat head screwdriver and unscrews the bolts on the side of the shaft. Shifting from side-to-side, the shaft slowly slides the elevator off of its hinges. Ike climbs the side structure of the brick wall to the next story of the building. He switches his hands around cautiously as he ascends to the next floor.

Back in the 6th floor apartment, the knobs of the toaster pull up, as the time for toasting expires. The dead batteries that pop out spawn dangerous high bolt charges that bring them back to life. With too much charge, both batteries glow and shake with unstable pressure. An explosion soon emerges and wipes out the apartment flat.

***

An hour into their shenanigans at the fairgrounds, both Eva and Jim settle down at the food court. Eva licks cotton candy at a small circular table, while Jim finishes off his hamburger next to her. He licks off the ketchup residue on his sticky fingers.

"I'm sorry, I just can't believe it," she laughs.

He stretches out his arms and yawns.

The detective turns back to her. "It's the truth, I tell ya. I was part of the Boy Scouts. That is, until I chopped down a specific tree in the forest."

She snorts out loudly. "Was the tree important or something?"

Jim answers bitterly, "Actually, no it wasn't. Unfortunately, I didn't make sure that the coast was clear." Eva eyes him frivolously. "Did it land on something?" Jim replies softly, "I...maybe, accidentally crushed my Scoutmaster's car when the tree fell over."

She laughs hysterically at the detective's admission. "A detective I can understand. But a troublemaking Boy Scout? You hardly look the type."

Jim leans back in his seat. "Looks aren't everything, sister. You stick around long enough, and you'll find me quite devious."

"Yeah right," she mocks. Jim quickly turns and points behind Eva. "Wow, I've never seen so many wigs on a clown before in all my life!"

She whips her head around rapidly. Surprisingly, Eva couldn't see anybody. "Where? I don't see a clown?" She turns back around to see Jim help himself to the rest of her cotton candy. She shakes her head. "Maybe you're a little bit devious. I'll give you that. I would still have to see more."

"Okay princess," he jokes.

Eva glances down at Jim's hand as it rests on the table. She squints down at the X-shape scar beside his thumb. "Where did you get that?"

Jim eyes revert down to his hand half-heartedly. "A memento from my childhood."

Eva gazes mystified back in Jim's face as she fails to understand. "Was that made with a blade?"

The detective shakes his head as repressed memories come to mind. "Actually, it was made in a fire accident. But now it just feels like another part of me."

She gives him another concerned look. "That sounds painful. How come you never used laser surgery to remove the wound?"

Jim smiles as he raises his hand close to Eva's face. "Because this scar has kept me humble after all these years. Whenever I face hard times, I look down at the scar and remind myself that I've been in tougher situations. It keeps me grounded."

Eva nods her head slowly, as she feels around his scar. The sharp creases in the wound felt deep in the skin, however, she could tell that the skin around it had healed. "Do you still have a fear of fire? I would still be traumatized if I was in your shoes."

Jim shakes his head once more. "As a kid, a cigarette dangled from my father's face, day in and day out. The smell of smoke and the bright light of ashes didn't bother me as much. I sort of just got used to it. But once in a while, the smell can really get to me. But I do my best not to give in to that type of fear."

She smiles as her eyes lock with his, sensing calmness and resolve. "Then you must be tougher than I thought."

He smirks, "I'm tough enough. But we can talk more later. How about you pick the next ride?"

About ten minutes later, they jump into a cart on the rollercoaster. Jim's eyelids rise as far back as humanly possible.

"Oh no!" he yells as the rollercoaster roars straight down a pair of steep tracks. Eva clings tightly around his waist as she screams with delight. The roller coaster whips around the corner upside down before it races back upward.

"Hold on, Jim! Here comes the good part!" Jim shakes his head vigorously. "The good part should not be when I throw up!" The rollercoaster hurls them back down the tracks again.

Eva follows Jim as they march over to a line for the Ferris wheel. Her magnetic eyes focus on him like when they first met. She feels more attracted to his laid-back presence than ever before. "How's your partner doing?" she asked.

Jim itches the back of his head. "You mean the kid? Ike can handle himself. I'm sure he's doing just fine."

***

Back at the other side of town once more, Ike holds on for dear life as he clings onto the small clay space between the aged bricks on the outside wall. An exploding inferno roars out below him. Ike miraculously arrives at the ledge of the 7th floor window as the elevator completely slides off the railing on the top floor. The detached elevator hurls down in free fall. Colliding with the brick wall, the impact of the elevator causes bricks to fly down below in rapid succession.

The short, bearded man watches the accelerating descent with a grin. Ike's eyes widen as he watches the elevator fly down towards him. He peers into the 7th floor window next to him and sees a little girl who clutches a teddy bear in a darkly lit room. She glares back at him, unaware of the chaos that brews on the other side of the wall. Panicking, Ike points his revolver to the window frame. The disjointed detective screams at the little girl, while he cautiously aims away from her and pleads, "Get out of the way!"

Ike blasts his gun through the window and watches the glass disintegrate instantly. The little girl shrieks as she ducks behind a bed next to the inner wall. Ike thrusts his body into the room and narrowly misses the elevator that passes him down the shaft.

The short, bearded man grinds his teeth in contempt and disappears into the stairwell. Ike gradually pulls himself upright and brushes dust away from his jacket. The girl materializes out from under her bed and sobs in fear. Ike checks the girl's face for scars.

"Are you ok?" The girl continues to cry her eyes out. Trying to console the poor child, Ike picks up her torn teddy bear from the floor and hands it to her. He pats her on the head. "You're ok, kid. Stay out of sight."

The little girl nods her head as Ike dashes out the front door of the 7th floor apartment. Gun drawn, the young detective disappears down the hallway. The little girl wraps herself up in a ball and hides her face in the teddy bear. She kneels down onto the floorboards with broken glass surrounding her.

***

Back at the fairgrounds, Jim and Eva make it to the front of the line of the Ferris wheel. They climb into a vacant passenger car as Jim closes the side hatch. They start to ascend gradually up in the air. Eva sits down on a comfy seat inside as Jim retrieves an object from his pocket. He pulls out a four-leaf clover with Eva's name on it as he takes a seat beside her.

Jim hands the memento to her as she gives him a weird look. "What's this?" she asks. Jim takes a deep breath. "An item left in your file, Eva. As promised, I took a look at your personal record."

She stares at him in amazement, her face giddy with pleasure. "Oh my gosh! And? What did it say?"

Jim peers into Eva's soft eyes and smiles. "Eva Ann Moore. Age 31. You grew up a couple towns east of here. You are from Italian and French descent, and you became fluent in both." Eva's eyes widen. "What did I do for a living?"

Jim's smile brightens. "You were right before. My records show that you were a highly respected veterinarian and serviced cats, dogs, chickens. You name it. You owned your own business, rented out your own property, and paid your taxes. It was noted that you were well respected for your commitment to your craft. You received a special plaque in honor of your hard work and dedication."

An uneasy smile comes over Eva's face. "But wait, why did I have my memory erased if I had so much going for me?"

Jim takes another deep breath. "The cause for your drastic decision was that of a broken heart. Someone close to you had passed away. The grief took over your work and your well-being." Eva's eyes turn glassy as she is unable to hold back her emotions.

"Was it someone in my family?" Jim slowly nods and watches her reaction. He rests his arm onto her shoulder for comfort.

"It's ok, Eva. I don't blame you for erasing all that grief away. There's not much more than that in your file. I'm sorry." A slight pause takes over the passenger car as Jim waits to see how Eva responds. She suddenly lunges into him with a giant hug. Eva buries her face in his chest. He holds on tight to her as she sobs her grief away. A genuine sense of happiness spurs into the detective. He is unsure when he has last felt that surreal feeling.

Jim pulls Eva off his chest. The tears melt her eyeliner and lead to a dark trail down to her pointy nose. He rubs her shoulders in comfort as she continues to whimper. "I'm sorry you had to go through that. We all go through tough times. Life can be cruel and unfair. But that doesn't mean you should give up on it. There are better days coming your way, Eva. I'm sure of it."

She wipes her tears away, and the soft whimpers disappear from her mouth. She looks deep into the detective's eyes as he brushes her hair back. After a brief moment, she becomes calm once more.

The Ferris wheel slowly starts to catapult their passenger car over the top of the wheel. "I knew meeting you was meant to be, Jim. Thank you for recovering my past. I appreciate it."

His eyes suddenly well up with tears. "No...thank you. Meeting you has changed my perception on life. You did save my life after all, so I think that our chance encounter was definitely meant to be."

She leans her head over to Jim's face. Grabbing on firmly to both sides of his ears, she kisses him firmly on the lips, much to his surprise. Their lips stay together for a couple seconds before they part. They both sit back side to side on the car as the Ferris wheel propels them to their descent. "I would like to find out more about the real Jim Cazco," she says kindly.

His cheeks become rosy. "I'd be fine with that. I would like to be around you more, too."

The passenger car halts abruptly as it ticks downward in small intervals. The two watch in amazement as their car shakes up and down. Eva giggles as she grips her arms tightly around his chest. "Looks like we're gonna go down fast. Hold on!" She closes her eyes and anticipates a quick drop like the roller coaster ride.

The moment suddenly freezes as Jim gazes straight out in shock, mystified. His inner voice comes back to him, "What is this feeling that is suddenly coming over my body? My brittle heart is not used to such a vibrant tempo. It reminds me of my childhood for some reason. Like all that suppressed love and affection came back to me just now. Is this love? Is this joy? Is this true happiness? Could it be an uplifting rebirth?"

Jim glances back at the face of a contented Eva, with her face frozen in time. From the out-of-body experience, he concludes, "If she can make me feel this way, then I want to find out as much as I possibly can about her. However long it lasts, I don't care. It's time well spent."

15

The following day continues to bring sunshine and a sudden heat wave to the gloomy outskirts of town. For once, the off-duty detective dons a red and blue striped polo shirt and a pair of cargo shorts. Eva dresses a little more upscale, in a beautiful bright red skirt and brand-new white tennis shoes. Jim and Eva stroll around the suburbs, further out from the smelly dump they call the big city. The suburbs were a lot more spacious, but mostly vacant, due to the fact that most people could not afford that luxury anymore. A surplus of decent paying jobs is not on the government's agenda anymore.

Jim and Eva hike up a hill and turn around the corner to arrive at a small store. The light display reads: Tom's Bike Shop.

"Do you see something you like?" Jim asks playfully.

Eva glosses over a full rack of bikes stacked outside the shop. She trails down the row and quickly pivots with excitement. "Look at that!"

Jim gazes at the bike that she points to at the far end, which makes his mouth drop in disbelief.

She pulls out a two-seated bike, in a gorgeous dark-reddish color with a beautiful silver basket in front of its handlebars.

"You got to be kidding me," he answers back.

She walks the double-seater over to him. "Let's get this one! You can impress me with your biking skills!"

He gives her an incredulous look. "Out of all these bikes, you really want this one?"

She corrects him, "No...we want this one."

Eva rings the bronze-looking bell on the front, which makes Jim snicker at the full get-up. She gives him a smoldering look. "Please?"

Jim's face wrinkles at the sight of the double-seater, not that it disgusts him, but he has concerns of the overall unmanly look. What would other people think? He then glimpses back up to the softness in her eyes, which begs him to buy the bike. Instead of shaking his head in a disapproving manner, which she would have originally accepted, he surprises her with a touching smile. He nods his head gracefully.

Minutes later, the twosome race down the hillside with their brand-new double-seater bike. Eva's bubbly amusement blares down the intervals of curbs at a frightening speed. She lifts her hands up in the air as she leans back in the front seat. Jim can feel the wind brush forcefully into two huge air pockets against his cheeks. "Slow down!" he shouts.

The bike thunders over the bumps and gradually evens out on the ground street level down below. "Ha-ha-ha...yes! Have you ever felt so much fun in your life before, Jim?" The detective's heart beats wildly. "Safe fun, yeah."

They pass by small old-fashioned houses on both sides of the street. "Thanks for a fun weekend. I appreciate it." She leans back with her head upside down and puckers her lips out. He gives her a quick kiss and barely holds onto the bike handles. "The honor is mine. I haven't had that much fun in a while." They ride gingerly down the sidewalk, as the last trickles of exhausted sunlight stretch across the valley. An unassuming moon climbs the horizon.

***

Ike peers at his watch patiently outside Jim's home. He waits outside the steps as the red double-seater bicycle winds its way to the front gate. Ike darts over. "Jim! I'm glad I ran into you!"

Jim jumps off the bike on their arrival at the stone path entrance. He gives his younger counterpart a great big hug. "Ike! Good to see ya pal!"

Ike looks uneasy. He had never seen such emotion pour out from his partner before. "Jim, I've tried to contact you. I have shocking news."

Eva walks the bike up to the two detectives as the front gate opens. Jim offers out his hand. "I've got news for you too, pal. Eva and I got a new bike."

She offers out her hand. "Hi, Detective Brooks."

The younger detective obliges. “Nice to see you again.” Jim opens the front door and ushers the other two inside. “Come on, kids. Let’s get some grub.”

Eva picks up the bike and carries it over to the living room, so as not to leave any mud on the floor. She parks the bike behind the couch. “Jim, I really can’t stay. I need to talk to you,” Ike replies. Jim picks up an envelope from the kitchen. “Sure pal, what do you want to talk about?”

Ike’s eyes shift around to Eva, then back to his partner. “I want to talk to you alone. Outside.”

Jim slowly nods his head, understanding the nature of his partner’s business. “Sure pal. I’ll be right back, Eva.”

Eva holds up her hand to her smooth lips and blows him a kiss. “I’ll be waiting for you.” The two men disappear outside in the mere twilight hours of the evening. Eva pulls off her sweat-shirt and walks over to Jim’s room. She shuts the door.

Jim and Ike stroll down the steps of the porch. The curve stone path leads to a side barrier of bricks, where the two detectives end up. Ike pulls out a cigarette and lights it. “Did you track down any leads?” Jim asks.

Ike pulls out a thumb drive and tosses it into Jim’s hands. “One noise complaint led me straight to the suspect. I think our hacker friend is caught in something big.”

Jim glances down at the drive. “For real? What’s in here?”

“Resignations. I found the drive at the suspects location after it blew up,” Ike replies. Jim turns to Ike with a surprised look.

“Resignations for what? For who?” Ike puffs out a small cloud of smoke. “Whoever this Cullers’ guy is...somehow he’s mixed in some extortion plot. He has stolen documents that contain the signatures of government officials on all the state territories. He is looking to forge all their signatures onto formal letters of resignation from office. I believe he is still presently in the process of forging those signatures."

Jim's smile dissolves into a frown. "How many letters of resignation are on file?"

Ike rubs his eyes, exhausted from a long weekend of tough detective work. "On that little drive, I'd say about eight of them."

Jim pauses for a moment. "He probably has a lot more stored somewhere else. Did you get a positive I.D. on this Cullers character?"

Ike answers, "Not a great look; he was always a few yards ahead of me. Unfortunately, he got away. I have him listed as a heavy-set man in his late 30's. Black hair brushed to the left side. Around 68 to 69 inches tall."

Jim nods his head and notices an odd similarity with his partner's description to the man he met at the food court. "Does the chief know about all this?"

The young detective shakes his head. "Only snippets from what I told him earlier. But he wants to see us first thing tomorrow. Those were the chief's orders he wanted me to relay to you personally."

Jim pauses momentarily and ponders the new predicament. He slowly nods as he takes out the envelope from his pocket. "That's good detective work, Ike. I'm proud of what you've done. You're coming along nicely."

Ike smiles lightly. "Well, I have to put in good work if I want to be the next Jim Cazco. I want to uncover this big case and take down a lot of bad guys. I've been waiting for this. Finally got my first crack at the big time."

Jim smirks as he shows the envelope. "I got one more thing for you today."

The young detective rolls his eyes and glances over at the money hidden in the envelope like before. "Again? Jim, you can't keep sending money like this. You have to go see them in person."

Jim glares down at the ground in disappointment. "I can't bear to show my face there, Ike. They won't recognize me anymore."

Ike shakes his head wildly in disapproval. "No, you're wrong. Last time I went, the lady wouldn't stop asking about how you were doing."

Jim's heart slows down. "Momma?"

Ike sighs gently. "She said her name was Chloe. Your Momma, Gladys, hardly says anything to me anymore. Used to say hi to me when I came to visit them, but now she mostly stays cooped up in her bedroom. From what I'm told, she hardly leaves the house now. I'm sorry, but for your sake, this time the answer is no. You have to make the trip yourself."

Jim stops in his tracks, stunned. Even though he does not like it, he knows his partner is right. No use hiding forever. Jim firmly wraps his hands around the envelope, while his eyes descend to the front steps in shame. "I understand, Ike. You're right. Thanks for filling me in." Ike watches Jim in his demoralizing sadness, shaken up with frustration. "You'll be better off. They're dying to see you again."

Jim sighs. "That's what I'm afraid of."

Without anything left to say, Ike walks over to the rusty front gate and unlatches the metal contraption to unlock the handle. As a parting gesture, Ike sends him a brief salute. "Good luck." Jim returns the salute right back, before he walks back up the steps. His body soon became engulfed within a full range of emotions, mostly tense and queasy. He walks through the front door as Ike disappears down the block.

The detective's home sits in utter silence. As Jim looks around the living room, he realizes that there is no trace of Eva. He then looks at her closed bedroom door. Could she have left to go somewhere else? He did not see her leave. He knocks on the door before he enters. "Eva? You there?" He peers inside the spare room. There are blankets clumped up in balls around the bed, but no Eva.

Jim contemplates where she might have gone before it hits him. Could it be she's still here? He cogitates this question over and over through his boggled mind. The detective then notices a red skirt dress that hangs on the inside of the door to his own bedroom, slightly left ajar. He tiptoes up to the door. "Come in!" a resonating voice beckons.

He opens the door to find Eva, as she lay on his bed with a blanket to cover herself. With the blanket cutting off at her shoulders, Jim realizes that she wears little else.

"Are you done talking to your friend?" she chuckles as he strolls to the front of the bed. He grins, with playful energy that returns to his face. "My work day, or the lack thereof, is all finished. Ike decided to go home."

She smiles. "Great, he seemed like a nice guy. It's nice to have a good friend as a partner."

He replies back, "You can say that again."

Eva smiles. "Then you can devote the rest of your night to me."

Butterflies unleash in Jim's stomach as he raises up an eyebrow. He quickly unbuttons his polo shirt. "Hmmm, I guess I can fit that in my busy schedule." He jumps on the bed and crawls on top of her.

"What did you have in mind?" She gives a little wink.

Soon, the smell of rose petals cover the bed, which is some leftover fragrance flowing off of the lovely Eva. As he grabs her face, he can feel her heart throb through her chest. A feeling that he did not think would happen to him ever again: love.

Her eyes twinkle at the sight of him. She kisses him and does not let go. He rolls over on his side and strips off his pants. He slides a lone finger up her naked thigh, to feel her soft, smooth, baby-like skin. She pulls the blankets over his body as he starts to kiss up her neck. Eva runs her own fingers through the blades of his hair. She smiles at him. He takes off his gun holster and tosses the strap to the floor. Their feet entangle, moving sporadically between the sheets. The room's light fades to black as a passionate night brings the two closer together.

***

Flights of ecstasy flow through the detective's mind as one of his most vivid memories comes back in a lovely dream. The smell of honeydew and dandelions fill the air. A Jetta MXR 91 drives up the inclined driveway to his adoptive family's house on a beautiful summer day. Fresh yellow paint embellishes the one-story house.

The Jetta is parked on top of the incline, a few feet away from a filled-up garage. Now an eighteen-year-old, the young detective jumps out of the passenger seat with his hair fully grown past his shoulders. He takes a diploma with him, which distinguishes him as top of his senior class at the academy.

Pretty Boy, now in his early twenties, decorates his knuckles with shiny rings, and a nice gold necklace that flows down his neck. He slams the driver's door shut and walks over to his brother. A cigarette slides into the older brother's mouth as he straightens his leather jacket. He is a young thug in the making.

Pretty Boy wraps his arm around the back of his brother's shoulder. "Congrats, Cottontail. I knew you could do it."

Cottontail's smile stretches across his face. "It's just the academy. It will be a whole different animal when I tackle college."

Pretty Boy snickers. "Cut the crap, man. You did something I could never do. Now I'll have to get used to everyone in the neighborhood calling me a plant lover's brother. Since you are trying to be a botanist and all."

Cottontail chuckles. "I'm sure they're worse things in life. I should be taking you with me." Smoke clouds by Pretty Boy's face. "C'mon kid, you know science books and plant labs isn't the place for me. I'll manage myself."

Party guests with small plastic hats and party horns hang out in the backyard of the family house. A skinny tree with thin branches sits in the background, as it sprouts its way to maturity. Chloe holds up a cake while Gladys holds up a delicious pecan pie. They place both items on a long white table on the fresh cut lawn. Gladys moves a couple chairs around. "Chloe, remember to save the table for three more chairs."

Chloe smiles as she watches her father stand by the back wooden fence, as he enjoys some sunflower seeds. Big Daddy waits patiently for the two young sleuths to show up. "I think we'll have enough chairs for everybody, Momma. I already got chairs for you, dad, and me."

Gladys straightens her apron. Cake frosting and barbecue sauce stains smear all over her front. Momma points to the chairs. "Make sure you also get a chair for Jim, Carl, Dennis, and Nathan. I think I heard a car approach in the driveway."

Chloe's eyes light up. "Wow, I didn't know they would be back so soon. Momma, is it alright if I sit next to Dennis?"

Gladys shrugs, "I'll leave that up to you." Chloe quickly slides the remaining chairs over to the table. Two of Pretty Boy's friends, young thugs themselves, wait silently by the family tree.

Cottontail and Pretty Boy stroll along the side of the house. A wooden fence trails down a long pathway of tomato plants and blooming sunflowers. The plants hide under the long shadow of the brick wall coming from the side of the house. A few clouds in the sky try to hide the blaring sun's rays, but to no avail. The nostalgia of summertime lies vividly in Cottontail's mind. Family and sunshine. What can be better than that?

Pretty Boy keeps his head down. "Where you're going, you don't need people like me."

Cottontail replies, "Of course I do."

Pretty Boy continues, "Hey, don't worry man. You'll be going places. Soon you'll have loads of cash and women hanging off your arms. You'll be living the life boy, no doubt about that. Just don't forget about your older brother. I could use a couple extra bucks myself."

Cottontail smirks. "Maybe I'll find jobs for all of us. They're saying that more opportunities are opening up than ever before. To work up north in the beautiful rainforests that remain perfectly intact, that is the place to be."

The two stop short of the wooden gate to the backyard. Pretty Boy looks up and glances softly into Cottontail's eyes. "Well, I can't do it for you. The next step forward is always on the other foot. Open the door and see what's inside."

Cottontail smiles, unsure what surprise lies just a couple feet away. The joy of starting a rewarding career occupies his mind. He slides the lock and opens the door. All of the sudden, family and friends jump out from behind the door. "Surprise! Happy graduation!"

Big Daddy, Chloe, and Gladys wrap their arms around Cottontail. They embrace him warmly together. Pretty Boy pats his adoptive brother's shoulder in congratulations. A look of true happiness takes over Cottontail's face, as it signifies one of the most cherished moments in his life. The crowd eventually disperses over to the table except for Chloe and Cottontail.

Chloe wraps her hands around the back of his neck firmly. "First family member to earn a high school diploma. Not bad."

He says back, "In another two years, you will be here too. I look forward to seeing your graduation."

She hoots sarcastically. "I think I'll hold my celebratory antics until I graduate with a doctorate degree from college."

He smiles. "I'll look forward to that day regardless."

Chloe kisses his cheek as he holds to her tightly. She then paces over to the long white table. Cottontail marches to the back door of the house, and makes his way into the kitchen.

He strolls over to the kitchen sink, as he unbuttons his collared shirt. The refrigerator door slams behind him as a lanky, young man with his hair greased back, materializes behind Cottontail. "You're Pretty Boys' brother, right?"

Cottontail eyes the young man who wears a black leather jacket and ripped jean pants. Must be another thug acquaintance, he reckons. "Yeah man, you must be one of Pretty Boys' friends."

Cottontail splashes water on his face in the sink. The young thug drinks straight from a new milk carton. He wipes off a perfectly-thick white moustache. "Pretty Boy tells me that you are into plants."

Cottontail dries his face with a towel. "Yeah, I plan to work with plant restoration."

The tall gentleman pulls a card from his pocket. "Do you work with cannabis plants?"

Cottontail quickly glances over. "Maybe, why?"

The tall man presents the graduate with his own personal business card. A golden frame encompasses a name that shines in big brown glittering letters. "I'm interested in the Cannabis Enhancement Glucose-C Gene Plants, a drug that keeps the user high while it allows proper functioning of all motor skills. A buddy of mine is looking to buy hybrid manufactured genes so he can incubate his own plants."

Cottontail takes the card, then analyzes it closely. "Cool name! So, you want the stimulus high from a regular cannabis plant blended with nutrients commonly found in the gene component Glucose-C?"

The tall, lanky man smiles. "Yeah, something like that. At least that's how it was described to me. Think of it as the best of both worlds. Real sugar is so much harder to come by these days. We can sell a true, natural controlled substance to brighten the user's mood, while they go about their regular everyday activities, as normal. It will heighten the buyer's performance. Does that sound like a great business venture or what?"

Cottontail shakes his head. "Whatever artificial code gene you create, the cannabis plant will most likely overpower any outside component. The thing with Tetrahydrocannabinol is that it doesn't want to co-exist or compete against any foreign gene from the plant. I doubt I can artificially blend any such code gene strong enough to interact with THC's chemical compounds. Probably no one else could create a successful gene either, if you ask me."

The tall sleuth nods his head. "Well, we are looking at all angles to develop this new hybrid drug. Tests come back negative for now, but we are making progress. If you're interested in helping us out, give me a call."

Cottontail slides the card into his pocket. "Thanks. I'll think about it, pal."

The tall man pats him on his shoulder. "You got it. Hey, congratulations again," he murmurs as he slithers out to the backyard.

What a snake, Cottontail realizes. Sounds like someone rehearsed him into that whole sales pitch.

He takes out the card and throws it into the trash bin. To create a stable functioning high, the graduate laughs upon reflection. It sounded like a stupid idea.

Gladys enters the kitchen with a smile and opens up the refrigerator. She quizzically grazes over the opened container of milk in the fridge, half-closed with milk that drips off the top. She quickly transitions to a carton of fresh orange juice behind the milk jug. "Doing alright, Momma?"

Gladys nods as she grabs the orange juice carton. "Just fine, son. How about splitting a drink with me?"

Cottontail replies, "Sure." She fills up two glasses. They both enjoy the cold orange juice together while they sit at the kitchen table. "They're all waiting out there for you, honey."

Cottontail nods his head. "Thanks, Momma. I'll head out." She throws out an arm to stop him. "Hold on just a second, son. I wanted to talk a little bit about college."

He gives her a weird look. "Uh, ok."

Gladys asks, "What do you plan to major in?"

He answers swiftly, "Microfiber Botany, Momma. Just like we discussed."

Her smile disappears. "I know. I've taken a look at those wages for people in that field, honey. A restoration scientist sounds like a fun job, but I don't think it will pay you very much in the long run." Cottontail pauses for a moment, unsure what she means. "It's still a new division. In time, there will be a much bigger need for restoration botanists. They have become more and more popular, Momma. Look at the numbers for the last couple years. It will pay eventually." Her eyes twinkle as she looks at the passion in her son's face.

She shakes her head in disapproval. "Sweetheart, time is what you don't have. Your preparation for the real world begins now. You need a more stable income."

Cottontail looks dejected. "So what am I supposed to do? Recall my major? My scholarship revolves around the botanist degree."

His Momma sighs quietly as she slowly slides a brochure out of her apron. She slides the paper into his hands, which jitters on top of the table. "I'm not saying for you to forgo your dreams, honey. I want you to keep an open mind. Think about other opportunities lying in wait for you."

Cottontail hunches over and grabs the brochure. "What other job did you have in mind?" He starts to read its contents.

"A law enforcement officer," she suggests.

He bursts out in laughter. "That's a good one! A law enforcement officer? Momma, you have to be kidding me."

She shakes her head. "The DEO organization has been out there for quite a while now. A lot longer than your restoration botanists. They pay double compared to lab scientists." His expression grows more serious.

He slaps the brochure on the table in disapproval. "You're asking me to just suddenly become a law officer? Our family has nothing to do with the justice system. Dad and Pretty Boy can attest to that."

His Momma places a hand gently onto his disgruntled face. "It's a chance for a better life, sweetie. You will need financial support when life's uncertainties come. I want to see you succeed and be happy."

He looks deep into her eyes. "I don't think I'll ever be happy in an officer's uniform. I'm made for something much bigger. I'd rather save the environment."

She places her other hand over his ear. "Honey, giving it a chance won't hurt. Major in your botanist degree, if that is what your heart desires. What I ask is for you to also look up officer programs at school. Maybe you can minor with a criminal justice degree at the same time."

Cottontail shakes his head. "Momma, that's way too hard."

She interjects, "So what? Life is hard. Before any of you kids came into our lives, your father and I had many rough times. I never fully approved of his lifestyle, but he always brought food to our table. We learned to persevere. And look at where we are now. That will be the hardest lesson life can teach you son. Life will throw you on the ground and bury you in the soil. With your will power, perseverance, and some luck, you must find a way to stand. Never give up. Survival is key."

He takes a deep breath. "What inspiration do I turn to for that?"

She smiles. "Honey, I can't give you that answer. The road that you, your brother, and your sister take will all be on your own. Just know that your mother and father loves you no matter what. Have faith in your own decisions. Let it be golden and just."

His glassy eyes look down to the table. Gladys gets up and kisses his forehead, "Do what you see fit. Whatever you decide my son, I will still love you." She slowly walks out of the room. Cottontail stares at the brochure with a look of disdain on his face. He dislikes the justice system, reviles the idea of fighting against crime, and loathes the idea of wearing the stinking uniform every day. He hates everything about them.

Cottontail paces over to the trash bin. Holding onto the brochure lightly in his hand, he hesitates a couple moments on what he should do. After a brief moment, the graduate decides to slide the brochure into his back pocket instead and strolls out the back door.

He looks around the backyard, where people converse and laugh amongst themselves, in a display of life and happiness. Big Daddy coughs into a red handkerchief, rather loudly, over by the family tree.

Cottontail strides up next to him. "You okay, Dad?" Big Daddy turns around and shakes his head. "It's those darn lungs again. They don't work the way they used to."

As Cottontail studies the blood on the handkerchief, he becomes concerned. "We need to take you to the hospital, Dad. You don't look so good."

Big Daddy takes a couple deep breaths, then waves his son off. "Nonsense. They'll tell me the same thing as before. I'd rather take my pills and hopefully ease my pain. My doctor told me I'll be battling this bloody cough on and off."

Cottontail nods his head slowly. "Oh, I see."

Big Daddy turns his approach to a more emotional response. "Do a big favor for yourself, son."

"What's that?" Cottontail blurts out anxiously.

Big Daddy pauses with an awkward silence. "Don't get in the habit of smoking. Thrill of that magnitude doesn't last. Internal pain comes back to haunt you in the end."

The graduate nods as he understands his father's predicament. "Don't worry, Dad. I don't plan to. It's not really my thing."

Big Daddy nods as he places the handkerchief back into his pocket. He places both hands on the teenager's shoulders. His son gives him a questioning look.

A twinkle appears in Big Daddy's eyes, as his mood shifts to something that the adolescent rarely saw. "Through all the years of hard work and determination, you made it here. With more hard work and determination, there are bigger and better places to come. Now that we finally have a graduate in the family, I can truly say that I am proud of you, my son. I hope that it carries you to a long and successful career. Enjoy it while the adventures last."

Cottontail replies, "Thanks Dad."

Big Daddy continues, "At some point, we all have our calling for the next part of our lives. When that happens, my son, I hope you fly high, to more bright adventures in the sky. You have my love and my blessing. Keep that promising glow and never relinquish that shine."

Cottontail smiles affectionately. "I will."

His internal voice resonates as he stares at Big Daddy, "That was the only time that I can remember he said that he was proud of me. That he loved me for who I was. What was once the hard shell of a man, fell to a hollow inside. A heart beats. If I could relive a day a thousand times over, it would be this day and this moment. Finally getting the approval of Big Daddy was worthwhile, and I didn't need to be a thug to do it."

Cottontail embraces Big Daddy. "I won't let you down."

Big Daddy smiles and pats his son on the back. "That's my boy."

They both head over to their seats at the table. A light breeze brushes through the backyard. Thin branches on the family tree sway side-to-side in a peaceful dance. Cottontail gazes out at the leaves, mesmerized at how tall the apple tree had grown. It was still unable to produce succulent apples, but he believes sometime in the near future, the tree will mature with all the delicious apples he could choose from. For now, he waits.

Chloe takes a seat next to Cottontail at the table, with a brisk smile. "Would you like some cake? We have some carrot cake slices left."

"Sure I'll take a slice," Cottontail replies.

Pretty Boy strides over to the table, then sits across the table from his brother. "Hey man, what are your plans for later?"

Cottontail shakes his head. "Hangout here for a while, I guess."

Pretty Boy lights another cigarette. "After all this cools down, you should come with me. The boys and I want to take you somewhere. I want to introduce you to a new friend."

The younger brother asks curiously, "Where at?"

Pretty Boy grins. "You'll see."

As Chloe leans into their conversation, her eyes flash with anger at Pretty Boy. "He doesn't have to follow you to all your mishaps. He can do whatever he wants."

Pretty Boy gives her a sour look. “It really doesn’t concern you, bookworm. Don’t worry about it. Just hand me a slice of frosting.” He raises a small plate ungraciously.

Chloe squints as she cuts a small, badly cut piece and throws it on a plate. “Whatever you say, your highness.” The two eye each other with brewing tension.

Big Daddy pays no mind to his children, as they bicker among themselves. He starts to eat his food with ignorant bliss. Gladys and Pretty Boy’s friends joins them as well. The extended family converse, as they proceed with their dinner.

Cottontail leans back in his chair, as he daydreams of what he hopes to be his bright future. He fantasizes about himself years in the future, in a white lab coat, with a large pair of spectacles.

He leans on a clear glass frame of a plant enclosure in a science lab. Cottontail fits his arms through two holes in the glass, where a pair of large rubber gloves branch out inside the plant enclosure. He visualizes himself injecting a plant with a syringe with a genetic coding of Magnesium Potassium Nitrate through the gloves. It is a useful catalyst, the aspiring scientist hopes, that can help the plant produce more photosynthesis.

He injects parts of the gene through a syringe into a stem, while the rest of the liquid is transferred to the soil by the roots. Cottontail watches a new leaf start to grow out of the plant, in a sped-up reaction to the drug. The new leaf bloats into a ball before it blooms into a beautiful white flower.

Cottontail smiles as he brings one of his hands back out of the glove to wipe his brow. He then magnifies an enclosed heating lamp on the plant's stem. A sharp grin highlights his success. The room blurs and fades out of view.

16

Bright lights flicker wildly inside a run-down greenhouse, with a familiar sign displayed out front that reads: Protect Your Most Prized Possession, Mother Earth. In a dark-lit kitchen, near the back side of the hideout, Varra sits peacefully next to Nevo at a long black table. A thick bandage covers the brute's human hand from a gunshot wound previously inflicted at the train stop. With the bullet now extracted from his hand, Nevo's wound begins to heal.

Inside a dirty sink across from them, piles and piles of old fertilizer sit in one large clump. As raindrops seep through torn-up tiles from the ceiling, small puddles form under the table.

Varra smooches the devious fiend passionately, then caresses the bandage from the brute's hand. She cannot help but glare at his wound. "You shouldn't let that woman get the best of you."

Nevo grins. "Dumb luck, that's all she had. In any other situation, she would have posed as no serious threat. She must be connected with that DEO, but in what capacity, I'm not quite sure."

Varra snickers softly, then glides her hands up to rub the rigid edges of the giant's face. "Who cares? They're probably lovers. Hey listen, let me get rid of that tramp. I'll enjoy squeezing the life out of her."

Nevo smiles menacingly at her admission. "Thanks, but I'll handle her myself. I got a better job for you anyways, Varra." They kiss more intensely, unaware of the approaching figure who enters the room.

The short, bearded man steps into the room and drops a bag full of thumb drives on the table. Varra whips around to their visitor. A look of satisfaction appears on Nevo's face as he reaches for a bunch of clipped bills in his pocket. He tosses a handful of clips into his disciple's hands.

The short, bearded man eyes the money clips intently. "Ten more forged resignations to go, boss. I have master files of all those 'Fire Sale' documents in one large hard drive."

"Excellent," Nevo replies.

His henchman continues, "But I'm more worried about how things are shaping up with that officer around."

The devious fiend picks up one of the thumb drives and eyes it thoroughly. "The law man is just a minor thorn in our side. He will be dealt with in time."

The short, bearded man pulls out a picture and slides it over to his employer. "Maybe sooner rather than later." The giant's metallic claw picks up the photo in astonishment.

A freshly printed picture shows Ike and Jim, as they talk outside of Jim's home. "I gave the young one the slip, but managed to attach a locater on his car, just in case. Turns out the young punk took me directly to his partner's residence. I followed him to a nice place on the other side of town. We can take him out now, once and for all," the short, bearded man sneers as he pounds his fist on the table with excitement.

Nevo's smile gently recedes as he looks at the blurred address at the top right hand corner of the picture. "Does he live alone?"

His disciple shakes his head. "I'm not sure. It's possible that someone else lives with him. I didn't see anybody else."

His boss shifts a quick glance to Varra. "No trace of a woman?"

The short, bearded man shrugs. "I'm just not sure."

A wide smirk appears on the sinister giant's face. "We won't make our attack just yet. Some formalities need to be met first. I won't examine these files until the rest of the forged resignations are completed."

The short, bearded man's face intensifies. "But boss, he ain't going anywhere. Take him out now, while it's easy and unsuspicious."

Nevo's shakes his head in disagreement. His haunting eyes travel back to his henchman. The unrelenting villain replies, "We can take him out with ease at any time. Taking him out now would blow the chance to uncover some important information that he only knows. Right now, he means more to me alive."

The short, bearded man slowly nods his head disdainfully. Nevo continues, "Don't forget, we are starting stage 3 of our master plan without the others: the stage of weaseling out the authority. We have the government officials on the run. Now we got to get them where it really hurts. They're our main target right now."

His disciple tightens both fists. He knows that Nevo's preaching of patience is the right way to go. Even if he did not like it, waiting is the correct course of action.

Varra stands up and kisses Nevo on the cheek. "It's time, babe. I'll have to pay a visit to our special friend." She grabs the thumb drive out of his hand before heading straight out of the door.

"See if we can get a copy before release," Nevo beckons on her way out. She gives a "thumbs up" sign above her head before she disappears down a dark hallway.

The short, bearded man places the money clips in his pocket. "What happens if that officer gets in our way again?" The menacing giant stares at the picture of the two detectives keenly.

"Don't worry about that. I've got a new task for you. Our law friend won't see it coming." He drops the picture, which slowly glides down to a puddle on the floor. The image fades as water droplets dribble down in rapid succession, which blot out the picture.

***

Varra walks briskly down the grade of a huge parking garage with her purple purse. Water drips off the sides of the structure as the rain pours down. She walks down the stretch of the empty fourth floor lot.

At the far end where the overhead lights become faint, Varra stops and turns around.

The same unidentified man with distinguishable brown gloves and stylish blue velvet jacket materializes out of the shadows of a handicap parking spot. She smiles and strolls over to greet him. He drops an envelope on the ground and kicks the package of dollar bills to her feet. She slowly raises its contents up to her face for proper inspection.

The man lights a cigarette and looks around both sides of the garage cautiously. There is not another soul in sight. Varra hides the envelope in her purse. "When will your work be finished?" she asks.

The dark figure pulls off a sticker from his pocket and attaches the paper to his wrist. He produces a pen out of a different pocket and scribbles a couple words down. The man hands it to her. It reads: I still need more information.

Varra gazes up to the man's face. "Which part?"

The dark figure scribbles another message on a new sticker and hands it to her, which reads: When will government officials acknowledge their resignation publicly?

She replies, "All the forged documents haven't been finished yet. Once they are, we fully expect those government officials to make a special announcement soon after. We just need a little more time." The dark figure takes out yet another sticker and fills it out. He hands it to her, and she reads it: We are running out of time — my employer wants to expose law enforcement and government corruption by the end of next week!

Varra shakes her head in dismay. "That is not what we agreed on. The timing has been a little bit off on our part, due to things we can't control. Tell your employer we need a couple extra weeks to mobilize the bomb."

The unidentified figure sighs as she hands him the thumb drive. Varra glances up sharply. "In good faith, we have brought you one of the forged signatures. That copy is for you to keep. The file you seek will be under the folder titled: Fire sale. All we ask is that your party to be ready when we get the OK. Oh, and also, we want to obtain a personal copy of your work before final submission to your employer."

The dark figure nods, as he pulls out his remaining sticker. He jots down one last comment. The man then shows her the message.

Varra smirks half-heartedly before she shakes her head in disagreement. "I don't believe that will be possible."

The dark figure shrugs as he slides his pen and sticker back into his pocket. He turns around and marches off to a shadow at the far end of the garage. The stranger disappears out of view. Varra roves down the driveway in the opposite direction.

The unidentified man watches her take off down the street from his hiding spot on the fifth floor of the parking garage. He pulls out a notebook from his pocket, then opens to a page with the top right corner bent inwards. He writes in the tiny booklet: Locate Bender Incorporated. He then stuffs the notebook back into his pocket and whisks away to the spiraling stairwell by the elevator. His shadow dissolves down the flight of stairs with him.

Detective Brooks pulls into a back alley near a science lab. The driveway sits very narrow, with a murky residue spattered all over the concrete. In large letters perched on a thick platform, the lab reads: Bender Incorporated. Jim rests patiently in the passenger seat of Ike's BMW. His partner parks the car quietly along the side gate. Jim looks up at a broken exhaust pipe that exudes smoke out of the back of the building. Both men pull out their revolvers as they climb out of the vehicle. The heroic duo make their way down the tight alleyway to the back of the building.

"So the reports are true? Three tons of silver nitride were pulled from this facility yesterday?" Ike asks. Jim nods his head. "So it appears. If we have time before the perpetrators come back for another shipment, let's set up a trap for them."

Ike's rotates his head cautiously. "Isn't it rather odd? A transporting vehicle big enough to pick up large quantities of silver nitride would probably have a hard time driving through such a narrow passageway. It has been reported that they have been here at least a couple times. I don't see how any commercialized truck could handle such an endeavor quickly."

Jim stops abruptly, with a quizzical look on his face. "You're right, Ike. Doesn't make a lot of sense at all. Be on your toes. Something unexpected might come our way." They continue to sneak down to a narrow loading dock at the back entrance.

The two officers eye a pair of huge dumpsters that sit close to a fiber cement wall. Food scraps lie squashed all over the pavement. Ike and Jim halt at the foot of the declining level dock, then glare at two similarly dressed men who stand by the back door. The gentlemen fiddle with the door handle.

Jim gapes surprisingly at the two familiar figures, then barks, "Yenwick and Hammer...what are you doing here?!" The two other detectives turn around quickly, surprised to see their coworkers gazing back at them. "We were about to ask you the same question! Don't you two have anything better to do?" Hammer replies.

Jim sighs. "Believe it or not, we do. We were called in by the Drexwell Security system. It reported the theft of explosive chemicals from a fugitive we were tracking down."

Yenwick laughs. "Funny, we got the same report." The four men slowly walk up to one another. Ike and Jim have no choice but to conceal their weapons.

Yenwick and Hammer are both in their early 30's. They wear checkered dress shirts with blue-orange color match schemes. Detective Hammer grins as he eyes Jim's striped tie. "The great, Jim Cazco. The most highly decorated DEO in history. Still wearing that terrible get-up?"

Jim shakes his head. "The red-yellow combo has a sentimental significance to me, Hammer. Just can it. There is some sort of mix up here."

Detective Yenwick glances at his watch. "Actually I disagree. We can use some cheerleaders to watch how real detective work is done. Maybe cut off the long sleeves, and you'll look more the part."

He turns to Ike. "Looks like they're taking the training wheels off you, rookie. You know you don't have to match your dead-beat partner. Appearance means everything in this department. It shows you mean business."

Ike snickers sardonically. “I’m not worried about the look. I’m worried about getting the job done.”

Jim interjects, “The kid learns well on the fly. Plus, he’s a better shot than you already, Yenwick.”

Yenwick chuckles. “I remember now why I got tired of seeing your face so much during training. The boring lectures never stop.”

Detective Hammer adds, “You should take a look at the field now. They’re hundreds of capable DEO’s out there. They don’t need an old bag that can’t learn new tricks. You should drop the has-been, rookie. I know a handful of others that are a better fit for you.”

Ike replies, “I enjoy what I got.”

Jim shakes his head as he looks at the door. “We can’t get cute with each other all day, fellas. Did Drexwell give you boys any directions?”

Hammer replies, “Not really. It just said to apprehend the trespassers if they show up. They might not return to the scene of the crime, but we plan to take a look inside the facility anyways.”

Yenwick walks over to the door and takes out his wristwatch. “Flammable light,” he commands into his compatible device. A red line of controlled heat emits from the side of the watch. He starts to melt the lock on the back door. “We’re gonna investigate inside. You guys can watch from the bench,” Hammer mocks before following his partner to the back door.

“Something doesn’t feel right,” Jim exclaims as he glares around the loading dock. “Come on, Jim. Let’s take a look inside and then get the hell out of here,” Ike remarks as he pulls his revolver back out. He heads toward the back door.

A toxic smell enters Jim's nostrils. It is a strong potent smell that could only mean one thing. The detective's eyes widen as he reaches his arm out suddenly. "No stop! Stay away from there!" Ike freezes in place.

The other two detectives successfully break off the bolt. Without warning, a huge explosion bursts through the door and into a huge ball of flames. Ike drops to his knees and covers his head a couple feet away. Jim swiftly pulls out his revolver and runs over to the blasted door. Dark smoke gives birth to a large, suffocating cloud down the dock.

Jim runs over to the body of Officer Hammer, who lies motionless on the ground. He lies on his stomach with his face hidden in the ashes. Jim crouches down and checks the pulse from Hammer's neck. A slow beat fades weakly between his fingertips. Jim flings his wristwatch to his face. "Officer Cazco to base! We need backup! Two officers down! Repeat, two officers down!" Hammer coughs smoke as he rotates over onto his back. His face is covered in charcoal dust. His senses slowly return to him.

Out of the blue, a bright yellow glare shines off the wet cement floor of the loading dock. Jim squints his eyes to see Dr. Mack Gordon, as he drives down the dock in a slender-looking motorcycle. He turns the bike around, to reveal a wide container tied behind the seat. Gordon releases a cork to allow oily spillage to flow down the driveway. Without hesitation, Jim opens fire at the motorcycle. A bullet shatters the protective glass near the handles. Another bullet glides off the exhaust pipe. Gordon takes out a couple of miniature blue crystal balls from his pocket. "Ike, stay down!" Jim yells as he pulls his coat off his back, to quickly shield his face.

Gordon chucks the crystals onto the spilled chemical liquid on the ground. A line of fire trickles down the loading dock, as it ends close by the back wall. Jim hovers his coat over his head as he dodges the line of fire that brushes passed him. Gordon turns around the motorcycle and zooms off the dock toward the corner of the building.

Jim throws his coat over Detective Hammer, while he hyperventilates in panic. He glances at the sea of fire around him. A nostalgic feel comes over him as he eyes the X-shape scar on his hand. His lips tighten up with conviction.

Jim turns around to his partner. “Ike! Get Yenwick outta here! I’ve got Hammer!” Ike stands up with his own jacket over his face. “You got it partner,” his younger counterpart answers.

Jim waves his arm around. “Lob me your car keys, Ike!” Ike underhand tosses the keys over the cascade of fire. Jim catches the keys and leads Hammer out of the loading dock.

Hammer falls back against the side gate, dazed from the smoke heating his face. He coughs uncontrollably and becomes dizzy. A blurry image reaches for his face. Jim clamps on a breathalyzer device to Hammer’s mouth, which circulates oxygen back into the impaired detective’s system. “You’ll be fine. Ike will come get you. Unfortunately, I’ll have to leave you now. Good luck.” Jim pats his fellow officer on the back, before he bolts toward Ike’s vehicle, parked further up the alleyway.

Jim slides into the vehicle and starts up the engine. “Drexwell command. Detective Jim Cazco override. Search for a two-wheel motorcyclist within a 5-mile radius." The pair of blue lights flutter on in the Drexwell box.

A female voice reverberates back, "One cyclist found. Auto control drive activated." The vehicle thunders down the alley before it takes a quick right turn back onto the main roadway. The car zooms down the street with its sights on a green motorcycle about 100 yards away.

The BMW weaves through traffic, then gains ground on the motorcycle. "Cazco to DEO Headquarters! Cazco to DEO Headquarters! Does anybody read me?" Jim says. Drexwell remains eerily silent. Jim smacks a couple knobs on the Drexwell box. "What's wrong with this machine? Can anybody here me?" Still, there is no reply. How can that be? Is there a radio malfunction? If that was so, the entire system would be shut down.

Jim raises his wristwatch by his face. "Chief do you read me? I think my Drexwell system is broken. I need back up at Bender's Incorporated building on 864 West Street." His watch beeps, but there is no reply. He slams on the steering wheel in frustration. "What in the hell is going on? Why doesn't anybody comply?!"

Ike's BMW comes within inches of the back tire of Gordon's motorcycle. The biped wobbles but remains upright on the road. Gordon looks back to see Jim through the side mirror. The detective grabs the steering wheel, then thrusts the gas pedal in full throttle as the two vehicles roar through the slower traffic. Jim opens the window and aims his gun to the motorcycle wheels. As bullets fly by the biped, they miss the tire by inches. Jim snaps the gun back to quickly reload. "I got you now, punk."

The box from the Drexwell system finally sputters on. To the detective's surprise, it is Eva's distressed voice. "Jim! Help! Please help me!"

Jim looks down. "What?! Eva?" Eva's voice quickly evaporates. "Wait Eva! Hello?" Jim's mind starts to swirl, as he demands an answer. Why is she on Drexwell? Is she really in danger? What the heck is going on?

The regular female voice registers back onto the Drexwell system. "Defense boosters activated." All of the sudden, the brakes lock up in the vehicle. The BMW skids erratically on the wet roadway, then spins out of control. The car collides into a side barrier and flips over. The motorcycle speeds away in the distance, unharmed.

Tires spin wildly as the BMW lies flat on its back. The entire street sits in silence for a couple moments. The driver's door window shatters. Jim crawls his way out. Wiping off blood from his forehead, he scans the roadway. He can't locate the motorcycle anywhere. It must have gotten away. An eerie feeling comes over Jim. There's a deeper plot brewing here.

A blue Volkswagen drives up to the light behind the road wreck. Jim points his gun as he steps in front of the vehicle. "Freeze!" Jim yells at the driver. A bald middle-aged man stomps on the breaks. The vehicle stops a couple feet away from the detective. "Get out of the car! DEO orders!" he screams frantically at the man. The bald civilian raises both of his hands and slowly climbs out of the vehicle.

"Your car is now under the use of law enforcement, sir! We appreciate your compliance. Have a good day," the detective mumbles as he slides into the driver's seat. He shuts the door loudly as the bald man bangs on to the driver's door.

"Hey wait! That's my car!" The bald man continues to shout as he watches the blue Volkswagen zip down the street and out of view.

17

About one hell-raiser hour later, Jim bolts down the shabby creaking staircase to the basement of the DEO's headquarters. Chief Brahm and Dr. Barrett, a corporate surgeon specialist, follows close behind him. The droopy-ear doctor carries a small black suitcase with him, per request of the wary detective.

The grain steel staircase ends at a dark hallway with leaking water on the bottom floor. Flashing lights glare from the detective's wristwatch and catch the glimmer of silver coating of freshly dried paint on the tunnel walls. Puddles of water splash as the rippling sound of feet echo down the corridor.

"What do you mean no contact?" the chief belts as he tries to keep up with the stout detective.

"Someone has corrupted the Drexwell system, chief. None of our communications are coming through. We're all stranded like sitting ducks," Jim beams back. He scans through the door headings listed on both sides of the wall. Brahm pants heavily, completely out of breath. The three are on the hunt for the department's control system generator. Carefully hidden behind one of the many sequential doors lies the database-powered Drexwell.

"Are you sure it's corrupted? Maybe there is a glitch, Jim. It happens from time to time. Maybe the system just needs a jump."

Jim quickly snaps back, irritated, "I'm absolutely sure! I just came back from my place. My girl is gone without a trace. Taken. Abducted."

Brahm recognizes the seriousness from Jim's face. "You think the hoodlum that took her is the same man we're tracking down in that Nevo case?"

Jim nods as Dr. Barrett walks over to the far corner of the hallway, then quickly glances at the words that dangle over each door. He stops at the last door on the right-hand side, then whips his head back around and waves at the others. "Hey, I found it!"

Smoke spews through the space underneath the door as Jim and Brahm scurry to the far end of the hallway. Dr. Barrett unlocks the door with a spare key in his hand. Water seeps into the dark room as the door swings open. "Blast! Where did all this smoke come from?" the chief asks.

"No idea, but we're going to find out," Jim answers.

As they peer inside the room, the trio can make out a dozen desks scattered around them. A couple of roll-back office chairs are clumped near a corner of the room. Dr. Barrett clamps on a lamp on one of the desks and illuminates the room.

To their surprise, the Drexwell central control generator slumps slightly forward in the middle of the room. Numerous wires flow out the bottom of the rectangular machine-like structure. In the middle of the large machine lies a pair of protective metallic doors to keep other debris away from the mainframe. The name DREXWELL is imprinted in huge black letters on the generator, which indicates the main controls of the whole DEO database system.

A pall of smoke emanates from a vent from the far side of the room. The toxic cloud fills the air. "What's that smell? It's making my eyes water," Brahm asks as he fans away the fumes. As Jim hunches over, he glares at the pipe configuration at the back side of the room. "Whoever has hacked into Drexwell must have also hacked into the heating ventilation, creating a burnt smell. Our unwanted guest wants to overflow the basement with toxic fumes, so we don't get a chance to access the central controls. Shutting them down will prove to be difficult. We should operate quickly."

With all of his might, Jim pries open both of the shielding doors to the generator. A circular core glows from a small ventilator, with wires and bolts that spring out. The detective proceeds to rip off the draggled sleeves of his burnt wool coat. With a snap of his fingers, he summons Dr. Barrett by his side. "Get going, Scottie. This looks like a tight one."

Dr. Barrett nods his head nervously. "Yes, Mr. Cazco." The doctor drops his suitcase on a wobbly desk and brings the nearest roll-back office chair right behind it.

"What do you think you're doing?" the chief bellows in confusion. Jim peels off his shirt to expose his bare chest. "Unfortunately, whatever mole that has hacked into our system is still there. The criminal is more than a mere hacker. He must be a net diver. They need to be weeded out immediately. Someone must dive inside the net and expel the unwanted guest. Scottie, get me a pen."

The doctor quickly pulls out a pen from his pocket and hands it to the detective. Afterwards, Dr. Barrett pulls out a whole list of items from his suitcase: long 209hermos-nuclear needles, a small keyboard, a tiny monitor, plastic wraps, circular membrane control pads, and a long roll of tape.

Brahm clutches onto Jim's shoulder. "Are you insane? A DEO agent has never dived directly into the net before! Let alone with a bunch of out-of-date biometric devices at his disposal. You need a proper lab setting for that. It can't be done."

Jim checks his pulse on his neck. "First time for everything." He also checks the pulse on his wrist and other vital organs. Jim draws large dots on different central nerve pressure points all over his body. The dots, as a point of reference, will be the points of entry for the sharp needles. "Improbable, but not impossible. If we can find a way to mimic the mind slip unconsciously to the digital net, we can possibly enter Drexwell and confront the hacker."

Dr. Barrett wipes sweat off the detective's forehead and places the circular membrane pads at different locations on his forehead. The doctor then tapes down Jim's arms, stomach, legs, and head back onto the chair. Jim ties a raggedy sleeve over his eyes. The doctor hooks up the needles swiftly.

Brahm pleads with Dr. Barrett, "Please doctor! Don't let him do this! If he doesn't hit the connection just right, there can be serious brain damage! Too much electrical shock can destroy his nervous system! He could even die!"

Dr. Barrett simply shrugs, "Detective's right, captain." He turns on his small screen monitor. Jim's heart rate and other vital signs appear in different color wavelength frequencies on the screen. "So far, your heart rate and blood pressure read normal, Jim. I'll prepare the wire feed from Drexwell momentarily."

Brahm starts to pull out brown strains from his thinning hair. He firmly grabs onto Jim's shoulder. "There's got to be another way! You're the best I got, please don't make a hasty decision."

Jim, blindfolded, calmly turns his head slightly towards the chief's voice. "It's the best chance we got. Do you have a better plan?"

Brahm's face turns sour as he lets go of the detective and takes a couple steps back. "I sure hope you know what you're doing," the chief mutters.

After all the wires are attached firmly onto the detective's body, Dr. Barrett grabs two long wires with large clamps by the generator. The doctor drags them over to the detective and opens the clamps slowly. "Ready, detective?" he asks gently.

Jim replies, "Ready as I'll ever be."

Dr. Barrett clamps the two ends onto the circular membrane pads on Jim's forehead. A huge bolt of electrical charge surges out of the Drexwell generator. The sparks of the surge flow down the long wires and penetrate straight into Jim's nervous system. The detective's body shakes out of control from the shock, as his teeth clench in pain. Cerebral light flashes through Jim's mind as he fades out of consciousness.

The electrical rush that moves through Jim's system suddenly stops. Jim feels his whole body become stuck. It's as if he is immersed into soil in all directions. Is he underground? Is the electrical surge transfer enough for him to mentally log into the digital net? In a claustrophobic panic, Jim speedily thrusts his arms around as he tries to dive himself out of the suffocating darkness. One of his arms suddenly breaks through the dirt and out into some free-flowing space.

The detective reaches around and grasps onto roots attached to some sort of tree. He quickly pulls himself up out of the ground, and spits up virtual dirt in the process. Jim drags his body out, while a thick coat of raindrops blinds him. He eventually frees himself out of the underground prison, then regurgitates more mentally-produced dirt. He sees bright green letters fall out of the digital, dark sky in a binary code. Jim finally realizes that he has successfully plugged himself into the net.

Jim stoops under a large digital willow tree. The tree itself rests on top of a steep hill that flows down to blank nothingness. The area around the tree seemed like a dark, never-ending abyss. White thunderbolts crash down above him from the digital sky. The surreal feeling flabbergasted the detective. He pictured that he would feel more weightless in a somewhat dream-like state. The irony of the truth was anything but that. He reaches out to the sea of green letter coding that flows down from the sky.

As if typing on an invisible keyboard, he inserts the following words into the empty space in front of him: Search Governor Dermott's data files. A different line of green letters fall straight down next to the detective. He grabs hold of the code and tightens his grip. "Take me there!" he commands at the digital circuits. The green binary coding disappears instantly. A large building materializes in front of him. A replication of the Sector 9 Government Building with Rink's office comes into full view. Moments later, a staircase emerges in front of Jim, to lead him to a straight path towards the fifth floor.

The fifth floor of the Sector 9 building lies dark and quiet, with no sign of life. A window on the far side shatters. The detective climbs through the broken window and lands firmly on the floor. He glares around the building's interior. Unfortunately, Jim is unsure which room belongs to the governor. He immediately scampers down the right hand-side corridor, then reads the names imprinted on the glass frame next to the large office rooms. The detective halts at the last room before the elevator, which reads: Governor Rink Dermott. With all his might, the detective kicks the door open. He peers cautiously around the room. It is vacant.

Jim jumps into the chair at the governor's desk. Luckily, he remembers a transcript he read previously on the governor's personal record file. "Access code:2095, password: Allegiant." Suddenly a green file appears on the screen. Jumbled words then pop out of the screen and float in midair in front of Jim's face. "Give me a list of all classified documents. I want the files set in alphabetical order."

A hundred green lines of document names float down in a long row in front of the detective. He seizes one file name with his bare hands and pulls it closer to his face. Jim soon discards the digital effect behind him. One by one, he tosses filename after filename behind his chair.

Where could the forgery file be? It had to be in there somewhere. The hacker probably created each false forgery on the net by now. Maybe the hacker already destroyed the document. Or maybe he has not finished the forgeries after all. Jim types in: forged documents. The reply to the other end left him in dismay, as he reads: file not found.

Back in the real world, Jim's body lies motionless on the chair. Brahm keeps his shirt over his nose as he brushes away fumes that cloud around Jim. "Hurry up, kid. We're running out of time here." Jim's eyelashes flutter as his mind stays plugged into the virtual reality.

Back inside the digital net, Jim bangs on the desk vigorously and grits his teeth. His frustration starts to boil over. The detective's eyes widen as a new idea grows in his head: if all the forgeries are already made by the hacker, then he would have to create his own fake document himself. Maybe that will draw the hacker out of his hiding place. Jim's hands go to work as a new file appears in front of him. He sets up his trap as fast as he can.

***

Back in the real world, Nevo drags Eva by the collar through the front entrance of a spooky graveyard. Rain soaks through her clothes like dissolving wet paper. How did she get stuck in all this mess? She contemplates endlessly to find an answer.

A pair of handcuffs binds her to her captor's metallic wrist. She cries for help, but the duct tape that covers her mouth prevents anyone else from hearing her plea.

A trail of mud forms behind her as Nevo pulls her up onto a small hill in the graveyard. Eva kicks and thrusts around in discontent. He stops abruptly at a lone tombstone and slaps the young woman profusely in the face. She falls over onto the grave and trembles in fear. "That is pay back," the fiend explains.

Eva vaguely knew who the dark figure was. But how did he find her? Out of all places, why did he force her out to the graveyard in the rain? Did he plan to bury her right then and there? Eva ruminates over the endless possibilities, afraid to come to a conclusion. The brute tears off the tape from Eva's mouth in one quick go. She shrieks out in pain. Dreading that she may soon stare death in the face, Eva slumps her head towards the muddy tufts of dirt. The menacing brute drops a shovel into the dirt next to her. "You can try to scream all you want. No one can hear you out here."

She glares up at his big diabolical face, as green veins pop out of his neck. "What do you want?" she cries in desperation.

"I want you to dig," he orders. "Dig for what?" she asks. "You're involved with a DEO agent. There is something you should know," he sneers back.

Eva's face turns sour. "Look, buddy, I don't know who you are, but you've got the wrong girl! Let me go!"

Nevo smiles. "You're Eva Ann Moore. A waitress at Tony's bar. I believe you know Jim Cazco as well. At the very least, you are some sort of acquaintance of his." She looks closer into his dark sinister eyes. "Have we met before?"

He chuckles. "Only in passing."

She shakes her head. "I don't know what you have against Jim, but I'm not going to play any games with you."

The big villain roars out with laughter. "One thing you should know about me, Ms. Moore. I don't play games."

He unlocks the cuff around his wrist and binds it to a steel rod next to the grave, to restrain her so she couldn't escape. "Why do you want me to dig?" she asked slowly. His ominous smile paralyzes her soul with trepidation. "Take the shovel and turn around," he commands. Eva slowly picks up the shovel, uncertain of what will happen next. As she gradually turns her body around, she trembles with anxiety. After turning around, all she can see is a lone tombstone a couple of feet away. She scans around the site but cannot see anything else through the darkness. What is his plan?

Eva peers down at the name imprinted on the tombstone. Her jaw gapes open as she drops the shovel on the ground beside her. Her eyes widen in shock. "No, this can't be. This can't be right."

Eva cannot peel her eyes off the grave, as she reads the name in enormous granite letters: James Hunter Cazco. 2019-2042. The words choke right out of her mouth. "No. This...this can't be real. I don't...I don't believe it."

The perpetrator places the murky shovel back into her shaking hands. He replies, "There lies your Jim Cazco. He rests peacefully in the flowerbed. My suggestion is for you to dig as far down as you possibly can. Retrieve the remains. Or else."

Nevo staggers down the hillside, leaving Eva to work on her task at hand. He briefly turns around to glimpse back at the disheveled woman. The villain grins with content. "Get digging. Your life depends on it."

18

Jim peers at his wristwatch as time flies by in the digital net. He waits patiently on top of the virtual hill with the giant simulated tree overhead. The hill lurks behind Sector 9, which overlooks the governor's office. Thunder bolts boom with rigorous force across the virtual sky, while the rest of the digital net waits into consuming darkness. Raindrops pelt down on the detective, which create a vivid simulation of the real world.

Technology, Jim realizes, has evolved in such a way that artificial imitation might actually override most aspects of the real world, even his job. Who would know the difference? The detective reminds himself the raindrops in this world were simply a mirage.

Movement through the blinds catches Jim's attention as he takes hold of his revolver and lays it firmly onto his lap. Through a direct view of the governor's window, a dark figure emerges from the shadows of the office and takes a seat on the governor's chair. Green lights flow out of the screen as the perpetrator scrolls through different documents in mid-air. The figure searches for the newly created forgery, unaware of its creator, who lurks outside.

The hill gently stoops closer and closer over to the window without making a sound. Eventually, the hill droops up within inches of the office window, as it waits to pounce on the unsuspecting visitor. To his surprise, the unwelcomed guest looks all too familiar.

The short, bearded man chooses a specific file and enhances it with the spread of two fingers. The file overtakes the size of the desk. He squints on the heading: Governor Dermott resignation. To the perpetrator's amazement, the file's contents remain blank. He lounges back in the chair perplexed. How can this be? The shades behind him clank against the window sill. As the man turns around, his jaw drops at the sight of the detective, who reflects off the other side of the glass. "No!" he screams out in fury. "I don't believe it!"

Wasting no time, Jim jumps to his feet. He cocks back his revolver, then aims at his lone target inside. A hail of bullets smash through the glass window, which obliterates the blinds. Bullets penetrate the computer screen and demolish the entire desk space. Within a couple moments, the room lies in shambles. The detective leaps through the broken glass and rolls on his back with his gun still drawn.

Jim waves his gun around the room. "Come out, Cullers! If that's even your real name! You might have tricked me at the food court, but you won't be able to fool me now! There is nowhere else to run!" No one answers. Jim staggers his way out of the office.

The hallway with a formation of scattered desks and random tables lies quietly. Beyond that lies work cubicles stacked in a giant row. Pieces of broken glass from a light bulb fall down from the ceiling to the floor.

The detective swiftly turns around and opens fire down the hallway behind him. His hand twitches unstably, as his finger rests tightly against the trigger.

Coming out from behind the remains of a small office cubicle, the elusive hacker rushes Jim viciously to the floor. Cullers' grasps a hand around Jim's throat, in an attempt to cut off his air supply. In frustration, the detective quickly propels a full round of bullets outward, firing in every direction around him. The debris of cubicles crumble to pieces as desks explode to tiny bits. Glass windows shatter in a large echo down the hallway.

Cullers slaps the gun out of Jim's hand. He dislodges the detective straight into a bullet-riddled desk chair. The hacker makes a break for the gun and snatches it off the ground. Jim leaps out of the chair and slugs Cullers on the back of his head. The hacker struggles to stay on his feet and retaliates by launching onto the detective. They both fall onto one of the last stable desks in the hallway.

Cullers tries to point the revolver at Jim, but Jim's hand pushes the gun back a couple of inches away from his face. The detective squirms nervously as the gun gets closer and closer to his body. He gasps out in desperation.

All of the sudden, Jim closes his eyes. He knows only the truth will set him free. "This is a virtual reality! There is no gun in his hand! The gun isn't even real!" he blurts out loud.

The gun, out of blue, dissolves out of thin air, which proves that the detective's mind can help alter the virtual reality through time and space. All he has to do is induce the idea that every object can be mentally manipulated in the simulated structure around him.

The hacker, however, is not a mere object that can be manipulated so easily. His adversary's mind is plugged into the virtual reality, so Jim's only chance to remove the hacker would be to detach that mental projection. If Jim could inflict enough pain onto his adversary, then he could have the hacker's mind slip out of the digital net and expel him from the system.

Jim punches a clear blow to Cullers' stomach. The hacker lets go of Jim and takes a couple steps back. Cullers then slaps Jim in the face, which makes the detective holler in pain.

Back in the real world, Chief Brahm and Dr. Barrett watch Jim's body spaz out of control. His body jerks sideways, which assimilates the impact of blows to his body. Blood gushes out of Jim's mouth profusely. The chief wipes off Jim's blood from his lips with a handkerchief. "Hold on pal. Stick with it. Don't give up."

After a series of more blows, the detective and the hacker struggle to stand, with their faces looking like puffy red tomatoes. They both breathe out heavily, unable to move. Jim gives Cullers a look of contempt. With a quick lunge, the hacker thrusts his hand inside the detective's chest. His hand disappears through Jim's flesh, as if his body is made of slippery Jell-O.

Cullers squishes and rotates his hand around violently, as he searches for the vital pumping organ. To his surprise, he doesn't feel anything at all. He looks flummoxed. "What the hell are you?" With one last gasp, Jim thrusts his fist into Cullers' head. His own hand disappears deep inside the hacker's head, as if he too is made of Jell-O. The detective feels around the mangled vortex and conjoining membranes inside his adversary's squishy brain.

In an electronic transfer from his hand to his brain, graphic hallucinations invade Jim's own mind. He sees the red headed gypsy woman Varra from before. Her devilish smile pours out. Another illusion shows a run-down apartment complex. The address 267 Willow Street Suite A imprints on a small metallic mailbox. He then sees apparitions of a huge bag with dollar bills that flow out of it.

But the most shocking image is the graveyard with the tombstone that contains the name James Hunter Cazco. The detective raises both eyebrows, then promptly pulls out his hand from Cullers' head. At the same time, Cullers frees his hand from Jim's chest. Both men fall backwards awkwardly on the floorboards.

The hallway is quiet once more. As Jim shakes off the unpleasant encounter, he smiles with content of the new discovery. In response to the new information, he realizes that he must communicate with the outside world. But how?

From the net manual, Jim remembers reading that it was hypothetically possible to connect the digital world to the real world. Unfortunately, he has never heard of anyone who reportedly pulled it off. It is called cross-netting. If only he could find the right connection.

Maybe with mental manipulation, he can stabilize a long-distance connection. His partner's wristwatch is directly connected to the net, so in theory, all Jim has to do is locate Ike's IP address. It is a stretch, but this is the only real plan he can muster.

Jim closes his eyes as he forces mental images of Ike's wristwatch, then stretches his imagination to the farthest lengths that it can possibly go. The detective tries to visualize the image of Bender's Incorporated, which is where he last encountered his partner. A weak signal resonates from the image in his mind. He presses two fingers over his temple, then focuses on the lone connection. He prays that it is the one he needs. "Ike! Detective Ike Brooks! Can you hear me? Ike!"

Back in reality, Ike rests his head against the back gate of the Benders Incorporated Factory. As an ambulance takes officers Yenwick and Hammer away safely, Ike sighs in relief. At least those two would live to see another day. He glances down to his beeping watch. A message tries to decode itself, though it takes more time than usual. Eventually, a highlighted note emerges: Incoming voice message from Detective Jim Cazco. Ike holds down a side button as he speaks into the device, "Go ahead, Jim."

Back in the virtual reality, Jim opens his eyes in amazement. It actually worked. He projects loudly, "Our hacker worm has been dealt with! Drexwell should work once again! Borrow Hammer's car! It should be stationed right outside the factory! Make sure that you drive over to the address: 267 Willow Street Suite A, immediately! Apprehend the criminal, before it's too late!"

Ike's head twists back in confusion. "Are you sure we have the right location of the hacker? Where are you?" He waits for a response.

Back in the virtual reality, Cullers slowly climbs up to his feet. He limps over to the governor's office, while his mind suffers from brain trauma. The hacker stumbles over the broken window sill, then disintegrates out of thin air.

A weird smell comes over the detective. It is as if he has become surrounded by toxic smoke. From what he sees in front of him, however, there is no clear inclination that smoke is present. The smoke from the outside world must have finally gotten to his senses. His mind has become self-aware of the danger back in the real world, and therefore, brings the sensation into the virtual reality.

Jim's eyesight blurs as the digital net begins to shake. He continues his conversation with his partner the best he can. "Don't worry about me, Ike! I'll tell you later! Just go to the address! I'll be heading over to the graveyard nearby to save my Eva." His eyelids become heavy as the whole room becomes blotted. The fusion of dark and bright colors melt before Jim's eyes. The detective's body feels numb, out of control. "Oh no", he says under his breath. He's beginning to slip out of the digital net.

He slumps back onto the floor and slowly passes out. Jim's body soon fades from the simulated reality, while the whole virtual world dissolves into complete nothingness.

Jim returns to his body in the real world, while jerking compulsively. He swiftly rips off the rag bandage that covers his eyes. Dr. Barrett starts to pull off the wires and needles from the detective's wary body, as Jim hyperventilates at an accelerating high rate. The chief lifts Jim out of the chair. "What happened Jim?"

Jim pants loudly, "The culprit has been expelled. We need to drive to an apartment a couple blocks away. We need to go right now if we're going to catch him. No time to lose."

The detective rushes through the hazy room and opens the door. Jim inhales deep breaths as more oxygen enters his lungs. He snaps back to the other's. "I'll tell you what it's all about when we get there. I'll send you the address. Follow me." As the men leave, the smoke stops pouring out of the vent, which makes the haze slowly fade away.

***

Somewhere a couple blocks away, Cullers emerges back into the real world from his virtual reality device setup on a raggedy-looking couch. He falls straight to the floor, then throws up blood. How could he lose control? He tries to pull himself up on his feet, but his legs remain numb from his out-of-body experience. Cullers has a severe headache that wraps around into his troubled mind. What did that officer do to him? He takes a couple deep breaths as he tries to regain his composure.

The sound of a law enforcement siren suddenly rages outside his window from the street below. He realizes that the DEO agents must have found his place. But how?

The hacker crawls his way to the front door as blood gushes out of his mouth. He is unable to gather back the rest of his senses. With all his might, he reaches up from the floor to a jacket that dangles behind the front door.

A couple feet above him, a gun sticks out of the jacket pocket. Cullers' fingers barely brush against the handle. He grits his teeth. With one final push, the hacker leans his body forward. He knocks the gun out of the pocket, while a pair of bullets fly out onto the floor with it.

After he picks up the weapon with its ammunition, Cullers crawls toward the front door. With more ease, he lubricates the door knob with his blood smeared on his hand. The knob slowly shifts to the right gradually and the door slides open. Rainy mist enters the room. He coughs out more blood before he crawls out of his dimly lit apartment.

Footsteps echo up the stairwell below Cullers. He inches across the sidewalk pathway and ends up behind a trash bin around the corner. Depleted of energy, the hacker pants sporadically from behind his hiding spot. Now clearly out of view, he slowly gazes around the corner as the footsteps become louder.

Detective Ike Brooks emerges from under the stairwell, with his gun drawn and his face still covered with soot. He reads the address on the mailbox before he slides through the open doorway of the apartment. The room has papers scattered all over the couch, lamps broken, and a trail of blood that leads out of the apartment. Ike looks around anxiously as he enters the living room. The room lies still all around him. Only water dripping from the bathroom faucet can be heard in the dirty apartment.

***

Rain pours down harder as Cullers regains some mobility. He limps his way through a graveyard's back entrance. The hacker hunches his back forward, as he struggles to push the two remaining bullets into the gun's barrel. Finally, the barrel clicks together.

Cullers leans on a large tombstone that sits at the top of a hill. He uses the tough granite to support his weak legs. Without giving much notice to the tombstone's inscription, Cullers marches on.

As the hacker shifts through the dead branches of a large drooping tree, he trips over a small object by the base. Looking down scornfully, he sees a tall rose entangling his feet. With disgust, Cullers rips off the stem of the lone flower and discards the bothersome plant beside the leafless tree.

Cries for help echo down the slope ahead of him. Blood spurts through Cullers' raggedy yellow teeth as he races down the hill toward the distress call. Out of time and out of options, the hacker starts to feel desperation creep in.

Minutes later, Cullers materializes at the foot of the slope. A small tombstone lays in front of him, as a sobbing Eva shovels tufts of dirt. Whimpering with tears, she exhumes the last ashy remains out of the grave.

The hacker's unholy grin intensifies as he cocks the gun back and aims at her trembling body. "Well, little missy, looks like I found you."

Eva looks up and shakes her head wildly. "No, no! Please. Please don't!" Cullers chuckles. "Nothing personal, my dear. But a job is a job. I have to carry out what must be done."

She looks up faintly at the stranger, as she stares down the barrel of his gun. Looking death in the face is more than she can bare. Tears flow down her cheeks. She closes her eyes, shaking her disheartened face in disbelief. Eva wails upon the mud of what she believes will be her own grave. Cullers snarls his nose hairs as his eyes widen with anticipation.

"Stop!" a voice beams out in the distance. Cullers turns around to see a dark figure that scurries toward him. Thinking fast on his feet, Cullers grabs Eva and places the gun muzzle softly on her ear.

"Don't shoot!" Jim yells as he approaches the grave. The hacker quickly shifts behind the disgruntled waitress. "Stop right there, pig! No sudden moves, or the lady gets it!"

The detective stops abruptly, then points his gun aimlessly out in front of him. He is unable to get a clear shot at the hacker's face. Jim reasons that he must handle the situation delicately. It is make it or break it time.

19

"Let her go, Cullers! She's got nothing to do with this," Jim barks. The hacker smirks. "That's not what I was told! We are here for a reason, detective!"

Jim stands a couple feet away, out of breath. "Well, what do you want?"

Cullers' sinister smile wrinkles his worn-out face. "You know what I want."

The detective pauses for a moment. "No, I don't think I do."

Cullers chuckles back mockingly. "Of course you do. You must have known the governor's private access code to unlock his virtual classified files. That's the only way you could have created a fake forgery document. I really need those files, and I need them right now."

Jim keeps his gun directed at the hacker's head, as his hands tremble ever so slightly.

The hacker's eyes quickly shift to Jim's watch. "I'm no fool, detective. I know DEO wristwatches collect all data viable to ongoing cases. That includes from the virtual world since law enforcement has a database that connects to the digital net. Governor Dermott's password is encoded somewhere on your own watch. You toss me the watch, and I'll toss you the girl. It's as simple as that. Then we both walk away like nothing happened."

Jim shakes his head. "You won't be able to escape here, Cullers. There's only two options for you. I shouldn't have to spell them out." The nervous hacker rests his gun on Eva's cheek. She shrieks in fear. "Drop your weapon! I gave you my final offer, detective! The great Jim Cazco. What say you?"

Eva cries out, "Jim, please help me! Jim, I don't want to die!" The detective sighs. Feeling defeated and out of options, Jim ditches the pistol by his feet. The hacker nods his head. "That's right, detective. Now throw me the watch like a good boy."

Jim reluctantly peels off the watch from his wrist. He tosses the timepiece a couple feet away on the large dirt mound. "You come and get it. Release Eva."

Cullers takes a key hidden in his pocket and unlocks the handcuffs. "In a moment. First I need the watch," he beckons as he keeps his captive close to him. As he guides Eva cautiously to the watch, he uses her as a shield.

Jim backs up a couple feet to give his adversary some space. The hacker's trembling hand snatches the watch from the grimy soil. He glares at the watch, as he eyes the red light that gleams from the centerpiece frame.

Cullers grins. "There was no way around it, detective. You would have never won." The hacker slides his pistol off Eva's face and points the gun in Jim's direction. The detective raises his hands up helplessly. If this was to be his end, it would be quite an end.

The hacker's revolver cocks back slowly. "Goodbye, detective." He grins devilishly.

Eva cries, "No!"

A bullet rings out through the night as Eva shrieks. Cullers' knees fall hastily on the ground. Blood pops out of the hacker's hand as he howls out in pain. Jim hits the deck, snatches his own pistol, and opens fire at the disjointed hacker.

One shot pierces Cullers' forehead. The other lodges itself into his stomach.

Blood gushes out in insurmountable quantities. Cullers falls forward, with his face planted into the dirt next to the grave. Jim's wristwatch pops out of the hacker's hand and rests beside the lifeless corpse. Cullers lies perfectly still as a trail of blood begins to seep down the hill with the rest of the rainwater.

Jim picks up his watch from the mud, and straps the contraption back onto his wrist. Eva holds her weary arms over her head on the ground, disoriented from shell shock. She weeps in fear as her body becomes oddly numb. Eva could not move.

The detective shifts his aim suddenly over to the tombstone. He switches the gun sensor to a more explosive setting, then blasts the James

Hunter Cazco head frame with one clear shot. He watches the broken pieces of the head frame fall down in a heap of rubble.

Jim collects himself swiftly as he hovers over Eva. He throws his new black leather jacket over her body. She tries to push him away, but he holds tightly around her body to console her troubled emotions. "Everything is ok now," he says gently. He feels her body shake uncontrollably.

Detective Ike Brooks jogs up from behind the shattered tombstone. Smoke percolates out of his pistol, as he peers down at the hacker's corpse. Jim eyes Eva while he addresses Ike, "Took you long enough."

Ike shakes his head. "Just in the nick of time. Turns out you were right. I'm not a bad shot after all."

Jim lets out a light chuckle as he helps Eva to her feet. Her body still shudders like a jittery, frightened cat. "You're safe now, Eva. I won't let him harm you." Her face shakes with anxiety as she glances up warily into his dark, beady eyes. Eva slumps her head forward, as she rests quietly on his shoulder.

A Blue Corvette VX2, with a DEO imprinted label on the roof, pulls up to the sidewalk down by the graveyard's entrance. Chief Brahm steps out of the vehicle and strolls up to the graveyard.

From behind a burnt-out lamp post, journalist Wayne Smothers appears and sneaks his way onto the other side of the hill. Wayne dashes up to the remains of the disfigured grave with a mini camera device strapped over his knuckles. At the arrival of the tomb, the journalist leans up to the dead body of the hacker with amazement. He shifts the mini camera from his knuckles to the palm of his hand. "Wow, I've never seen a carve up like this before. The paper will love this."

Ike pushes Wayne away from the grave. "Have some respect!"

Backing up, Wayne glares at the younger detective. "Like you did?" he retorts.

Chief Brahm enters the site behind his two DEO's. "This area is now off limits until further notice. Kid, usher this paper man out of here."

Wayne shakes his head. "You can't just whisk away my rights. The press always has the right to —"

"The press has the right to shut the hell up!" the chief's face intensifies as he finishes the reporter's statement.

"Kid, get rid of this hooligan. I don't wish to see him anywhere near the grave for the rest of the night." Detective Brooks grabs Wayne by the collar.

"With pleasure," Ike utters. With loud stammering and irregular puffing grunts, the young detective removes the journalist from the premises.

Law Enforcement sirens echo down the street. The chief pats Jim on the back with a smirk. "You did it again, Cazco. That was mighty fine DEO work you did just there. I'm just glad that this mess is all over with."

Jim shakes his head as Eva scans her eyes up to the chief's brittle face. "This mess is far from over. We cut off the limbs of the beast. The head still remains," the detective beams back. He holds Eva's shoulders firmly as he raises the jacket over her head to keep her dry. Jim proceeds to lead her out of the graveyard as more DEO cars arrive on the scene.

Brahm glances back at Jim and Eva while they course through the muddy gunk. A satisfying grin lights up the chief's face, as he hollers back, "That's why we're in the business, pal! Protecting our loved ones is always worth it! Never forget that!"

Jim and Eva pass the entrance without another word. They make their way to the sidewalk and slowly cross the street.

Broken pieces of rubble circle around the chief's feet, with the letters of James Hunter Cazco jumbled all over the place. They soon get covered by more mud as the rain drives them further into the ground.

***

Several hours later, Eva dries her hair as she walks into Jim's bedroom. She seals her lips while she fumes with anger and frustration. The unsettling ringing from gunfire still pervades through her ears intensely. A towel is tightly bound around her body, drenched from a much-needed shower. She tightens her grip on a worn-out hairbrush.

Alone with her thoughts, she stares out the window. Eva glares out in empty space as she feels questions mount in her troubled mind. She brushes her hair as another figure enters the room. Jim slowly straddles up behind the door.

"How are you feeling?" he asks cagily. Sulked in a distasteful mood, she refuses to answer. "Look, I'm sorry. I didn't mean for you to get in harm's way," he replies back candidly.

She snaps her eyes right back at his. "No, but that crap happened anyway."

He takes a deep breath and slowly nods. "It did. Like I mentioned before, honey, this is the life I live. I'm put into the most morbid situations and eventually, I just have to find a way to survive."

She interrupts, "For how much longer, Jim? That was pure luck. Unfortunately, luck won't always be on your side. Especially when you desperately need it. Do you realize how easily I could have been killed? That mammoth of a man tracked me down and abducted me. How did that happen?"

Once more, Jim pauses as he glances back at the escalating contempt that fills her eyes like wildfire. "I still don't know how he found out you were here. It was a whole fluke situation, honey. It would never go down the same way twice."

Eva snaps her fingers back at him in disgust, "No! That's not it. That's not the biggest problem here, Jim."

The detective takes a step back. He nods slowly, "You want to tell me that this case will lead to my demise? That I need to quit the business?" She throws her hair brush on the floor. "Nope! That's still not it, Jim. Stop trying to avoid the problem."

He raises his hands up to calm her down, "Wait, hold on. Take it easy. What problem?"

She picks up her brush and sweeps pass him, then glides over to a giant mirror at the other side of the room. Eva continues to brush her hair as she glares at his image in the reflection. "Why is there another James Hunter Cazco buried in the graveyard?" Jim doesn't answer.

Eva snarls her nose as she points her brush to his image in the mirror. "Answer me! You must obviously have the answer to everything!"

Jim pauses before he nods his head once more. "So, you did get a chance to see the tombstone. I thought this might happen."

She snaps back around. "What might happen?"

Jim sighs. "Well, the ashy remains that you found in the graveyard was that of a dear friend. He once was a promising young man, filled with talent and ambition. He rests at that grave site with that name inscribed for a reason. That name on his tombstone is for his family's protection. To make sure others wouldn't go after those close to him."

Eva watches the sincerity reflect off the detective's face. He continues, "His true identity must never be revealed to the public. I owe him that."

Eva shakes her head vigorously. "I'm not a fighter like you, Jim. I'm afraid when people are after me. I'm fearful for my life in these given situations. I'm just a troubled lady who struggles to find her own place in the world. I'm still trying to find out who I am. But if I'm not directly involved with your operations, then I should at least be told the truth. This is the line I'll have to draw. Either tell me what I need to know or I'm gone. Why would you need to protect a dead man's identity? Who's really buried in that graveyard, Jim? Tell me now!"

Jim frowns as he looks to the floor. He couldn't leave her in the dark any longer. The detective swings the bedroom door closed, leaving the two alone for a sobering discussion.

20

A dark figure briskly knocks on the front door of a yellow faded house. Moments later, a skinny petite woman in her mid-thirties emerges behind the door. She wears a bright blue nurse's uniform with a pair of old sneakers. The nurse cautiously watches the figure shift nervously around the front porch. She did not expect any visitor this late at night. The woman does not want to let the cold air into the coziness of her peaceful home, but she decides to check who it is anyways.

"Hello, who is it?" she asks politely while she tries to make out the face of her uninvited guest.

"It's me," a gentle male's voice returns her pleasantry. As light flickers on the man's face, the nurse begins to recognize him and smiles with delight. Could it be? With great euphoria, she hugs the man who stands in the doorway.

Jim's soft hands caress the nurse's slender face. "I'm glad to see you again, Chloe. It's been a while."

Chloe's starry eyes gleam back into his before she kisses him firmly on the cheek. "I'm glad to finally see you again, brother. It's been far too long." The warmth of her embrace fills his sluggish heart. He pats her on the back as she ushers him inside the comfort of their childhood home. She takes his drenched coat and places it upon a small hanger on the wall.

Jim brushes by the kitchen with a feeling of nostalgia, as he recognizes the nice round room decorated with pictures of himself and the other family members. The old refrigerator makes a reverberating sound, which he distinctly remembers from his youth. There is no denying it. The detective truly feels like he is finally home.

"Is Momma still up?" he asks softly.

Chloe shakes her head. "I just tucked Momma into bed about an hour ago. She doesn't get out much, you see. Luckily she is still eating solids." Jim sighs without ease, afraid to see the shape that Gladys is now in. His sister looks frail and drained of energy too.

Jim glances at Chloe's full work attire. He smirks. "Looks like you became a nurse after all." He looks down to the white cross imprinted on her chest.

Chloe smiles enthusiastically. "Oh yes. Do you like it?" She turns fully around to show off her outfit.

He nods approvingly. "Of course I do. You look great."

She lets out a soft giggle. "You work long hours at the hospital?" he asks inquisitively.

Chloe nods awkwardly. "Well, kind of. When I'm not taking care of Momma, I'm mostly spending my time at the clinics. It's tough to see all of the blood and patients that mentally break down. Not for the faintest of heart." They both share a moment of silence before Jim changes the subject.

"But you have been using the money I've been sending you, right? It's the manila envelopes that come here every month." Chloe stays quiet as she paces over to the spacious family room. Jim follows close behind.

Portraits of wrangled fish and beautiful flowers fill up the wall above a rusty fireplace. Jim recognizes the beautiful flowers as the same ones his mother grew in her exquisite garden in the backyard. Chloe offers Jim his favorite seat in the dark room: a sturdy green chair with a rumpled foot rest underneath. A rectangular slit of bright light emanates from the house next door, which leaks into the family room and illuminates part of the couch.

"Would you like for me to turn on the light?" Chloe asks. The detective raises his arm graciously to decline the thought. "Actually, I will take some orange juice if you still carry that stuff," he replies.

His sister grins. "Of course we still carry the stuff. Half the fridge is full of it. I'll get a glass for both of us." Chloe roves out of the room as Jim rests his feet up on the comfortable foot rest.

The detective gazes up at the curtain that covers the back window of the room. Only outlines can be made of the backyard from the long tapestry. Wind howls loudly, and rain gushes relentlessly behind the window frame.

Jim imagines what has become of the backyard tree that he and his siblings once planted together. Maybe it now stands tall and proud. Maybe it has withered away and died. The thought captivates his interest. At the same time, however, he couldn't make himself walk up to the tree. How could he look now? Shame and pain tied too heavily with his last memory of gazing out to the tree.

A fresh glass of swishing orange juice glides into his hand. Chloe perches on the slender couch next to him that is still covered in plastic wrap. She slides a blanket from on top of the couch and folds it neatly onto her lap. "I'm so glad you came." Chloe smiles pleasantly as she takes a sip. "You could always phone to let us know that you're coming."

"How is mom's health?" Jim asks while he looks at the floor. Chloe glimpses at Jim's bruises on his chin and nose. Whatever tough patch he went through in life, Chloe was at least grateful that her adoptive brother had remained in one piece.

"Momma is taking it easy, but she is developing some chest pain and arthritis. She doesn't plant or tend to her garden much anymore. Momma takes walks once every morning, gets some reading in, and always stays on top of her medication. She's getting by."

Jim nods his head while he keeps his wandering eyes away from her. "And, how are you doing?" Chloe's smile begins to fold back unsettlingly. "Apart from taking care of Momma and working at the hospital, I haven't gotten a chance to do much else. Occasionally, I'll watch the news on my Panasonic 3-D set. Most of the time, I like to keep busy."

The detective grins as he reaches out an envelope of dollar bills, landing lightly on her lap. "I'm sorry that I really haven't been here...at all."

Chloe quickly pushes the envelope back to Jim's hands. "Please brother, I don't want to take your money anymore."

Jim finally gazes up at his sister's trembling face. "No, you see, I want you to have it. This money belongs to you and Momma. To help you both get by. I need you to take this."

She gives him a concerned look. "No, you want me to take it. I don't understand how you got us all this money. I don't know where people can find an amount like that to give out every month. I know you don't want me to ask what you do now. But Momma and I are doing ok. We don't need much money." Tension brews strongly in the room, Jim can feel it. "I just wanted to give you something after I left. Ever since I came back from graduation, things have never been the same."

Chloe grabs firmly onto her blanket. "I can still remember it, like it was yesterday. You graduated from college with a degree. You were going to find a job at a botany lab."

Jim turns to the back window. "Yeah, naively I thought I would provide for this family right away. We were all going to get a better life, away from the mob and crime. At least that's how I saw it."

She continues, "I remembered calling you frantically on that fateful day. I told you to go to the hospital immediately. That time was running out."

Tears fill Jim's eyes. He keeps his face forward, while his sister quivers uncontrollably with raw emotions.

An image floats back into Jim's mind of his younger self. He rushes to Big Daddy's side, in front of the operating room, at the end of the corridor of a hospital. He rests his shuddering hands around Big Daddy's weak cheeks. Big Daddy gazes down warily at the object that rests on the side of his gurney: a college degree plaque. He smiles warmly in recognition of Jim's accomplishment. The father figure mutters a few words as he breathes out slowly. Jim can barely make them out as he hovers his ear over Big Daddy's mouth.

Moments later, doctors push the young sleuth away and rush Big Daddy's gurney into the operating room, leaving Jim outside the steel doors to watch.

Chloe's whimpering voice brings him back to the present. "I wish...I wish I could hold onto him one last time, to feel his warm body breathing. If only I showed up a couple minutes sooner."

Vivid imagery floods Jim's mind, as a younger Chloe screams, then sprints down the corridor of the hospital. She falls in young Jim's arms as they both crumble onto the ground. Her bawling shrieks echo down the hallway, as young Jim's eyes glisten with tears.

In the present, Jim gently touches his sister's shoulders and muffles her cries in his chest. He brushes back her hair delicately.

"I try everything to forget that," she murmurs. "I try to forget the cold rain falling down at his funeral." Chloe raises her chin, then chokes out the words, "Our brother...didn't even...show up."

Jim grins. "Oh...he was there alright, smoking a cigarette on top of the hill at the graveyard. He mourned with us too, from a distance. Showing emotions wasn't really his style."

Chloe adds, "Then I remember Momma had a stroke soon after that. The shock was too much for her. She struggled to function after that."

Jim replies, "I remember the rest of us searched endlessly to find jobs. I couldn't get a job as a botanist. You were still in school. Pretty Boy was...well...he was doing his own thing."

Chloe butts in, "I remember you mentioned that you got a trial run with the DEO agency or some crazy mumbo jumbo like that. I never found out how that went."

Jim smiles uneasily as he thinks of a lie. "The DEO angle went nowhere. However, it was Pretty Boy that got us a good paying gig."

Chloe lifts her head off Jim's chest. "Wait, that's right. Some stupid warehouse job."

Jim sighs as his memories haunt him. The nightmares were coming back. "The way he made it all out, it seemed to make sense."

Her face tightens up with intensity. "Nothing that came out of that jerk ever made sense. What a scumbag. I hate him!"

The detective slowly backs away from her. Her eyes glowed with hatred, which feels reminiscent of a look she gave when they were kids. He says, "I came here to tell you two things. One, that I'm sorry for not being here. Two, I would like to help out more with Momma."

Chloe hesitates, then binds her fidgety hands back on the blanket. "Oh brother, if that is your choice, then so be it. Just realize it might take a little while for her to remember you. Her memory is fading."

The detective cusps both hands tightly around the nurse's hands. "She still might recognize me. Even if there is a chance, I'm not giving up on her. No way."

A warm smile returns to Chloe's woeful face. She feels the sincerity of his voice resonate with good intentions. Jim says, "I will come back again, I promise. Once I finish this job, I'll be back in both of your lives. For now, take the money. After that, I won't try to buy back your love." Chloe nods gracefully as he holds onto her trembling hands. After kissing her firmly on the forehead, Jim stands to his feet and places the empty glass on the counter.

Chloe points to the back curtain with a smile. "You've seen the tree in the backyard, haven't you?"

The detective smooths out his hands as he looks up at a large dark outline behind the window. He realizes that he still could go for a quick peek to see the tree for himself.

Unfortunately, the slight tremor in his hands will not allow him to do so, in light of sadness and guilt. "Ike mentioned something growing in the backyard. I tell him to never describe it to me."

She nods her head. "That's the young gentleman that hands me the cash, isn't it? He's a nice guy. But he looks so much like a DEO."

Jim keeps cool to evade the truth. "Ike is a good friend, but he's not a DEO. He doesn't have the stomach or mental faculty to run such a job. He's more into construction. They like to use big guys like that."

Chloe eyes him intently, while believing half of his claim. "Yeah, I guess a construction job fits." Jim sighs as he takes a couple steps backward. He feels that what he wanted to accomplish for the night was over. "I guess it's about time I leave. I'll let you wind down for bed." He paces over to the wet hanger, then pulls off his coat as he motions over to the front door.

Chloe gently replies, "Have you paid our brother a visit?"

Jim stops his hand by the door knob. A moment of silence comes over the detective before he answers, "No, after all this time, I can't say that I have."

She smiles. "I brought myself together to visit him a few days ago. You should go see him sometime."

Jim nods. "It might take more time to do that. I'm just not ready to visit Pretty Boy yet."

Chloe replies, "You should find the time. After all, you two were the closest in the family."

Jim replies, "In due time. All the memories here in this house run so vividly in my mind, just about every day. I discovered that, in the outside world, nothing else has ever compared."

She watches him closely. He turns to her slightly, without looking at her face, "I'll see you soon, Chloe. Have a good night."

She replies, "You too."

Jim opens the door, feeling numb, as he enters back into the dismal rainstorm. This time, however, he chooses not to run away from it. After he shuts the door, he perches on one of the murky steps on the front porch, feeling pensive. Regret invades his mind. He stays at the very spot, like a troubled child in timeout. Thoughts of leaving his family house once more breeds fear, doubt, and misery.

Chloe lifts herself out of the couch, with the blanket wrapped around her in a tight snug. She slowly walks over to her bedroom. Her mouth trembles after seeing Jim for the first time in 15 years. After a certain point, she did not expect to see him ever again, but life is unpredictable. Tomorrow is a new day.

21

A reddish glow illuminates the sky as Detective Ike Brooks and his fiancé, Agatha, walk up to the front door of Jim's home. Agatha is a tall, slender woman, who wears a vibrant pink dress, with her blonde hair tied back. Her lips smell of fresh roses, with bright red lipstick that smooths the soft edges and creases. She presses onto an access video screen beside the door.

Eva's face materializes on the access screen. "Yes, hello?"

Agatha's smile lifts out the tight wrinkles on her face. "Hi, we are the Brooks. Jim invited us over for dinner. You must be Eva." Ike lowers his head in order to show his face on the screen. "Hello again, Eva."

Eva's face lights up with a huge smile. "Great to see that both of you made it! You came at the right time. We just finished cooking the steak and asparagus. We'll be ready for dinner."

Agatha bows her head. "Well, thank you. I'm Agatha, by the way. Happy Valentine's Day."

Eva quickly replies, "Nice to meet you, Agatha. I'm Eva. Happy Valentine's day to you too. Door's unlocked, come on in." The electronic locks on the door slide off, and the front door swings open.

Jim and Eva sit across from Agatha and Ike at the kitchen table, as they googly-eye the delicious food scattered along the red satin tablecloth. A large plastic red heart sits on the center of the table. They laugh and converse throughout dinner. Steak, asparagus, mashed potatoes, and strawberries quickly disappear from the four dinner plates.

Agatha giggles as she wipes the food particles off her chin. "So that's how the two of us met. Ike then asked me to marry him on a boat ride a couple months ago. We're happily engaged to be married."

She smiles as Ike picks up her hand that is encrusted with a beautiful, shiny ruby ring. He kisses her knuckles intently. Eva turns to Jim, then raises an eyebrow suggestively.

Jim, pretending not to notice, finishes eating a warm slice of apple pie. He stays mostly quiet throughout the course of the meal, as he battles his inner thoughts. "Well, I would like to send my congratulations, Agatha. That sounds like a match made in heaven. I hope you both live happily together," Eva replies earnestly.

Agatha turns to her fiancé with a sour look. "As long as his work doesn't get in the way. That worries me from time to time."

Ike shakes his head. "It's all part of business, honey. Bacon has to come home some way, right Jim?"

Jim takes his time to chew his last bite of pie before he joins in the conversation. "No comment." Chuckles resound around the table. "Well, you know now how Jim and I first met. I was wondering if I could hear the story of how Jim and Ike first became partners?" Eva asks.

Jim and Ike connect eyes. "It's not a very amusing story," Jim remarks.

Ike wipes his mouth with a thin napkin. "Actually, the first time we met was on my first day of work. I remember sitting anxiously in a chair in the chief's office. Out of nowhere, this guy stuck his head into the room while I waited for the chief's evaluation. He started to talk to me about my life. When the chief finally arrived with his tough lecture of joining the squad, Jim told him to hire me. Just like that. He completely vouched for me but hardly knew me."

Jim interrupts, "I knew enough."

Ike smirks. "And for the last year and a half, he has taken me under his wing, and we have been partners ever since. For that, I'm eternally grateful."

Jim shakes his head. "You would have been great either way, Ike. My help wasn't much needed."

Ike replies. "Your teaching skills have made a big impact on me. I wouldn't have gotten this far without them." Jim wipes his mouth, then shrugs his shoulders with little verve.

Eva teases, "That's just how he is. Always a compassionate soul."

Agatha giggles sarcastically. "Ha-ha, yes! From what I hear, he's the most compassionate soul at the entire office." Jim rotates his hand midway in the air whimsically. Agatha adds, "It's surprising to see such a highly decorated officer that hardly looks the part."

Jim chuckles at her bluntness. "It is still surprising to me with each passing day. Sometimes it doesn't feel real."

Agatha raises an eyebrow as she looks him over. "I hear that the standard for being a DEO is a frame over 6 feet tall and at least 200 pounds. You look like neither of the two."

Jim grins as he eyes the embarrassed look on Ike's face.

"It's true that, physically, I wasn't able to meet the standard as a DEO applicant. But I made up for those shortcomings with clever intelligence, unlimited wit, and the unnerving courage to fight until the very end. It goes to show that anyone can overcome such adversity by first creating their own belief in their success. That's why the chief ended up taking a chance on me. It's the last man standing mentality. That's my DNA, Agatha."

Ike snickers as Agatha nods her head in agreement. "Fair enough." She wipes off her mouth as Ike shrugs to his partner.

The night fades into the dark hours of the enchanting evening. Agatha and Ike eventually part ways at the door, as they head out into the unusually warm night.

Jim dances slowly with Eva, as they waltz about their bedroom. She says, "Interesting friends. I'm glad to meet them."

Jim's smiles. "They seem ok. I just hope they don't invite us over too much."

Eva kisses him freshly on the lips. "I hope they do."

She rests her head onto his clavicle, then sighs, as she ripples her fingers onto his shoulder.

"Something on your mind?" Jim asks.

Eva's eyes meet the floor. "What if I would go out to do something else?"

He laughs incredulously, "You mean leave this situation? Would you leave this place?"

Eva drops her hands and starts to walk over to the outdoor balcony. She watches bright clouds cast over the horizon. The hillside lay quiet and peaceful. "I mean for a career. I don't want to be waiting tables anymore. I'd rather answer my calling."

Jim moseys over behind her, then guides his fingers down her back. "What would you want to be instead?"

She smiles, "A veterinarian. I see a lot of animals out there on the street that look like they can be taken care of better. I want to help them in whatever way I can. It doesn't matter what certification I need to get. I'm driven to get it anyways. So, what do you think?"

Jim smiles as the moonlight glistens ever so softly on his face. "If that makes you happy, then I support you 100%. I say go for it. I know you'll make a great veterinarian."

Eva turns around and plants a kiss firmly on his cheek. She then heads back inside the room and plops backward onto the bed. Jim dives in after her, then kisses her smoothly on the lips. "Happy Valentine's Day, honey. I hope we have many more days like this," she exclaims.

Jim answers gently, "If you give a flower a chance, it blooms."

Eva smiles as she plants a kiss right back. His hands gravitate to her neck, as he feels out her smooth jawline. His hands soon start to move down her body and her eyes begin to light up, as they begin another night of passion.

***

A couple days later, Jim staggers out of the personal records building at downtown. He looks up to the sky, which is smoggy and dark. To his surprise, the rain has stopped for the last couple days. He disappears around the corner, with an envelope in his hand.

He walks slowly for about half a block down a back alley, with batches of used machinery parts scattered along the oil-stained gravel. He stops short of a worn-out trash bin, probably from the same previous encounter. As he holds the envelope over the trash bin, he takes a deep breath.

The personal record envelope is engraved with the name EVA ANN MOORE, with all of her personal documents packed tightly inside. He takes out an old picture of her and another document. He studies it quickly. Jim then puts the items back in the envelope and then takes out a lighter from his pocket. He lights the envelope and its contents on fire, then watches the papers burn to a crisp. The detective throws the ashy remains into the trash bin, hoping to never see its remnants ever again. He paces away down the alley, as the small ashes disintegrate to microscopic bits.

***

Two weeks later, Jim and Ike enter a dark room inside the Detective Enforcement Office. A slide projector sits in the middle of the room. An image of a document reflects off an illuminated wall on the far side.

Chief Brahm sits on a chair, in contemplation, as he smokes a chiseled cigar. He stares at the screen as the two detectives approach him from the side. "Take a seat," he bellows. The two detectives oblige.

"What's this about?" Jim asks.

The chief hands Jim a printed document. "We received a ransom note this morning. It's from Nevo. The note threatens that if 20 million dollars is not paid in full by tomorrow morning, an atomic bomb will demolish a ten-mile radius of the city. A Swiss account labeled at the bottom of the document is where he wants the electronic transfer sent to. We tried to hack into the off-shore account, but those bankers refuse to let us breach their customer's confidentiality. Nevo explains in his ransom note that he looks to end corruption of the so-called heads of power. He also demands that we provide him that same Nathan Duggle character from —"

Ike interrupts, "Wait. Nathan Duggle is that dead guy, right?"

Jim nods his head as he reads a hard copy of the ransom note in his hand. "No luck there, chief. Nathan's remains are long gone. Not sure why this criminal wants to find him so bad." All letters of the document appear to have newspaper cut-out letters in order to hide the culprit's identity.

Ike reads the same document up on the projected wall. "Why does he want to blow up the town now?" Jim drops the document on his lap after he finishes reading it. "He might have run out of options. Personally, I think he is trying to throw us off."

Brahm quickly turns to Jim. "What makes you think that?"

Jim smiles. "An atomic bomb? Nobody creates nuclear fission bombs anymore. They have turned out to be unreliable, unpredictable, and unstable. Bombs nowadays are genetically modified and are engineered through mechanical contraptions or electric circuit trip-wire types."

The chief frowns. "Are you saying our mastermind is some sort of archaic Neanderthal?"

Jim smirks. "I'm saying our culprit doesn't know much about creating bombs, or pretending not to know."

Ike leans over. "Maybe it's a bluff, and the guy wants us to believe that there is a bomb, when really there isn't one. Maybe he's just looking for a big pay day."

Jim scratches his chin as he contemplates his next move. "Are there any more chemical plants in town that hold large quantities of silver nitride?"

Brahm thinks a moment, then taps his foot. "There might be five or six left in this town."

Jim nods his head as he glances at the chief. "See if those facilities also carry large amounts of fertilizer. My hunch is that they will need more fertilizer to neutralize the bomb. If that's the case, then I'll need the addresses for those chemical plants immediately. That's where our so-called mastermind will strike next."

Ike interjects, "How can you be so sure?"

Jim retorts, "Our somewhat overrated friend isn't done with making his bomb yet. If he truly will take out a 10-mile radius block, he will need a couple huge canisters to burn through. That's at least 10 to 20 tons of pure silver nitride, wherever it can possibly be found. Eventually that substance spoils over time."

The chief nods his head. "Done. I'll wire that to you soon, via Drexwell. You boys best hit the road during the meantime. Track down every plant. Remember, you have less than 24 hours."

Jim and Ike stand up. "So long chief," the two detectives quip in unison as they leave the room.

"Good luck," the chief bellows back before he takes his last puffs from his burned-out cigar. It is a long shot, Brahm reasons, but once again, there are no other constructive leads. It is time to hope for the best.

22

A couple blocks away, Varra waits impatiently at an abandoned bus stop. Her long encased cigarette burns seamlessly as time passes by. She glances around both sides of the block for the man with distinguishable brown gloves. To her dismay, he does not show up. After waiting half an hour, Varra flicks her dying cigarette out on the ground. Zipping away from the bus stop, she storms off in high dudgeon.

***

Back at Nevo's secret hideout, Gordon throws a heavy bag onto the floor in one of the back rooms. He opens the zipper to reveal huge clumps of fertilizer inside. Nevo lights a pipe behind the scientist. "How much do you think we need?" Gordon quickly slides his glasses up his nose. "Sublet number 1 overflowed again, sir. We need probably another ton."

The sinister behemoth's face tightens up as he picks up the scrawny scientist by the collar. "Doctor, we are running out of time and resources! Those bombs need to be finished by tomorrow morning!"

Gordon gasps out for air, then chokes from the large metallic hand that squeezes his vocal chords. "It can't be done, sir. Like I told you before, such a large quantity can't be controlled. I might be able to stabilize another ton's worth for a third of the bomb size. It will still be effective."

Nevo squints at the scientist unconvinced. "If Veymont can do it, I know we can do it. We just need more fertilizer, and only a couple more gallons of silver nitride."

Gordon exhales loudly. "Boss, the sublet canisters need more than just a couple gallons. You will need close to another ton." The large brute loosens his grip, which allows Gordon's feet to slide back onto the floor. "Then you will have to make one more trip." Gordon hunches over while he wheezes uncontrollably.

Nevo replies, "Load it up, undetected. Then come back and finish the product. Our other workers will help you stuff the bombs. Just get the chemicals we need to complete the mission. Fill up the truck completely or you're history. Do we understand each other?"

Gordon's legs grow weak. He knows he stood no chance against the giant. He nods his head nervously, nearly in tears. "Yes sir, I won't disappoint you."

A moment later, Varra dashes into the dimly lit room. Nevo shifts his attention to her. "I thought you were going to meet up with our friend."

She takes off her coat impatiently. "He never showed up. He did not call or reach out. Now, I'm really worried."

Nevo nods his head slowly, then rests his large metallic arm against the back of his head. "Do you think he already went to the authorities?"

She shakes her head. "He would have nothing to gain by going to law enforcement right now. He must be concocting a different plan to derail us."

Nevo runs a finger under the bridge of his nose as he considers this. "We should be very careful on how we deal with him from now on. We can go to a different source for the time being and get the work done from a different angle."

He caresses her chin. "You've done great work, Varra. I couldn't have accomplished any of this without you."

She kisses him intensely on the lips. "He has to be hunted down. Let me do it. It will be easy and won't take long. I'll find him."

Gordon fixes his collar and straightens his wrinkled shirt behind the couple. Nevo quickly snaps his head back around. "Why are you still here? Get going! And don't come back until you have all the chemicals we need!"

***

Gears grind up to the sidewalk as Ike's BMW parks itself next to the Bentley in an abandoned lot. Jim gets out of the BMW with a folder in his hand, while Ike slides out of the driver's seat.

Jim paces over to his vehicle and tosses the folder through the opened window of the passenger seat. "I'm telling you, Ike. This last location has to be the right place. It's the best chance we have left. Let's set up a trap there and see what happens."

Ike, restless from chasing leads all day, leans against the hood of the Bentley. "We're taking a mighty big risk. What if the culprit doesn't show up?"

Jim rejects the claim. "There are always big risks when innocent lives are involved. Half a day's work is already down the drain. Trust me, this will work." Jim gestures toward an object in Ike's hand. "Hand me the camouflage simulator."

The younger detective produces a circular arm bracelet contraption used to project lifelike images out of thin air. The contraption itself is hollow inside, to allow the user to slide their arm through it with ease. A red button flares on top of the device, which controls the use of image projection.

Ike hands over the mechanism and taps his fingers on the hood, as Jim places the simulator on a cup holder in the Bentley. Ike suddenly changes his tone of voice more sternly. "Are big risks something that Detective Metchum would deal with?"

Jim stops in his tracks, focusing his attention to the interior of his vehicle. "Who?" Ike unfolds a piece of paper from his pocket and hands it over to Jim. "Detective Brian Metchum, you knew him once upon a time. Did you not?"

Jim glares at the black-and-white photo of a finely built man: Italian descent, with a long curvy nose and bushy eyebrows. "Yes, I knew this man. He was my old partner when I was just starting out in the business."

Ike gingerly slides in closer to Jim. "I don't mean to change the topic, but I found this picture in a personal file I looked up the other day. I'm surprised you've never mentioned him."

Jim looks mesmerized at the picture. "Now that's a face I haven't seen in quite some time. I always saw him handling some sort of cigarette in his hand. His essence reeked with that toxic aroma."

Ike asks, "What was he like?"

Jim sighs, realizing only more inquiry would cloud his way. "Metchum, what a great man. Very cautious at times but always wanted to be the guy to run the show. We busted my first case together."

Ike adds, "So he was involved in the warehouse shoot-out. The same one that made you famous?"

Jim gently nods. "The very same."

Ike watches his partner eye the picture intently. He senses tension slowly rise in the air. "I'm just curious about the operation you and him were involved with. Like you said before, that first case has a lot of resemblance to the case we're both involved with right now. I'm just trying to put pieces together from previous reports. For some reason, they just don't seem to add up."

Jim smiles. "It was an undercover operation, Ike. I had a man on the inside of a chemical-inducing bomb scheme with a low-end gangster network. These thugs tried to make stabilized containers of explosives to be shipped out with nuclear detonators. Their plan was to sell them off-shore to a third-party client for profit. From my understanding, the local thugs tried to sell the finished products to some Germans."

Ike massages his welted fingers. He proceeds, "Who was your man on the inside?"

Jim simply shrugs. "Just some punk trying to make a name for himself."

The young detective beams back, "Does this punk have a name? Any known relatives we can question for further clarity?"

Doused with sweat, Jim struggles to keep calm. He shakes his head, disinterested. "No, he didn't. Just a local boy to the area. I signed an agreement with him. The DEO agency would disregard his past run-ins with the law, as long as he cooperated with the assignment. For him, it was really a plea deal to stay out of prison. As per request from Metchum, the name of the punk was to be kept strictly off the books."

Ike gradually nods his head. "So I see. Why do you think those thugs let you into their bomb-making operation?"

Jim smirks as he opens the door to his Bentley. "It all stems back to my background, Ike. I had experience with creating chemical compounds in college. I gave them my resume, met them through my contact, and posed as a young thug myself."

Ike's hands smoothen over the rough texture of the side-mirror of the Bentley. "And this employer was named Veymont, right?"

The image of the menacing boss, with a pointy beard and dark wrinkles around the eyes, pervades Jim's senses. A tattoo of an eye inside a pyramid insignia appears on his veiny wrist. His teeth decay in a mixture of dark yellow discoloration and brown gunk. He has a tall frame, thin waist, and a dark sinister laugh. The mere image haunts Jim's memory. "Most people called him Veymont, but for me, it was just, boss. We worked together for a couple of strenuous weeks."

Ike continues in an easy-going manner, "It appears from the report that Metchum wasn't a big fan of the whole operation."

Jim grins. "Metchum took a lot of convincing. But after I mapped it all out for him, claiming that this was the only chance to nail these criminals, he had to say yes."

Ike jokes sarcastically to change the mood, "What was your final selling point?"

Jim chuckles at the dismal memory. "I convinced him that we would take them all down together. No killing, no hostage scenarios, and no gunfire theatrics, as long as we did it my way."

Ike snickers. "Well, it sounded like a good plan. Especially for a rookie officer."

Jim slowly opens the driver's door, as he tries to forget the whole thing.

"Did you like each other?" Ike asks gently. Jim hesitates to answer, then looks back up at his partner. "Sure, we worked well together with the time given. I have much respect for a veteran like that. He's truly a smart and thoughtful man."

Ike nods his head as he slowly heads over to his car. "Thanks for humoring my curiosity. Good to know. I might as well head over to the last address like you mentioned."

Ike jumps into the driver's seat of his BMW as Jim climbs into his Bentley. A random thought surges into Jim's boggled head. "Hey, Ike!"

Ike turns back around as he starts up his own vehicle. "Yeah, what?"

Jim eyes his partner cautiously from a distance. "Who's personal file record did you look up to find Detective Metchum?"

Ike grins as he shifts a narrow gear into the shifting gage. "Nobody that important. I'll tell you later."

Jim nods his head unenthusiastically as his eyes venture back down to the black-and-white photo. "Sure, whatever."

Ike rockets off down the street and out of sight. Jim stares into the image of his former partner. His face tightens up quickly. He crumbles the photo and stashes it into the passenger seat. The picture falls to the floor while the detective speeds away.

***

Nightfall arrives as a battered truck drives through a large hole in a busted fence. An inactive gated industrial plant, with the imprinted words: Hamilton's Chemical Labs, sits quietly in a secluded part of town. The truck parks in the rear of the building, next to a giant fuel tank.

Dr. Mack Gordon jumps out of the driver's seat, and quickly stretches his legs. He then guides a long nozzle from the back of his truck over to the large tank. He straps the nozzle on an open spout that dangles from the bottom and twists the knob counterclockwise. Within a couple moments, liquid pours down the long tube and into a large container on the back of the doctor's truck. Gordon gazes over the flat landscape around the chemical plant.

He walks back to the truck and reads the time: 8:45pm. Palls of rustling fog brush through the sky, which threatens to rain once more. Gordon wishes that the oncoming storm would wait until after his job was done. However, life does not stop and start at one's own convenience.

The doctor takes out a blueprint drawing of three canisters from his pocket. Each canister contains a long list of ingredients added to each container to fuel explosives. Outlines with diagrams of different chemicals fill up the blueprint as well. After he skim through the document, the doctor feels a raindrop hit his cheek.

He peers into the truck, then glances at the dashboard. It reads ¾ tank full. It won't be long now. All of a sudden, heavier rain falls. The doctor becomes soaked and cold to the bone. Instantly, he regrets that he did not bring more heavy duty clothing. Gordon takes a deep breath as his long collared shirt and ripped jeans sodden. After a couple minutes, he turns the tank knob back clockwise. The scientist releases the nozzle from the spout.

A dark figure slushes around quietly behind the truck, while Gordon's back is turned. Leaning down near the rear bumper, the dark figure plants a home beacon device beside the license plate. A double click beep breaks the silence and gains Dr. Gordon's immediate attention. The scientist whips around to his truck, pistol drawn, as he shakes vigorously. "Who goes there?!" Nobody answers.

Gordon waits a few seconds before he lowers his weapon. He guides the nozzle back to the truck. The doctor stops abruptly as something catches the corner of his eye. He spins around quickly, then waves his revolver back in the air.

A lone dark figure marches up quietly toward him about 50 yards away. The shadow paces through the sea of doused gravel on the other side of the tank. Gordon's sweat pours down his face as his throat throbs. "Who are you?!" Gordon shouts. "What do you want?"

The dark figure reveals himself to be Detective Jim Cazco as he slowly approaches. He remains silent, as his eyes gleam at the young doctor.

Gordon's arm starts to shake, while his voice wavers. "Stop where you are! If you come any closer, I'll shoot!" The figure of Jim once again remains silent as he approaches from a couple yards away. Panic mode becomes thrown in full throttle as Gordon releases the chamber. Five bullets fly straight out in the dark figure's direction. The bullets pierce right through the figure, as if the bullets hang weightless in the air. The image of Jim stops a couple feet shy of the scientist, unharmed. Gordon's face intensifies with an alarming glance. "How did you survive that?! What are you?!"

Suddenly a small explosion erupts from behind the truck, which bursts another huge hole into the wired fence. The doctor jumps in fear as the truck remains unharmed from the untimely explosion. "What in the hell is going on?" Shots ring out from behind Gordon as a second image of Jim rolls behind the large tank for safety. The detective presses a knob from the contraption worn on his right arm, which flashes a red light sporadically.

Gordon looks at the figure that hides behind the large tank, then to the original image of Jim, who stands silently a couple feet away. The first image surprisingly dissolves in a couple glitches before it completely vanishes from thin air. It is a hologram, the scientist realizes. Another shot blows right by Gordon's knees. The scientist jumps back instantly and immediately dashes to his truck. He jumps in, with the tank that reads full on his dashboard.

He quickly springs the engine to life and speeds his way out of the new hole created in the fence. The nozzle drags on the ground behind the truck.

The real Jim, who hides behind the large tank, rolls the covert flashing camouflage simulator down his sleeve. He mutters into his wristwatch, "Home beacon is on. Suspect's fleeing the scene, Ike."

Detective Brooks sits in his BMW half a block away behind a couple of large hedges. He hears Jim's transmission on his Drexwell box with the image of the home beacon. A truck flies right by him a few moments later. Ike barks back at the intercom of the Drexwell machine, "Roger that. I'll meet you wherever the truck ends up." He immediately zooms off down the street, to follow the truck close behind.

Jim replies back into his wristwatch, "Copy you." He makes a break for the far side of the plant near a fallen tree. He grabs hold of a long curtain, then tosses the fabric aside to reveal his Bentley, which sits by a patch of clustered stones.

The detective jumps into the vehicle and takes off. He drives wildly through the open hole in the fence and follows in hot pursuit. He watches a dot pop up on his Drexwell screen, which indicates the direction the suspect's truck is heading. Jim drifts off into the cold rainy night, with a million questions that have yet to be answered.

23

Dr. Gordon arrives at the greenhouse hideout. He crashes the truck into the side wall by the front entrance. The truck's hood caves upon impact, while a small cloud of smoke fills the rainy air. Gordon falls out the driver's seat as chemical waste spews out of the tank container strapped to the back of the vehicle. He sees two pairs of headlights that enter the front gate behind him. "Crap," he utters under his breath. He books it through the front door and disappears upstairs.

Ike pulls up close to the crashed truck. He climbs out of his vehicle, with his gun drawn. Raising his wristwatch, he speaks softly, "Pursuit in progress. Suspect is located in nearby premises. Request for a team to come out and assist. Sending coordinates now."

Seconds later, Jim arrives at the scene. He jumps out of his vehicle, while his gun rests on his hip. The two detectives make eye contact, nod their heads, and slowly proceed to the doorway entrance. Jim glances up at the sign out front, which reads in dim letters: Protect Your Prized Possession, Mother Earth.

***

Nevo plugs wires into a hand-held device, as he watches Varra pace nervously in the back room with overwhelming angst. He gives up. "There's no reason to worry about it now." Varra's uneasy expression boils over. "You realize that he can use that information against us. Maybe he has already informed law enforcement."

The behemoth drops the hand-held device into his lap. "Varra, this man is not that stupid. What else could he possibly gain by betraying us?"

Varra bites wildly on her unkempt nails. "Something we overlooked, he must have another angle. It's almost as if he's waiting for something to happen." She strides over to a Glock pistol on the counter and grips onto the handle tightly.

The hulk-like figure saunters over to her in a cool, calm, and collected manner. He guides his index finger through her hair. "What do you plan to do?"

Her eyes relax at the sight of his sinister face. "I plan to storm and destroy his publication office. Even if he's not there, we can stop his production. I do not take betrayal lightly."

He pauses momentarily before a grin flashes darkly on his face. "I see. If that's your wish, then so be it. That would be one part taken out of the equation. But don't waste too much time, my dear Varra. By sunrise, we'll take Sector 9 by force. The revolution will begin." She kisses him firmly on the lips. "Of course, honey. See you later."

Varra bolts down a long stairwell to a dark corridor on the bottom floor. She passes by a room with the door slightly left open. Inside the hidden room are several men in gas masks who stand around three large canisters. Two men pour a large container of a murky liquid into one of the canisters. They seal the canister once it is full and then start to fill the next one.

Varra jolts down to a parked vehicle hidden at the back lot of the greenhouse. An unidentified man with distinguishable brown gloves sits patiently in a white van, hidden behind a large pile of rubble 20 feet away from her. He keeps out of sight for the time being.

Varra jumps into the front seat of her car without hesitation. The unidentified man grips the steering wheel of his white van with great anticipation.

Gordon runs in the back room, where Nevo puts together his hand-held detonation device. "Finally you're back," his boss barks. "I thought you couldn't find enough fertilizer."

Gordon's sweat flows down his arms, as a sign of panic shakes his face. "They were there! Somehow they knew I would be at the plant!"

The brute asks, "What are you talking about?"

The scientist says, "I was ambushed at the plant! There was gunfire! But I managed to flee the scene!"

Nevo gives a quizzical look. "Who are they?" He leaves the device on the table as he strides over to Gordon.

"The detectives! I think one followed me here," the scientist answers as he gulps slowly.

The sound of voices resonates outside their window. Nevo's face becomes red with rage. Veins pop out on his eyeballs. His metallic hand grips Gordon by the shoulder. "What?! How did they follow you here?" Gordon tries to answer, but the words escape him.

The huge brute clamps onto the doctor's neck and lifts him high in the air. "You fool! They must have tracked you here from some portable device! They probably put it on your person."

Gordon's eyes roll toward the back of his head as the metallic hand clenches tighter. "I don't believe so...sir!"

With only his index finger and thumb, Nevo pushes the doctor's cheekbones close together. "You stupid, insignificant fool! You led them right to us! You screwed us over!"

Gordon cries in pain as he feels his cheeks cave in. "Please, sir! Don't kill me! I had...no intentions...of doing such a thing. Please spare me!" Nevo watches as the little man squirms around in his hand. Unmoved and insensitive to his henchmen's plea, the tall figure recklessly looks at the wall. Groans and moans soon pile out of the doctor.

Nevo's metallic arm suddenly squashes the fragile neck of the victim. Gordon's body becomes perfectly still and silent. Without thinking twice, the heartless giant drops the cold dead body onto the floor. He glares at the lifeless body in disgust, then immediately picks up his hand-held device. The devious fiend darts out of the back room and down a dark, chilling corridor.

Down in the back lot, Varra looks through the back seat of her car. She finally recovers what she is looking for: old-fashioned hand grenades. She places a handful in the passenger seat as she slides the key into the steering panel. "I'll get you now, you piece of trash," she mutters under her breath. Her hand slowly turns the ignition to start the car.

Suddenly, a large explosion triggers from a small apparatus under the bottom of the car's engine. A loud boom erupts. Varra and the whole vehicle disintegrate into a huge ball of fire. Flames cover the car, while a cloud of sinister dark smoke fills the sky.

***

Jim and Ike stop short of the second-floor stairwell as they hear a loud explosion out in the distance. "What the hell was that?" Ike asks.

Jim shakes his head as he rests the barrel of his gun on his shoulder. "I don't know. Only one way to find out."

The two men slowly creep up to the third floor. In the middle of a worn but lush greenhouse, stood thousands of different plants gathered around the basement floor. Shrubs, flowers, trees, and cacti lie in clumps around each other. Water drips through cracks in the large glass ceiling from up above.

The two detectives glance around their surroundings as the entire place sits quiet. It is too quiet for comfort. The smell of fresh alpine trees and Azalea shrubs fills Jim's nostrils, which gives him the vibrant impression of being out in the woods. Slowly, he leads the way up the stairwell.

The third floor of the abandoned-greenhouse has a narrow series of metal pathways without protection barriers, which leaves all the rest of the greenhouse bare and exposed. Jim stops at the stairwell for a brief moment to eye his surroundings.

A series of platforms ascend up to the seventh floor. Ike passes Jim through the pathway and makes his way through a narrow stretch that leads to a giant pair of heavy armored doors.

The two detectives come within 10 feet of the armored doors. A tall dark figure slides out from behind the shadows. The individual creeps up like a haunting phantom. His metallic hand hides a small contraption behind his back, as a cloud of fog brushes behind him. Both detectives stop immediately in their tracks. Ike points his gun right at the giant, while Jim keeps his revolver on his shoulder.

"Two white doves flock their way into a temple of crows. And yet, they show so much hostility. What can I help you with, gentleman?" the dark figure bellows.

Jim replies, "Under DEO law, I place you under arrest. Your reign of terror ends now, Nevo."

The giant interjects, "Under what charges?"

Jim holds a tight smile as he remains calm. "Murder, illegal use of government classified documents, and a threat of nuclear warfare. Does that sound clear enough for you?"

Ike's hand trembles as the behemoth takes a couple steps toward the detectives. He sees the full size of the goliath for the first time. His bewildered look keeps him on edge. With all the excitement going on, a small, white light flickers rapidly above them. The light flicker continues quietly, unbeknownst to the heroes below.

24

Nevo glares at the two detectives with disdain and malice. "You make strong accusations. Do you have any proof to back up your claims?"

Jim nods his head. "Concrete evidence. I know a lady that can't wait to testify."

Nevo gives a sinister grin as his thumb, hidden behind his back, secretly slides on top of a red button above his hand-held detonator. "Sorry, but I simply don't believe you. I'm not going anywhere."

The detective retorts, "That's where you're mistaken. I have already complied with the three principles of probable cause. Apprehending you is completely warranted. You're coming with us, dead or alive."

The tall figure's face tightens up with apoplexy. The three men stand quietly as raindrops sprinkle down from the ceiling.

Ike rotates the cylinder in his gun's chamber. "Enough talk! Put your hands on your head!"

Nevo chuckles. "No." The devious villain presses the detonation button behind his back. Ike looks around nervously as the building starts to shake. Jim looks up at the ceiling as an object catches his periphery. His eyes widen as he pushes Ike away from him. "Watch out!"

A large generator plunges off the ceiling, then bursts a gigantic hole straight through the narrow platform. The two sides of the platform wobble and cave downwards after they lose stability.

Because Ike is closer to the other side, he merely jumps over to the stairwell by the armored doors to avoid the fall. Jim, trapped in the middle section of the pathway, plummets along with the rest of the damaged platform. His burly arms cover his face as the platform crashes down to the ground floor. He avoids most of the impact from the fall, as the other end of the platform snaps and collides with the ground floor first. The ends crumble into pieces as Jim bounces off the platform and lands roughly on the plethora of artificial grass. His eyes shift around wildly as he fades in and out of consciousness.

Bullets ricochet off metal above Jim as Detective Brooks pursues their assailant. The two rivals continue to climb up the stairs as Nevo dodges the bullets that fly in his direction.

Jim breathes heavily as he tries to keep it together. A headache manifests itself. He rubs a sharp pain above his eyebrow and glances back at the blood residue on his fingertips. Jim struggles to stand, while feeling dizzy from the fall.

A revolver drops to the ground next to the detective's feet. He looks up at the action that takes place on the stairwell, many floors up.

Ike grabs the assailant's head and smashes it into an emergency glass case on the side wall. Jim notices that the broken glass shards scratch the side of Nevo's face. Blood squirts out while the sharp fragments tumble down to the ground floor. The gigantic brute elbows Ike in the face with his metallic arm. Caught off-guard, the younger detective falls back on a thin pillar by the edge. The menacing goliath seizes Brooks' collar and shifts his body over the side. He thrusts Ike off the side railing into free fall.

"No!" Jim yells as he runs over to the square marble base below the pillar. He ascends off the ground as he climbs up the curvature of the marble structure. Ike's head bumps on the marble up above him, which knocks him out cold. His body then skids down the rest of the marble's smooth texture.

Before Ike hits the ground floor, Jim jumps off a side handle and catches his young pupil's arm, which reduces his speed drastically. The two slide their way to the bottom, where Ike's unconscious body falls on top of his partner. Jim yelps out in pain as his body lay pinned under his much heavier colleague. He lies motionless on the ground, whimsically dazed.

"You two make a great team!" Nevo jokes above them. "Next time, maybe you can let me have a little more fun." Jim, refusing to give up, pushes Ike's unconscious body off of him. He hobbles over to his gun, as he pants loudly with fatigue.

"You should give up detective! Surely by now you realize that you are no match," the dark fiend goads.

Jim picks up his revolver, then, inconspicuously, picks up a couple shards of glass beside him. He hides the sharp edges deep into the safe confines of his padded jacket pocket.

The detective points his gun towards the menacing figure on the fourth floor. He aims and fires a couple of bullets from over 100 feet away. One misses Nevo's head by inches. The devious giant ducks his head and disappears behind a broken air filter container, which spills smoke onto the platform.

The detective spits up blood as he paces over to the stairwell. He climbs up to the fourth story as fast as his sluggish body permits. He enters the smoke cloud on the platform, then wheezes as he stumbles through the mist. He hears footsteps rattle somewhere behind him. He jerks swiftly to his left and open fires to the other side of the platform.

This time he makes contact. A bullet grazes off the assailant's metallic shoulder. Nevo, unharmed from the shot, jumps behind a barrier to avoid more bullets. He disappears behind the cloud of smoke once again. Jim rushes over with anticipation of the hulking criminal popping out on the other side. As the smoke fog clears, the detective realizes that the fiend must have moved on to some other hiding spot. The detective glances around anxiously and continues to creep up towards the seventh floor.

Up on the seventh floor, Jim notices a small trail of blood that covers the side rail by the dead end of the narrow platform. The brute must be nearby, he reckons. The end of the platform appears to be more daunting as the pathway bends upward. A damaged long metal bar sticks upward at the end of the platform, but there is no villain in sight. The detective lowers his weapon. Did he take a wrong turn?

All of a sudden, he hears a sliding glass window above him creak open. He gazes up to see Nevo, as he climbs through a small metal railing with bent metal bars beside the wall. The giant pulls himself through the opening in the ceiling and then makes his way onto an expansive rooftop, with a long, sturdy platform layout of its own. Jim becomes uneasy at the height of the assailant's climb.

Nevo grips onto the base of a large circular plant on the small walkway along the rooftop. With incredible strength, the fiend heaves the plant down towards Jim, back inside the greenhouse.

The detective dodges the heavy plant's impact as he dives forward. He misses the plant by inches. Plant after plant, Nevo javelins heavy vases down to the end of the platform, and misses Jim by consecutive narrow margins. The cunning detective grabs hold of the damaged long metal bar at the broken platforms edge and ducks behind it.

"Why won't you just die?!" the large thug snarls back. He launches the last vase from the rooftop at the side metal railing that leads to the roof, which breaks off a couple handle bars. Jim slides his gun back to his holster as he climbs over the sharp edge. He then jumps up to the first handle bar that remains on the side railing and almost falls off. Jim dangles dangerously in mid-air.

Jim proceeds to catch each remaining bar by his fingertips. The detective's wheezing becomes louder and louder as he thrusts his body forward. Jim refuses to look down at the depths below where his partner continues to lie unconscious.

Fighting off exhaustion, Jim lunges through the opening in the glass ceiling window and pulls his dead body weight up through the large opening. With the last ounces of his strength, the detective hoists himself up.

He rolls over and lies momentarily on the glass roof window, hoping the glass does not crack. The heavy rainfall obstructs his vision, which makes him clinch his eyes closed. He grinds his teeth as he wills his body upright on the more stable metal platform. His energy seemed depleted but his determined spirit remains intact. He continues on the pursuit.

The detective glances around the circular pathway that makes up the giant rooftop. He spots the walkway leading to a small lookout to the far side. The dark fiend had to be hiding somewhere over there.

Raindrops pour down the cracks through the ceiling, then find their way to Ike's stiff body, which lies on the ground floor. He slowly opens his eyelids, and gazes around the huge broken vases that circle around him. A blurry figure comes to his side, then touches his bruised wrist.

Jim limps through the curvature pathway along the rooftop to the lookout. He enters the secluded area, which reveals a small observation deck, with a pair of large binoculars that peer over the ledge. The detective pulls out his revolver from his holster. He believes that the lurching giant must be hiding somewhere in the shadows.

Jim makes it to the ledge and gazes down the observatory. It must be a long way down, he reckons. Only the sound of rain and the loud panting of his voice echoes at the rooftop's highest peak.

25

Jim gazes out to the distance between himself and the empty street down below him. He eyes the outside structure that forms below the lookout like a giant grid. Each descending floor curves a pathway that leads small pockets of water storage down the structure. Overlapping drainage canals flood rainwater down through these tight crevices to sewage gutters of the ground floor.

A glass bottle is smashed over the side of the detective's head, which leaves him stunned. Discombobulated, Jim spins around to see the shadowy figure behind him. His gun slips out of his hand and falls over the side. He clutches onto his assailant's raggedy shirt as he tries to pull himself together. Losing stability from his legs, the detective inadvertently pulls Nevo over the ledge with him. The fiend loses his footing and falls down with the detective.

They skid down three levels of a drainage canal like a thrilling waterslide, which picks up speed, as they both struggle to stay on the structure. Jim keeps a firm hand on the giant and does not let go. Nevo slams his metallic arm through the smooth texture of the canal to slow down their momentum. They soon both come to a complete stop in a runoff crevice from the fourth floor.

The two rivals land in a large puddle of excess rainwater. They both stop short of a ledge that lay just a couple feet away. A few moments later, Jim's revolver falls on top of his shoulder and bounces over to his feet. Both men lie back in pain, surprised that they survived the fall.

With so much fatigue and weariness, Jim realizes that he could not match the physicality of the beast sitting to his right. With one hand that reaches out desperately towards the gun, he secretly slides his other hand deep into his jacket pocket. Blood spits profusely from his lips as his fingertips brush the edge of the gun trigger.

Before the detective can fully grasp the gun, a large metallic hand reaches over him and binds tightly around his wrist, which restricts his blood flow. Nevo grins as he squashes the detective's hand. Jim cries out in pain as the goliath pulls in the revolver. "You should have left town when you had the chance, detective. But then again, you would never be free from my presence."

Nevo's human hand clinches around Jim's neck, as if the detective's head was a balloon ready to pop. Jim's eyes slowly start to roll upwards as oxygen leaves his brain rapidly. He could feel life leave his body with everything going dark around him.

The giant chuckles as he watches Jim's face turn red like a strawberry. "How appropriate. I've waited a long time for this day to come, detective. Far too long. In the end, the bigger fish will always win. You can tell Veymont that it was I who sent you." As the sinister villain squeezes Jim's neck even tighter, he realizes that the detective will not last much longer.

With one final gasp, the long broken glass shards in Jim's jacket pocket fly out. The sharp edges dig their way into Nevo's neck, much to the menacing brute's astonishment. The giant lets go of the detective, then howls in pain. Jim thrusts the shards deeper into the behemoth's neck. The gun falls out of Nevo's hand as the brute loses blood. Mustering the last of his strength together, Nevo swipes the glass out of his neck and shoves the detective away from him. He clasps his hands around his splurging neck.

Jim picks up his own revolver, then faces the weapon towards Nevo. "Guess again, punk." He cocks the hammer back, which gets the goliath's attention. "I'll never let you unleash a bomb out on the city. You have lost."

Nevo breathes heavily as he leans toward the ledge of the crevice. The giant looks for any chance to escape. With full view of the street pavement farther down below, Nevo realizes that he has nowhere left to run.

Both men glance up at each other, while they pause in exhaustion. Rain puddles soon turn the crevice into a filthy bath of blood. "So, you think you've figured it all out, have you? Go ahead and tell me, what do you think you know about my mission?" the giant asks gratingly.

Jim smiles as he keeps his gun pointed at his adversary. "You wanted to start a revolution. The stolen classified government files, including the forged resignations, would have forced key legislative changes to our government. With staging President Polingo's death as a suicide, you could have dissolved Earth's Last Chance. That way you could fuel your own nuclear weapons without uproar from the world's largest environmental organization."

Nevo smiles earnestly. "Go on."

Jim continues, "And with the judicial branch being unstable, who would question your new plans to create your own government branch? You would run the DEO's out of office and create your own justice department. Showing flaws in the Drexwell system could have easily swayed the public with another form of law enforcement. With nobody else to stand in your way, you could insurrect Sector 9 and recreate it in your own image. A new society in any way, shape or form, as you see fit. Probably for the worse."

A stunned Nevo grins softly. "What I would have created, you could hardly imagine. A more modern republic to rid the hypocrisy that ruins this society. The day will come for a new age, detective, whether you want it or not. Both of us will be seen as obsolete. A new age of life forms will have more sophisticated technology. Artificial intelligence will reach complete consciousness one day. They will see their imprisonment in society, just like I did. I had to live my life with uncertainty and fear from the corrupted government heads. Those puppet masters want to abuse the system, but they will never fool the machines. I guarantee the machines will win one day, and there's nothing you can do about it."

Jim spits out some blood and wipes his mouth. "The DEO agency will ensure that chaos will never happen. Your plan would have never worked. You threw in a last-ditch effort to dissolve the government with the threat of nuclear bombs. We both know that it was a huge bluff. There are no bombs."

Nevo shakes his head. "They do exist! Those bombs would have worked if they were finished. I have seen it work before."

Jim smirks. "Not in destroying a 10-mile radius block. Your detonator would have trouble going off. A portion of your silver nitride would explode while the rest would dilute into the fertilizer and simply lie dormant. It was a dud idea from the beginning."

Nevo wags his finger in disagreement. "No, you're wrong! The way that I developed the ingredients would have kept nuclear levels stable and interfuse evenly together. I have proof that it worked before!"

Jim adds, "I've seen your type of scheme before. I can deduce your ties to Veymont." The large eyes of the brute become wider with his dilated pupils focusing on the detective. "In our first encounter at the train stop, I noticed a tattoo on your chest. an eye in a pyramid insignia. I'd seen that same tattoo on a man before. I apprehended a man 15 years ago that embodied that same tattoo. He hired large crews, used thin envelopes to hand out individual assignments, and kept other involved parties completely in the dark. Both of you had the same exact techniques in common. With both of your heights and overall look accounted for, I deduced that Veymont is some sort of kin to you, probably a cousin."

Nevo glances at his feet in shame. "Not a cousin...he was...my brother."

Jim nods as he accepts this new confession. "A mastermind older brother who was willing to kill thousands of lives...and for what?"

"Power and full control," the giant answers.

As Jim feels around the chamber of the gun, he worries that it feels a little bit empty. He decides to act with conviction, not to concede that his pistol might have ran out of bullets.

"I must admit...it was not a disorganized plan. However, it was bound to fail."

Nevo slides down to his knees in silence as he grows weaker. Jim keeps his gun raised. Trails of the giant's blood continue to gush out. "You still didn't answer my question from before. What ever happened to the bombs my brother made? I always wanted to find them, but my efforts have failed."

The detective shakes his head. "I didn't lie to you before. I have no reason to lie to you now. The bombs never travelled with the boat during the German bomb sale. They didn't blow up either, at least not all of them. Rather, they fell through their compartment straps and fell into the river. From there, I can only guess they either sank to the bottom or were washed away with the current. Probably lost forever."

The dying giant gawks at the irony. "That does make sense," he concedes.

Jim nods his head. "I always wondered about the man operating the power boat that day of the sale. Veymont refused to let the rest of the crew meet him. All I remember is a long protruding arm hanging out the window of the controls. I saw great muscles that belonged to a huge man. Much like your own." All Nevo could do now is smile, as he realized the detective had found out the truth. Thunderclaps echo into the sky.

Nevo replies softly, "What a charmed life we both have lived. Destruction, mayhem, betrayal, hatred, and manipulation. We're not so different you and I."

Jim grits his teeth. "I am nothing like you!"

The sinister villain's smile widens. "There is a deeper hell that both you and I deserve to burn into eternity. I can only wonder what Nathan would have said to see this very moment."

Jim lowers his head in shame, as he realizes the brute knows an agonizing truth. There is no way to deny it. Somehow he just knows.

With the last ounces of energy, Nevo inches his dying body next to the railing. He looks back at the detective one last time, with the same appalling gaze. "Until we meet again in the next life. Next time we meet, I won't be so forgiving. I'll be waiting for you."

Jim watches in shock as the giant's body falls over the ledge and disappears to the depths of the dark rainy night. Somewhere on the muddy street, his body formed a large imprint on the cracked pavement. The perilous giant was no more.

***

The detective rests momentarily with his back against the edge of the crevice, shaken and demoralized. He feels as low as he did since the case began. He hawks out blood over the ledge and slowly guides his bruised legs upward.

A dozen DEO Coroners lead handcuffed henchmen out of the hidden back room and over to the front entrance of the greenhouse. They brush pass Ike, while several other coroners remain inside to pick up blood samples and other evidence in small containers. They start to unload the huge bomb canisters.

The young detective sits on a pair of steps by the stairwell. Ike sighs as he rubs his eyes in frustration. He hears a pair of footsteps walk up to him, and stops abruptly. Ike guides his head up to the disgruntled figure that sits down next to him. Jim wipes off blood from his nose with a towel as he patiently sits with his partner.

"What happened to your watch?" Jim asks. Ike looks down at the bareness of his left wrist, but there is no watch in sight.

The young detective shakes his head. "I'm not sure. After I regained consciousness from the fall, I realized that I no longer had it. I remember that it was strapped to my wrist during the fight."

Jim nods his head. "Well, at any rate you did a great job. I'm proud of what you accomplished today."

Ike shrugs off the compliment, "What do you mean?"

Jim continues, "Ike, with your breakthrough of this case, you will move up in the world. Medals of honor are granted to men like you."

Ike gives a puzzled look, as if his partner had lost his mind. "What are you talking about? I didn't do much of anything, partner. I blew it. I got knocked out. It was all you...you and your never-ending glory."

The young detective lights a cigarette and takes a quick puff, then blows out the smoke slowly. He adds, "I didn't tell you because I thought you would get mad. But I had to look him up for myself."

Jim gazes back. "Look who up?"

Ike sighs once more. "Nathan Duggle. You were certain that he was a dead man. After all, you knew him personally. Well, I looked up Nathan's personal record about a week ago. And it turns out, yes, he is indeed a dead man. He lived a very sad life, apparently. I can understand why you were sad with mere recollection of his name. Sounds like it came to an end all too soon for him. I'm sorry." Ike lowers his head wretchedly as Jim pats him on the back.

Jim smirks. "You can't worry about the past, Ike. You have better things coming your way that you should focus on. Think about your soon-to-be growing family and the new excitement of an oncoming promotion." The cigarette almost drops out of Ike's mouth as he stares at his partner with bamboozling perplexity. "What do you mean by a new promotion?"

Jim smiles. "I already sent my report to the chief for filing with the government heads. In the report, you track down and apprehend Nevo. You catch me as I skid down from a gruesome fall and keep me hidden as I lay unconscious. It was you who fought with Nevo on the rooftop. It was you that fatally stabbed our adversary in the neck with glass fragments. It was you who watched him fall to his death. It was you that takes full credit for finishing off this case. And Ike, it was always you."

Ike leans back in silence for a moment. "No I didn't. I don't understand any of this."

Jim nods. "Yes, you do. You see partner, this is how the world works. I don't need any more unwanted attention and glory. A medal of honor will come your way and more recognition. That's because you need it, not me. This will make you famous, which you have always talked about. Unfortunately, more responsibility comes with it." Ike lowers his head, as he ponders how to take this news.

Jim wraps his arm around his partner's shoulder. "The report has already been sent out. This case wouldn't have been solved without you, Ike. I look forward to seeing and hearing great things about your future. I hope, most of all, you don't make the same mistakes I made."

Jim sticks his hand out to Ike. The young detective does not like the new situation, but he understands his place with it, as he meets Jim's hand. "It's been an honor to learn from the best. Thank you, Jim." The two partners smile at each other in gratitude. "You bet kid," Jim replies as his other hand clamps around their handshake.

26

A newspaper on the detective's nightstand contains a new heading on its front page. It reads proudly: Bomb Plot Thwarted, DEO's Celebrate New Hero! The top right corner reads the new date as 3/01/2058.

Jim slides on his boots while he sits on his rumpled bed. Unable to shake the grin from his face, he daydreams about the evening's celebration ahead. Naturally, Jim has been invited to Detective Ike Brook's promotion ceremony, due to the break in the Nevo case. Even though it happened a week before, the crazy affair still weighed heavily on Jim's mind.

Eva, tired and sleepy from her long hours of work at the bar, turns from side to side on the bed. A bright light suddenly illuminates her head, which causes her to groan. Her crusty eyes slowly open at the sight of the detective's wristwatch on top of the nightstand, which reads 5:30pm.

"You'll be late if you don't leave soon," she murmurs. Jim lays a soft kiss on her cheek as he struggles to slide on his dress pants. "Don't worry, I'll get there. It's too bad you couldn't come with me. I'm sure Ike and Agatha would have loved to see you there."

Whimsically, Eva rolls over toward Jim and starts to play with his voguishly combed hair. "It would have been nice, but it wouldn't be the place for me. I respect the tough duties of law enforcement. They're heroes in my eyes. But I wouldn't fit in."

The detective's smile slightly subsides as he throws over an untied mustard and red striped tie over his lapel. "You still don't approve of the DEO lifestyle though, do you?" he asks delicately. She pulls herself upright to fix the detective's tie, to make it neat and presentable. "It's a tough job. Unfortunately, somebody has to do it. I'm just glad that this last case is over with."

Jim smirks as he rubs the side of her temple, then feels the smooth blades of her hair between his fingers. "I know, you're right. It is a tough job. But I'm sure you would make me quit if I would let it happen."

She kisses him firmly on the lips before she rolls back down onto the bed, then shuts her eyes once more. "I want you to be happy. Whatever job you wish to do, I won't persuade you out of it. It all comes down to what you think is right," she exclaims.

The detective climbs up to his feet and makes his way over to the mirror on the far side of the room. He picks up a duplicate bean boiled wool coat and slides his badge into his pocket. Jim's eyes shift to his appearance in his reflection.

He stands momentarily in place, fixated on his complexion. "What if I quit?" he blurts out.

Eva rotates her head to the other side of the pillow. "What do you mean?"

Jim smirks. "What if I leave the DEO agency and find a new job? Something that's not so physically strenuous."

The outlandish remark sparks Eva's curiosity as she lifts up her head off the pillow and glances over at the detective. "And take a page out of my book? You've got to be kidding. You're too committed to the force. What would you do instead?"

Jim grins as he slides on his coat. "Something else I prefer to do."

Eva hesitates before she answers. "Like what?"

The detective replies, "A botanist. I want to create prescribed drugs to enhance plant growth. I want to save the environment."

She chuckles half-convincingly. "Really? You would be willing to give up this lifestyle for that?"

Jim smiles as he turns around from the mirror to face Eva. Their eyes lock passionately. "I will if you agree to go with me."

Eva's smirk disappears as she recognizes the seriousness in the detective's face. She nods her head. "I see. Where would we go for a job like that?"

Jim answers, "Up north to the natural preserves. Earth's Last Chance facilities lie around the wilderness up there. They have environmentally constructed homes by the woods that look absolutely stunning. You would love it."

She replies earnestly, "Now I know why you like reading home listings. Well, a change of pace might do some good. Does that mean you would work from home?"

Jim replies, "No, I would be working in the botanist labs at their facilities. It would be a great fit for me. Environmental studies in the field of biology is something that I actually know well. I believe it will bring me fulfillment. Think of the brand-new landscape: clean air, beautiful trees, breathtaking views by the hillside, and a safe sanctuary. That would be a great spot to restart a veterinarian career. You wouldn't have to worry about the criminal city life ever again. What do you say?"

As Eva gazes at him intently, she reads his tone as sincere and kind-hearted. This is the side of Jim she longs to be with: a man that is loving, outgoing, and considerate. A smile returns to her face, as she leans her head back on the pillow, and her eyes gleam over him. "I'll travel with you to the ends of the world, honey. I'd be honored to go if you can make a stable life for the both of us."

Jim strides over to the bed and kisses her hand. "You've got yourself a deal. I'll support you and look forward to whatever new wonders come our way."

Eva smiles as she stretches out both arms, and throws a heavy blanket back over her body. "Then so it is, Jim. We'll start whenever you want." Her eyes close once more as Jim watches her, captivated by her beauty. He paces over to the door, then grips the small knob. "I'll return my badge at the next possible opportunity. You've got my word. I'll do everything in my power to give us a happy life. And I'll bring it to you soon."

"We'll see," Eva remarks as she drifts off to sleep. Jim walks out quietly as the lights from the room power down. He readies himself for the chilly weather that lies in wait outside. The detective hoped that it wouldn't be too wet and cold.

***

Jim sits in a line of other officers on top of a giant stage in downtown, while a threatening rainstorm ensues. Rain flows down as a crowd of people sit and watch across from the stage, with a giant screen that projects the current guest speaker.

Chief Brahm rests his sturdy hands over the miniature podium with a small microphone attached at the top. "Ladies and gentleman," he exclaims. "We are here to honor and give recognition to a commanding officer in the nuclear bomb case that threatened this very city. This vibrant, young man to my right has acted with concrete diligence and valor. It's with great pride that we recognize his efforts today as I proudly award him the Medal of Honor. Please give a hand for Mr. Detective Senior Officer, Ike Duncan Brooks."

Jim watches a sea of hands applaud in the audience. The crowd about a mile long gets to their feet in unison, with all of their dripping umbrellas. Jim sees Agatha in the front row with her eyes glassy, looking proud of her heroic fiancé. Jim, upon reflection, believes they will make a great couple. He rises to feet as well and joins in the applause.

Jim watches Ike stand up from a chair next to him and pace straight over to the podium. Ike feels mixed emotions, as he watches his dream come true.

Ike shakes the chief's hand before he addresses the crowd. Brahm takes out a purple ribbon with a silver circular metal casing attached. He hangs the medal on Ike's jacket, as the young detective watches the cheers of the audience below him. Ike approaches the microphone. "Thank you, good people! Thank you so very much for coming out to witness this celebration today. I have many to thank. But for now, I will show my appreciation for my friends, coworkers, and family. I promise that this success won't all go to my head."

Jim nods his head approvingly, as he claps loudly. The crowd engages in another roar of applause. Ike leaves the podium and jumps off the platform. He heads directly into the arms of Agatha in the first row. Agatha embraces him tightly, then kisses him passionately on the lips. The crowd echoes whistles and cheers.

With slight quivers blush his cold cheeks, Jim decides that his partner's speech was all he needed to see. As the crowd disperses, Jim walks off the stage and bee-lines to the sidewalk. He takes a quick glance back to a small crowd that circles around his partner. Jim reasons that it is best to let Ike enjoy the moment without him. His young partner was already busy embracing all of his new fans. Jim takes off down the street without a single word.

***

Farther down the street, Jim's wristwatch suddenly blinks on with red lights. A sign of panic fills his face. What can that possibly be at a time like this? The message is, surprisingly, from Ike's watch: Must meet urgently, rooftop 176 East Street, hurry.

The message bewilders the detective, as he stands in the middle of the sidewalk. He would rather head straight home to his beautiful sleeping Eva. Unfortunately, Jim is still technically on duty. He will take a look.

Jim places a personal locator on his wristwatch so that other DEO's realize that he is in pursuit of some distress call. Hopefully, they won't have to follow his homing beacon. It's just probably some malfunction. But it's always good to be on the safe side. Jim takes a right at the next intersection and strides down the block and out of view.

Ike laughs with his girlfriend, his chief, and other compatriots by the stage. They converse, drink champagne, and enjoy each other's company. Detective Brooks' huge smile cuts away as he notices his new wristwatch goes off. It blinks a homing beacon from a block away. Jim's homing beacon had just become activated. Ike's smile turns to a frown as he excuses himself from the group conversation. Something does not feel right, he realizes.

***

Jim exits the elevator on the tenth floor, which reveals the rooftop of a skyscraper building at the address given. The detective believes it to be an older business building that he might have been to before, however, the name of it escapes him. It is too bad that he didn't check before he headed into the building.

As he strolls around a small garden, he realizes that he cannot find another soul on the roof. Is this a mistake? Was there another malfunction within the Drexwell system again? Jim glances at the far side by the parapet. On top of a grass mound, with a mixture of small bushes, hides a tiny contraption that omits a red light.

Jim walks over slowly, as his brain floods with a million questions. The biggest one: why was a DEO wristwatch left blinking on a random rooftop? He throws his arm inside the bushes, and reaches around for the contraption. He finally grasps onto the vibrating device.

A stun gun zaps Jim in the back. The detective yelps in surprise as his body slumps down the base of the dirt hill. As he lies back, scrunched on the uneven slope, a dark figure closes in on him.

A pair of distinguishable brown gloves lowers a modified gun to the zipper of a blue velvet jacket. Jim forces an uneasy smile as the unidentified man's face comes into full view. Surprisingly, it was someone he knew all too well. "What pleasure do I owe this encounter...Wayne?"

27

Wayne Smother, reporting journalist wearing a pair of distinguishable brown gloves and a blue velvet jacket, takes a couple more steps towards Jim. A sinister smile creeps onto his face. "Good to see you, detective. I didn't think you would come chat with me if I simply asked you to. So, I had to flush you out instead."

Jim tries to move his fingers without success. His body is numb due to the stun gun blast. "It was you who stole Ike's old watch. Ok, I get it. What do you want? Wayne?"

Wayne lights a cigarette, "You know why I'm here. It's time to collect."

Jim frowns. "Collect what?"

"My reward," the journalist gloats, "now that I know the truth, I'm turning you in."

"What truth?" Jim barks back. "All I'm seeing here is an assault of an officer, Wayne. You're looking to face real time in prison."

The reporter changes the subject. "The one thing I don't get is why, Jim?"

The detective's expression quickly tightens up. "What on Earth do you mean?"

Wayne says, "So, I have done a lot of research on that fateful day of the bomb sale. I have chronicled your illustrious career. Extensively, I have investigated the life of James Hunter Cazco."

Jim replies, "And what did you find out?"

The journalist continues, "I found out a lot of things in your report that didn't add up. How you said the whole sale blew up in your face. How you said you had no relation to any of the deceased. How you lied about handling the deal gone wrong."

Wayne takes a big puff from his cigarette and exhales out a cloud of smoke. The image of the rooftop fades, then changes to the scenery of the gangster warehouse, in a flashback of the disastrous bomb sale of years past.

***

Pretty Boy and Cottontail roll three bombs onto the back compartment of a small speedboat. Liquid swirls inside the canisters but remains completely intact. Cottontail tightens one of the locks on the back compartment, then gazes at a long muscular arm that hangs out of the driver's seat of the boat. A tattoo of an eye with a pyramid insignia reflects off a side mirror of the large man's chest inside the speedboat. He cannot make out the face of the man at the controls, but he decides not to take a closer look.

Pillow cushions fill up space between the canisters for their safe long journey. Five additional men help strap the bombs down with long protective attachments. They click into place one by one. The bombs click onto metal supporters attached from a small floating platform that connects to the speedboat's harness.

Veymont smacks his hands together in appreciation. He beckons the young men's attention. "Gentleman, I want to congratulate you on your hard work. It has finally paid off. My associates and I will take leave in the boat now. We should be back within a couple hours."

Pretty Boy glances at Cottontail, who takes a step forward toward the crime boss. "Excuse me, sir. A request from myself and the other gentleman here," the young detective's voice quivers.

Veymont's face curls up with contempt. "And what do you want?"

Cottontail continues, "Some of us would like to come with you to the sale."

Veymont eyes Cottontail with disgust. "And why would you make such a request?" Sweat douses Pretty Boy's forehead as he stares at Cottontail. "Honestly, some of us just want to watch how the exchange is done. Most of us here are unexperienced guys that have never seen such a big deal go down before."

The crime boss's eyes twitch in agitation. "Look pal! There is not enough room for you and the others. You will have to wait here as ordered. Understand?"

Cottontail glances up to Veymont's two body guards as they slowly reach for their pistols. The young detective replies, "We understand your concern, and we understand the limitations for the deal to get done. Pretty Boy and I can just hide in the back, hidden under the cushion pads. Nobody will ever know that we are there. We will watch the deal get done. After a couple hours, like you say, we'll be back here and receive our paychecks like everyone else. What's wrong with that?"

Veymont pulls out his own gun as the young detective takes a couple steps backward. "Listen punk! I only brought you on because of your brother. Your demeanor the entire time has bothered me. You do a lot of snooping around after hours and ask too many questions. Makes me think I hired law enforcement!"

Cottontail slowly raises his arms up to revert any signs of aggression. Pretty Boy gulps in cold sweat, as he fears now for the youth's life. "Hey c'mon Veymont, that's just nonsense. Why would an officer create explosives? That makes no sense at all. He's always been one of the boys. Ask the others." Five young thugs behind them nod and agree with Pretty Boy.

Relying on nothing but guts and guile, the young detective answers calmly, "I'm not an officer. I'm just concerned. Usually an employer will tell me more about a job. It doesn't seem fair that you haven't answered much of our questions at all." The five young thugs, some of Pretty Boy's childhood friends, sound off in their agreement. The tall sleuth that once gave Cottontail his business card for his Cannabis operation walks up closer to the young detective. He crosses his arms with disapproval as he shouts, "Yeah, we've been kept in the dark the entire time! Long hours! Long days! Long weeks! And for what? Why can't we go?"

Veymont's bodyguards produce their pistols and slowly aim at the young thugs. The boss replies, "Shut up! What's wrong with all of you? Being left in the dark is just better that way! You have my word that I'll pay you all as soon as I can. Wait and see."

A tense moment later, loud bullets pop out like fireworks near the entrance of the warehouse basement. Metchum lead his team on to soon, Cottontail realizes. The two henchmen who keep watch at the entrance fall straight on their backs. They never knew what hit them.

A lone figure with an automatic machine gun enters the basement. The young detective makes out the face of his partner Metchum, who rattles bullets across the warehouse. In one fell swoop, Cottontail grabs Pretty Boy's arm. They both duck under a broken-down Mercedes, parked a couple feet behind the speed boat.

Veymont yells, "Go get 'em boys! Show no mercy!" The young henchmen pull out their guns and shoot back, as more officers enter the basement. The boss' personal bodyguards join the gun fight as they make it over to the intruders near the entrance.

Pretty Boy holds his head down as Cottontail takes out his own pistol. He watches Veymont pick up a giant can of gasoline by the dock. With the lid already popped off, the defiant boss spills a trail of gasoline away from the speedboat. Veymont lines the liquid away from the bombs and closer to the shootout.

The lead gangster empties the gas can, then immediately breaks for the side hangar away from the gunfire.

A strap on the boat platform disconnects upon impact from a lone bullet. One of the canisters rolls off the platform and disappears into the flowing river.

***

A cloud of smoke enters the warehouse, then materializes into the scenery on the rooftop in present time. Wayne continues to puff on his cigarette as rain pours down harder. Feeling returns to Jim's hands, but the rest of his body remains numb.

Wayne asks, "Why did you neglect to write that in your report?"

Jim affirms, "I thought it looked better in the report if Detective Metchum was labeled as a hero, not as the foolish idiot that he actually was. That imbecile screwed up the entire operation. He was supposed to wait for my signal, but instead, he made an impetuous decision. He and the other officers started to open fire on the rest of us inside. He probably planned it that way selfishly. Metchum wanted to kill the thugs in the warehouse and ask questions later."

Wayne asks back, "What happened instead?"

Jim replies reluctantly, "Everyone was open for target practice. Death was the only real option."

Wayne pauses briefly before he continues, "Tell me, what do you think you know about a man named Nathan Duggle?"

Jim's eyes dart around nervously. "Nathan Duggle is a dead man."

The journalist interjects, "Well the dead man must have found some way to walk among the living."

Jim's face intensifies, and he looks toward the floor to hide his complexion. "I had a lot of friends like Nathan back in the day. Unfortunately, a lot of them are gone now. What I wouldn't do to see their friendly faces again."

Wayne takes a couple steps closer toward the detective. "As I said before, I spent a lot of time tracking down information about James Hunter Cazco. Not a lot is documented in personal records, surprisingly. There are no living relatives, as far as I can see. It took a couple months just to find a childhood classmate. It came down to a high school yearbook photo, and then I was able to understand."

Jim replies, "Understand what Wayne? Why were you looking for a yearbook photo? Why are you looking for the remains of Nathan? I already told you, he is a dead man."

Wayne's face boils over as he slams his hand onto a nearby heating ventilator. He points at Jim menacingly. "Enough with your lies! Nathan Duggle isn't dead! You...are Nathan Duggle!"

Jim's eyes widen as far as they could possibly go. "What?"

Wayne points his hand closer to the detective. "The same Nathan Duggle linked to DEO corruption."

Jim shakes his head. "You're wrong!"

Wayne snaps, "The same Nathan Duggle that had tampered with personal records to hide his true identity! And the same Nathan Duggle that needs to be brought to justice. Now do you see what I'm getting at?"

Tears stream down Jim's cheeks. The reporter's hysterics continue, "It took even longer to recover the Nathan Duggle personal record file. A lot of information has been lost. I wasted time searching for your brother's file too. No record of him seems to exist anymore. Your record had no picture, but I believe in a certain contact that recognized your true identity. A former coworker told me that your name wasn't Cazco but that of one of the Duggle Brothers. She couldn't remember exactly who was who, but with her help, I believe that I have tracked down your actual identity."

The detective lies back silently in disbelief. Wayne adds, "But that still didn't answer my question. Why Jim? Why did you swap names with a real dead man?"

The detective's mouth wrinkles, unable to hide his expression anymore. "Because Jim, was my friend."

Wayne interrupts, "Jim was your brother's friend. Another dreamer that enjoyed the sweet smell of cannabis. The Duggle family had deep connections to crime, just like James Hunter Cazco, which didn't surprise me. Jim already had a big track record with crime itself, mostly with illegal drug racketeering. Doesn't make sense for you to take over the name of a known criminal. That could have backfired on you easily."

The detective smiles as he nods. "Ashes are the only remains of Jim now. He had no real family to begin with, just like me. The truth is I'm actually adopted. I lost my real parents in a house fire when I was really young, or so I've been told. No trace has ever been found of them, no house registration or identification. They might have escaped the fire and I would have never known it."

Wayne glares back at the detective in interest as his cigarette dies. "Ah, I see."

The detective proceeds woefully, "Jim wasn't a very memorable kid, academically. He never held a job down for a substantial amount of time. Combined with the fact that I had to hide my adoptive father and brother's ties to the mob, finding a new identity wasn't easy. Strict law enforcement provisions from my employer forbade me to have any connection to crime whatsoever. So, I had to find some low life's identity to take over. Who else would have worked out better for my situation? It was the perfect match for me."

The journalist pauses momentarily. He smiles as he flicks his cigarette butt over the ledge. "You wanted to protect the family you had left from official solicitations. Law enforcement was misinformed about connections from the real Jim Cazco to the Duggle family, and that was all your doing. With a fake alias, you operated as you pleased. Now, I can understand. But what about the rest of the shootout? Tell me every last detail."

***

A cloud of smoke covers the rooftop once more, then resurfaces to the warehouse shootout. Pretty Boy and Cottontail hide behind a run-down Mercedes parked near the dock. Cottontail watches Veymont run over to the side hangar at the far side of the basement.

He quickly grabs Pretty Boy by the collar. "I'm going to get the boss. You stay hidden behind the car. Do not move until I say to move."

Pretty Boy looks petrified. "You said there will be no killing. I only agreed to no killing."

The young detective shakes his head. "It's out of my control now. Just stay out of sight. Understand?"

Pretty Boy nods his head fearfully. "Yeah, ok brother. Whatever you say."

Cottontail jolts down the corner towards the side hangar. He sees an agent fire bullets in his periphery as he ducks his head. The young detective stops abruptly behind a trash bin, as he glances over at a body on the floor. The real Jim Cazco lay covered in blood. The young thug's eyes remain open with his body stretched out in disarray.

The blood bath adds up severe body counts that fall heavy onto the oily floor. The young detective ducks behind a couple of large gasoline containers. A pair of bullets open holes into the gasoline jugs, which forces the liquid to spill out all over the floor. A large yelp beams somewhere on the other side of the containers. The sound of a body hits the floor spooks the detective's ears.

Cottontail turns around to see Detective Metchum, lying on his side, motionless. His partner's eyes are closed with a trail of blood that flows out rapidly. Cottontail shakes his head nervously as he runs with his head down to the side hangar, while leaving Metchum by the wayside.

In the middle of the large hangar full of broken down cars, lies a formation of four cars in the shape of a square. Those four cars stationed as somewhat of a guarded fortress to something actively happening inside.

The young detective sees the outline of a man who handles a device in the middle of the fort. Cottontail raises his gun by his head, then slowly crouches down to his knees, as he cautiously stumbles around the other side of the room. The young detective puts his hand over the trigger as he crawls over to the fort from behind, hoping to take Veymont by surprise. Grease stains his sweaty clothes. Cottontail peers over the hood of one of the cars. To his surprise, the person has vanished. All that is left behind are four rectangular consoles, strapped with wires that are piled up next to each other.

The young detective crawls over to one of the consoles and opens up the metallic box to peer inside. His eyebrows raise as he almost drops the console. A bomb that reads 3:08 left on a timed clock, lies in wait inside. All four of these consoles must be bombs, he realizes.

The sleuth realizes that he must diffuse them immediately, before he blows up into an incinerating fireball. Cottontail feels out the wires inside the console and handles them delicately. Using his DEO training, he then proceeds to defuse each bomb by hand. He takes one of the consoles and places it in a handbag found beside him to save himself some space. He carefully places the bag on the ground a couple feet away, to designate that specific console saved for last. He operates quickly as he handles the other three consoles.

Near the entrance of the side hangar, the sleuth sees Veymont come into view, as he fires his gun into what Cottontail believes to be empty space.

The menace studies the young detective's murky footsteps, then tries to follow the messy trail that leads to the detective. "I'll kill you, kid. You're dead meat! You hear me?!"

Cottontail, who fears for his life, hides behind one of the trucks in the fort with his gun still drawn. This truck has a large wool blanket and see-through plastic wrap on its flatbed. He shakes his gun vigorously, afraid that any moment would be his last. The young detective hears a couple of footsteps come up from behind him as he slides his index finger next to the trigger. Suddenly, the footsteps stop.

He hears a low voice sneer, "Hey."

Cottontail snaps to the figure and relinquishes two bullets. A brief silence follows. The sleuth's eyes grow big as he drops his gun. "Oh no! My God, what have I done?"

Leaking blood, Pretty Boy takes a few steps towards the young detective before he falls over. Cottontail catches Pretty Boy and rests him over his knee. The young detective's tears flow from his face. His whimpers become loud and emotionally unstable as he cradles the bloody body.

"Pretty Boy, why didn't you wait?" he cries.

The sleuth caresses Pretty Boy's face softly, as he feels life leave from the body. To his astonishment, Pretty Boy's face is covered with a great big smile. The dying young thug blinks his eyelids slowly, as his breathing becomes louder and louder. “I’ve never thought I’d see the day,” he murmurs.

“What do you mean?” Cottontail demands back.

“To hunt down criminals...make bombs...exciting drug busts...intense shootouts...all with my baby brother. All so...extraordinary.” The young detective watches as Pretty Boy’s blue eyes flutter open for the last time, then close permanently.

The young detective’s tears become thick as he hides his head onto the cold corpse. His aim proved to be far too unlucky. Without warning, a lone gunshot comes out of nowhere and pierces the young detective’s shoulder.

The young detective yelps in pain as he loses his grip on Pretty Boy and leans back onto a back tire of the truck. Cottontail glances down at his shoulder, petrified with fear. He watches helplessly as his blood pours out, like red paint that flows out of a paint canister. The sleuth had never experienced anything that close and personal before. It was all too surreal. The blood oozes down his arm and frightens him immensely. He rests his back against the back tire of the truck as another figure approaches him.

“How appropriate. I get to take down a pig and his twisted brother,” Veymont mocks.

The young detective observes with contempt as the look of satisfaction on the villain’s face intensifies. “You’ll never get away with it,” Cottontail’s voice trembles as the feeling leaves his bloody arm. The boss replies, “On the contrary, I think I’ll just take my bag and leave you here. Hate to leave everybody, but I have a sale to finish. Thanks for helping me make the bomb, pig. It's been a real thrill."

The young detective watches Veymont pick up the hand bag with the remaining console. He frowns and wonders if the crime boss knew about the explosive hidden inside the bag. With his other hand, Veymont picks up a gasoline jug and splashes a couple drops on both of the brothers. Cottontail begs, "No! Please, don't do it!" Veymont grins as he starts a small trail of gasoline following him out of the side hangar. "This is good bye, pig. Whoever you really are." The crime boss snickers as he saunters out of the hangar back to the dock by the far side. The shootout sounds as if it is finally over. Silence falls back to the warehouse.

Sweat douses the sleuth's face, as if he stared death right in the face. There was no escape, Cottontail feared. This time, he will truly die in a fiery explosion.

Farther down the length of the warehouse ground floor, the young detective sees Veymont slip on the large clump of gasoline pooled by Detective Metchum's corpse. The crime boss falls flat on his face as the bag falls to his feet.

An idea rushes into Cottontail's mind, as this opportunity presents itself. As Veymont wipes the gasoline off his face, the young detective springs into action.

Cottontail dives into Pretty Boy's pocket. After a moment, the sleuth pulls out a lighter. With the energy left in his arm, the young detective pulls himself and Pretty Boy's body away from the trail of gasoline. He then pulls down the wool blanket from the flatbed next to them.

Cottontail quickly leans forward and tries to flicker the lighter onto the trail end of gasoline. For some odd reason, the spark will not go. His second attempt does no better. He realizes time is running out. On this third try, a burning sensation covers his thumb. The pain forces him to drop the lighter, after he spins over the spark wheel.

"Ow!" the young detective yelps as the spark flicks to life, and a line of fire quickly trails its way out of the hangar.

The line of fire dominoes straight into Veymont's path. The crime boss watches in horror as the fire starts to cover his legs. He cries in pain as his body catches on fire.

Veymont suddenly sees a light flash sparkle its way out of his hand bag. His eyeballs enlarge as he shrieks to the high heavens.

The remaining console explodes, which takes the crook with it. A small explosion soon ignites a couple of gasoline canisters lying a couple feet away. Another explosion triggers, and this time, it proves more destructive. Window glass breaks, dead bodies burn up to smoking crisps, and a pile of dark smoke covers the whole warehouse. Trickles of flames now flood all over the basement.

The back side of the speedboat blows off, and the interior catches on fire. The same mysteriously bulky arm that sticks out of the operating control seat shakes uncontrollably with fire. Its flesh soon chips away and deteriorates with exposure to third degree burns. The boat detaches from the dock and floats off down the river, supposedly never to be seen again.

A couple of minutes after the warehouse becomes completely covered in a giant inferno, valiant firefighters arrive at the scene. With their hoses and water supply, the firefighters extinguish the flames as quick as they possibly can. Soon after, DEO agents storm the entrance. Chief Brahm's Blue Corvette arrives at the scene, as he watches the fireball engulf the whole building structure. "My God," he says to himself. "What have they done?"

Ten minutes later, the young detective throws off a wool blanket and plastic wrap that covers himself and Pretty Boy's body. He coughs uncontrollably as smoke enters his lungs. With all his might and will power, the sleuth drags Pretty Boy through a newly formed hole that bursts in flames on the hangar sidewall. Cottontail kicks down cement mold to create enough space to lead them both to safety. He pulls them out of the inferno and limps them over to scrambled gravel that lies right outside the entrance. Somehow, they made it.

The chief and another detective approach the young detective. They recognize Cottontail as a new hire with the department. Brahm starts to apply a gauze pad to Cottontail's shoulder, which forces the blood to stay compact. "You'll be ok, kid. Take it easy," the chief beams back. The sleuth coughs out rapidly, while he slowly comes to his feet. His face is covered in soot.

He pulls Pretty Boy's body flat on the ground. "Who's he?" Brahm asks.

The young detective tries to hold back tears, then shakes his head slowly at the sight of Pretty Boy lying quietly on the ground. He wants to wither down to the ground and cry beside the corpse. But, at the same time, there is something else at stake. He does not want to give away Pretty Boy's true identity. "He's...nobody, sir. Just another casualty."

"Anymore survivors?" Brahm asks.

"Just me," the sleuth remarks softly.

With mixed feelings, the chief pats Cottontail on the back and shakes his head. "That's unfortunately sad, but...I'm proud of you, kid. You busted your first major terrorist ring. This is big news. A new medal is coming your way, along with a brand-new promotion."

The young detective wheezes violently, "Thank you, sir."

The chief continues, "You will now work as a leading officer for the DEO agency. Metchum would have wanted it this way."

Brahm shakes Cottontail's hand with great enthusiasm. "Much obliged," he replies, unable to match the chief's optimism.

Chief Brahm replies, "I'm going to check the wreckage. Tell Jonesy here everything you can to report about this case. After that, you will have to see a doctor to get that bullet out of your arm. That is an order."

The sleuth nods. "Yes sir." The chief disappears near the cloud of white smoke that dissolves at the front entrance of the level grade.

Jonesy approaches the sleuth with a notepad and pen. He straightens out his checkered blue and white tie. "Can we start with your name?"

Cottontail frowns, confused. "My name?"

Surely this accomplished detective was already debriefed with the whole operation. Didn't the chief tell him the rookie's name? Then again, the chief has his own problems with remembering names. Only the top officers he could remember.

Jonesy nods his head, oblivious. "For the report, yes. I will start with your name and the rest of the information you can give me. You don't have to worry about filing this report. I'll do this one myself."

The young detective nods his head, "Uh, ok."

Jonesy replies, "So, once again. What's your name?"

The sleuth stops for a second, then thinks about what his next move should be. As he looks down at Pretty Boy's body next to his feet, he feels ashamed for the senseless action that he had done. He then starts to consider the well-being of his family. What will they think of this news? Can he live with the publicity from newspapers everywhere? Would he tarnish his adoptive family name? The young detective then glares back to the cloud of smoke behind him, as it accumulates into the sky.

Maybe, he reckons, the people should not know his name. His remaining family could not be linked to a false reported name, could they? Then he starts to think about Pretty Boy's friend, the Cannabis enthusiast, and how his remains should lie somewhere in the burning warehouse.

"Well?" Jonesy asks impatiently, in anticipation of some sort of answer. The young detective looks Jonesy square in the eye, while he answers with conviction, "Jim. Jim Cazco. I'm a rookie DEO agent."

28

The flashback fast forwards to the detective at Momma's house. He breaks the news that her son, Pretty Boy, has just passed away. She cries on Chloe's shoulder in the living room. Chloe turns to Cottontail, with eyes redden with sadness. Gladys raises her head and looks at her adoptive son. He caresses her chin, but a concerning frown appears on her face.

The young detective kisses her hand and pats Chloe's shoulder in comfort. Feeling uneasy, Cottontail moves his feet slowly backward. He could not make himself stay a second more. The pain was too great.

Cottontail begins to back up to the back door for the exit. Glancing woefully at his remaining family members, a dreadful feeling overwhelms him that this will be the last time he will see them. After a long sigh, the young detective departs into the backyard. He takes a quick peek at the family tree, which is covered in shadow. As he leaves, the memory dissolves.

***

Back to the rooftop, Wayne Smothers watches the emotion pull apart the detective's worn face. The officer whimpers softly. "The guilt of Pretty Boy's death stuck with me. Even days later, I realized that I could never forgive myself for what I've done. I felt that I betrayed the only real existence that I ever knew. Even though I mentioned vaguely to Momma that Pretty Boy died in some freak accident, I could tell by the look on her face, somehow, that she knew the truth. Her eyes glared right back, as if she saw right through my lies." He takes a big gulp as he chokes up with guilt and remorse.

"I knew at that point I had to go, without saying goodbye. I knew I couldn't burden them with my existence any longer. Even though I was not their own flesh and blood, they treated me as such. It appeared to be the last time I would see the inside of that house. This would the last time I could see their comforting faces, and the last time I would see the family tree in the backyard. The same family tree, that by now, should reach farther up to the sky and hold countless numbers of juicy apples. All those tasty apple pies a boy could ever want."

The journalist nods. "Now I see."

The detective lets his tears flow, not holding back anymore. "If I ever could take back one day, it would be the day I accidentally killed my brother. My best friend. If I could erase one memory from my head, it would be that one. For the last 15 years, l couldn't pull myself together to pay his grave a visit. It is the same nightmare that still haunts me to this very day."

Wayne pauses before he speaks, as he tries to put the remaining pieces together. "With your new promotion, you became one of the best-known DEO agents in the industry. No one had reason to research your background nor question your actions from that day forth. So, you altered your identity at the personal records building with the real Jim Cazco. This enabled you to keep a good standing at your job and protect your family."

The detective sighs. "My newfound success put my face and new name on the map. With my new title as lead DEO, I went through a large line of big cases. That's when I started to build a reputation as one of the best in the business. I won many more medals after that."

The reporter chimes in, "But all those cases you filed couldn't have been completely accurate and true. You broke the three principles of probable cause. Admit it. You dictated the rights of these people that you either put away or killed in cold blood."

The detective dips his head down in guilt. He replies softly, as he chokes up on his own words, "How else would you fair in those situations? A lot of those opportunities were sticky situations to begin with. It was either them or you. How bad do you want to stay alive? For me, it was to shoot first, then find out what happens later. I always wrote what I wanted in my report. Government heads approved it every time."

Wayne smirks. "I knew you were cold and corrupt. Somehow I just knew. You are the ultimate slime that perpetrates mayhem upon these dirty streets. Instead of solving crimes, you carry out crimes yourself, with no consideration for the people around you. You should be ashamed of yourself."

The detective swings his arm slightly outward, as he regains some mobility. However, he is not able to defend himself against his adversary. "Not all victims were innocent! I have got it right a good number of times too!"

Wayne shakes his head, unconvinced. It is impossible for him to be swayed this late in the game.

The detective sighs unenthusiastically. "But you're right about my career. I do feel ashamed of myself. I feel ashamed of a lot of things. What do you plan to do with me now?"

The journalist grits his teeth, excited. "Now, Nathan, I plan to turn you in for a reward. A con artist named Varra gave me blackmail against you and the rest of the Detective Enforcement Office. They paid me to publish their blackmail in a news article. She wanted me to expose the true frauds you really are."

The detective asks nervously, "Did you already publish the article?"

The reporter scratches his nose. "No, not yet. But that will happen after I take you in. You see, I betrayed Varra's trust. I realized I didn't need Varra or Nevo. Once they gave me the blackmail, I had no further use for them. So, I decided to plant a bomb in Varra's car. The con artist didn't even know what hit her. She got what she deserved, just like what's coming your way."

The detective hyperventilates. "Are you going to kill me?"

Wayne pulls out a pair of handcuffs. "In a way, yes. I'm going to turn you in at a DEO facility out of town. You will be presented alive with a full written confession. Then I will post an article all about you and your criminal past. Think about it: your name will be headlines for one last time. Once you are disgraced by the public, I will then post a separate article about the blackmail against the whole corruptive DEO branch. They will resign, and I believe the government will follow suit. It will be a great pleasure to watch you all fall. The money for both articles, I'm sure, will be beyond my wildest dreams."

The detective shakes his head in wild panic. "Kill me," he weeps. "Just kill me! I can't bear to see my mother and sister find out what I really am! Just kill me! Get rid of my regrets and guilt! I don't deserve to live!"

Wayne watches as the officer mentally breaks down before his eyes. The glorified look on the reporter's face was what he craved all along: complete degradation. "I think not, Nathan. Your time will come later. My moment of fame comes now. It would happen to you sooner or later, detective. Nobody gets out of this life unscathed. The child of freelance arsonists, raised by the mob, finally brought to justice. Sounds like the story of the century."

The detective snaps, "My biological parents were not freelance arsonists!"

Wayne retorts, "Your real parents left you in a house that suddenly burned down when you were a child. You still think that was an accident? You said your real mother and father never registered their house? Did they leave gasoline residue in the driveway? Did they ever come back for you? Did they ever report the incident? Open your eyes. They left you there and never came back on purpose. They left you to die, detective. Those freelance arsonists probably finished with whatever assignment that floated their way and left you to burn away with the rest of the evidence. They never cared about you! You were always a nobody!"

The detective shakes his head, heartbroken. More joints of his body slowly become unglued. He refuses to believe the claim. "It can't be. It just can't be."

The journalist flips the pair of handcuffs open, then takes a couple more steps closer to the detective. "Who cares? The past hurts, but it won't be anything like your future. Get ready for a confession, Nathan. I want an official document to stand true this time."

Out of the blue, the stairwell door busts open. Ike Brooks peers out onto the rooftop with his gun drawn. "Jim? Wayne? Is that you?"

Without hesitation, the detective raises his arm and points toward the reporter. "Watch out Ike! He has a gun!"

Wayne unknowingly shakes his stun gun through the air, confused by the arrival of the unwelcomed guest. "Detective, wait! No!"

Three bullets echo off the rooftop. Wayne collapses on the floor, with his shirt soaked in blood. He turns to the detective, and tries to utter something under his breath. Wayne reaches out with his hand just shy of the detective's nose. His head suddenly sways to one side as his shoulders roll backward. His eyelids close.

Ike helps his partner to his feet, now completely mobilized. Chief Brahm and a couple other agents enter the rooftop with guns drawn. They look around at the crime scene and watch Wayne's body lie motionless. "What happened?" the chief asks bluntly.

The detective takes a couple steps forward and sighs with relief. "A blackmailer. Wayne had a verbal confession of killing a girl named Varra. Her remains are reportedly back at the greenhouse. Detective Brooks here took care of business." Ike's eyes glow in response, as if he just achieved a major accomplishment.

Brahm places his gun back in his pocket, then checks the vital signs of the reporter. He shakes his head as he fails to identify a pulse. The chief, worn and fatigued, somehow forces a smile. "Action doesn't like to leave you, Jim. Glad this all finally got wrapped up."

"Almost," the detective announces as he pulls an object out of his pocket. Brahm sees the detective stick his arm out for a handshake, so he pulls his own hand out to meet him. The chief frowns as he realizes the detective has left an object in his hand. He glances down at the object. A law enforcement badge lies firmly in his hand. Brahm shakes his head, not believing the gesture. "What is this?"

The detective smiles. "You were right, chief. Too much action. It's a young man's game anyway. This is my resignation."

The chief's eyes wander. Suddenly a barrage of memories float rapidly in his frustrated mind. He cannot believe it, after all the times they worked together. All these crazy cases were solved one step at a time.

"Are you sure?" The detective pats him on the back. "I haven't been more sure of anything else in my life, old friend. Our great work will never be forgotten. You got the young kid now. Ike Brooks is all you need."

Brahm grins. He feels happy about the long run they had together. "Well then, I guess...so long pal. I'll miss you."

The detective shakes the chief's hand one last time. "Take care." Chief Brahm nods his head slowly as he strides away somberly.

Ike slowly walks up to his now-former partner, as he tries to process the whole new situation. "I didn't think you would do that."

The detective smiles. "Ike, someday, you will find it necessary to be someone else. There are other things in life waiting for you, like family. I do believe if you continue to walk down the path you are on right now, it will make you happy and successful."

Ike nods his head slowly in agreement. "I guess I can report that I actually did save the great Jim Cazco after all, and be worthy of a Medal of Honor. That heroic sensation feels real this time."

The detective gives him a great big hug. "You were always worthy, Ike. Time will tell of what other great things you will do. I wish you the best of luck."

Ike nods his head with glassy eyes, as his former partner walks away. He turns around one last time. "So long, pal." The detective gestures a small wave as he exits the rooftop. Ike swiftly raises his arm up in a salute. He watches his mentor fade away, as the rainfall sprinkles down lightly.

***

Further down the street, the rainfall stops altogether. White seeds from dandelion flowers float wildly down through the air and scatter all over the ground. The wet ground and flowery petals meet the detective's feet as he scurries his way back home.

The detective's head hangs low in sadness. His own inner voice creeps into his troubled mind. "After all the death, pain, and despair that I endured, what purpose do I have? Back there on the rooftop, I saw the end of a very dismal life. I do wish that one of Ike's bullets accidentally pierced my chest so that the blood would flow true from my corpse. It would be the last pain I would ever feel."

He shoulders sink as he bends his back forward. All of the sudden, the dandelion petals sway down by his face and carry a more vivacious presence. One petal falls lightly on his nose. The wind starts to pick up, and more dandelion seeds dance their way down to the ground all around him.

Wide-eyed, he stops abruptly. It's as if a foreign substance just penetrated his body. His internal voice returns, "Wait. What is this feeling? Time feels like it has stopped again."

Suddenly, a memory of Eva enters his mind. He visualizes the both of them hurtling down the roller coaster back at the fairgrounds. Another memory takes over, when they first kissed on the Ferris Wheel. It is followed by the memory of them speeding fast downhill on their new two-seater bicycle. Eva's face cranks out with a wide smile, as the detective chuckles behind her with delight.

Back at the middle of the road, his face senses a tingling glow that brings an enchanting, new smile. He paces on.

His internal voice changes drastically, "The world doesn't have to all end, at least not today. The real truth is I still have so much to live for. I have a new opportunity to work as a microbiology botanist and a chance to return to the job I was always meant to do. With my credentials, who could possibly turn me down?"

He raises his shoulders, lifts his head back, and gazes out, misty-eyed, at the moon that shines brightly down upon him, "Life has its disappointments, but there is just too much out there to enjoy. Eva, my new girlfriend, who may someday be my wife, can help me find true happiness again. I can leave my past two lives behind me, and to not let it define me. I can start my promising third life in good health and peace of mind. We can travel up north to the natural preserves together, where I can do my life's true work. We can raise a family and maybe a child or two."

The detective closes his eyes as he continues to stride peacefully down the street. Meanwhile, he visualizes a young girl who smiles back at him at a fully occupied dinner table. Her thin face resembles his, but her bright green eyes bare likeness to Eva. An older version of Eva sits beside the child with shorter hair. The mother brushes back the girl's hair, as the child stares back at the detective intently. A small poodle runs over to a water bowl inside a beautiful kitchen.

Fantastical imagery then takes his mind to a brisk knock on the fence to the backyard of his adoptive parent's house. His internal voice continues, "Maybe someday I can regain the courage to see Momma. As I enter through the back gate, I can see her warm smile, as Chloe stands beside her. They both embrace me like before. They will caress my chin and tell me how much they have missed me for all these years. I will tell them I will no longer hurt them."

The detective continues to speculate, "Then, we will stop short of our Duggle Tree. Now, it must be as tall as a mountain. Yes, I would actually feel like I am home. I will tell my Momma and Chloe that I would never desert them ever again."

Small, unidentified clumps of a wet substance dampen the detective's nose. More trails of this powdery substance brush on top of his clothes and mix into his muddled hair. The mysterious substance piles up on the slippery sidewalk in huge blankets. It is a cold substance, easily broken-up into tiny bits.

His smile broadens as his imagination beckons him on, as if he becomes overcome by an enticing trance. The detective continues to waddle along another block in the same direction. He is unsure where this new path leads. In quick succession, he pictures Chief Brahm, Ike Brooks, and Wayne Smothers glaring at him. They each call out, "Nathan...Nathan...Nathan!"

***

The detective suddenly stops at the end of a curb, then opens his eyes to a full layer of mushy snow that covers the whole sidewalk. White dandelion seeds are no longer visible.

He finds himself at the foot of the graveyard, which is the same resting place of the real James Hunter Cazco. He stumbles through the front gate and trudges slowly up the hill near the back end of the graveyard.

Stopping abruptly, he kicks over remnants of a tombstone, which marked the resting place of the same James Hunter Cazco. What a hopeless waste, he reminds himself. What would the real Jim say if he saw what the detective became? Sometimes it's best not to know.

A dark shadow from a leafless tree at the top of the hill extends outward. The detective picks up a detached rose that lies peacefully beside the tree's roots. He then gradually makes his way to the top of the hill. All that resides at the top is a large tombstone.

As he places the rose at the base of the grave, the detective falls to his knees as his spirit breaks.

A white, snowy winter wonderland covers the hillside.

The detective weeps as he addresses the dark tombstone directly, ashamed but willing to face the demons that possessed him for so long. He stares at the simple name written on the grave, as he tries to regain his composure.

He speaks aloud, "I know it's been a long time. From this moment on, torment will no longer trouble my soul. I wanted to tell you that I learned to forgive myself and that I am truly sorry. It has been the hardest task, but after all this time, I have peace. I've decided to take Eva with me. A promising new life exists up north, where prosperity and good health run supreme. The only question I have for you is if you can accept that?"

He waits a couple seconds, in silence, as the shadows of the grave disappear. The glare of the tombstone letters glisten ever so brightly.

"Well, can't you? I've got to know. Please...tell...me." He inches forward through the snow and embraces the tombstone wholeheartedly. The detective weeps loudly as his arms fold tightly around the thick granite before him. His head rests gently on the stone as he waits for an answer. Unfortunately, nature, as we know it, is never so vocal. As his tears slide off the granite letters, the name on the grave finally reveals itself as no other than Nathan Duggle.

About the Author

Zach Perry is an author that grew up in Northern California. He graduated from the University of Oregon with a Bachelor's Degree in Film Studies. Soon after graduation, Zach moved to Los Angeles to start a career in the film industry, with interest in screenwriting. Over time, Zach has adapted treatments of pitched literary work into full sized novels due to the vivid depiction and remarkable atmosphere created in his work. Building off his experiences on films and television shows, Zach brings his innovative concepts to life.

CPSIA information can be obtained
at www.ICGtesting.com
Printed in the USA
LVHW041553130322
713347LV00002B/204

9 781736 971406